~~

# Neptune
# Love
# Affairs

~

~~

# Neptune
# Love
# Affairs

*Divinely Guided*

*a fictional novel based on a true story*

by Talia Grace

~~

*To my natal Neptune Sun,*

*thank you for the beautiful escapes, the highest*

*form of love and guidance!*

~~

~~

~~

# 1

# Grace

2010 - 2011

Grace appreciated getting out of Twin Falls, the little city where she was born and raised. It was home to 70,000 people, surrounded by agricultural fields, open sunny skies, and a few dusty hills to the south. This area was nicknamed "The Magic Valley" due to the Snake River's ability to provide fresh water to the arid desert, transforming it into lush cultivated land before slithering on towards the Pacific Ocean.

The captivating view often stole her attention from conversations with Matt, who'd swing through and pick her up from the comfortable Barnes and Noble cafe. Together they'd drive north, crossing the beautifully crafted steel bridge—secured by steep lava rock walls, where sagebrush and waterfalls sprinkled about. Over four hundred feet below and to the west lay a manicured golf course while upstream displayed the majestic Shoshone Falls—the "Niagara of the West." It was a sight to see after a winter's snow melt.

She admired the change in scenery as the flat desert morphed into a narrow valley, squeezed within the mountains where sagebrush and dry grasses turned to pine trees and white aspens. The ride was always enjoyable, ending in eagerness to get working as they approached Ketchum & Sun Valley. There, she'd hop out and guide Matt on where to park, then heave the resistant latch on the horse trailer as she had hundreds of times before—freeing the doors, like opening curtains to her stage, rubbing her hands together, ready to unload boxes of produce and display supplies.

They'd set up a pop-up tent and tables, neatly arrange organic veggies that would—by the season's end—expand out and beyond their tables and double tents. She cherished beautifying the farm's booth by adding colorful price signs for each product while keeping herself on schedule, even when friendly vendors interrupted with welcome waves and cheerful conversations.

Once the market began, off came her shoes as her bare feet grounded to the earth, and she proudly prepared herself for her audience—ready to interact with like-minded individuals and provide for them an honest product. Their busy lines and gracious shoppers made time fly. The social interactions were the best part of her day: exchanging healthy recipes, sharing cooking tricks and gardening tips with others gave her purpose and a sense of pride. They were more like confidantes than customers, which was great since Sun Valley was previously an intimidating place.

While growing up, she knew it was famous for attracting many wealthy and elite families: A-list actors,

Olympic gold medalists—it was even the last home of Ernest Hemingway.

But working at the farmer's markets changed her opinion of the place and people. She vibes with down-to-earth, health-conscious consumers who shared an appreciation for and knowledge of local food and healthy living.

Her second season on the farm was now in full swing. Last year, she donated her time on the farm since she'd wanted an opportunity to learn the ropes of a sustainable farming operation. What inspired her to seek out this experience was her upcoming two-year Peace Corps assignment in the Caribbean where she'd be helping farmers increase their sales. Her goal before leaving was to practice assisting a local grower to market their products more efficiently.

Fortunately, within a short time, she was introduced to Matt Haze, who provided her with a perfect situation, giving her hands-on learning experiences, freedom to run with her ideas, and the skills she needed to prepare for the two-year stint abroad. Haze, a laid-back, Hawaiian shirt kind of guy in his late 60s, was perfectly content being a family man and providing local, sustainable food. He'd offer food to anyone, if necessary —no questions, even when he was a man of modest means.

Grace admired him for his giving heart and strived to be that way as well, regardless of her lot in life. These character attributes made it easy and rewarding to do what she could to increase his sales.

After a full year helping Matt, her Peace Corps plans fell

through but were quickly replaced with a trip to Tanzania at the end of the market season. She was determined to satisfy her appetite for giving back. This deep desire to assist in Africa began in her early teens and only grew stronger over time. This year, she was gonna do it!

She had planned to donate her farm hours for a second season. However, Matt insisted on paying her for all her hard work. He also hung a flyer in their booth, informing customers about her upcoming journey and announced all winter squash sales would go towards Grace's excursion.

Curious customers wanted to know all about her service trip and helped pay for her flight into Tanzania. She set aside the extra cash for a donation to the orphanage once she got there. She'd have plenty of time to find a good purpose for it during her three-month stay, starting five days before Halloween and ending two weeks after New Year's—the perfect time to escape Idaho's winter and head to the equator.

When the last day of the market came around, she said goodbye to all her pals who'd wished her luck on her travels. Her friends and family threw a going-away party at her most beloved restaurant, Local Sprouts in Twin Falls. It was owned by a couple who served produce from their geothermal greenhouse gardens. They supported other local farmers and ranchers by using their ingredients in their cooking and selling it in their storefront.

Every guest sent her off with notes of positive encouragement on her journey, their messages would come in handy when she got homesick or when she needed a friendly reminder of home.

* * *

After a day or two of jet lag, Grace woke midday from the sound of repeating footsteps, circling the volunteer house. She was slightly dazed and dizzy, so she looked out the window to check it out, maybe get some fresh air?

A tropical Arusha scene surprised her with a beautiful mountain staring back at her. The house was empty, so she went outside to ground herself. Right outside the front door was a tall, skinny Maasai guard.

"Hi!" she said, holding her hand out to shake his.

"Habari," he said, lightly touching her hand, as though he wasn't sure he was supposed to.

She pointed to the mountain and asked, "Kilimanjaro?"

"Meru," he said, politely then pointed east. "Kilimanjaro."

"Oh," she said, able to now assess her location, remembering seeing it on a map of Tanzania.

Just then a vehicle came through the security gate and a voluptuous woman climbed out.

"Grace, how are you?" she asked with a heavy accent.

"Good, after some rest. Thank you!"

"Good. I'm Elsa. I manage the volunteers. You are the first in the new house." She raised both her hands to show it off. "Karibu—welcome. There's another house full of others in town. Don't worry, another volunteer will be coming in a few days and Monday will be your placement initiation. Pick any room you want. The house will be full by Christmas, and we are building a few rooms in the back for the boys. Your dinner will be ready at 5. Just don't go through the gate. Stay within the security walls!" She dropped some things inside and immediately came back out and said, "Bye, bye" and left.

Grace used her free days to make herself at home. She journaled, did yoga, walked around the dirt yard, and played solitaire until her first companion showed up. Sun was from Japan and would be there for two weeks. They had the same placement, but she only knew Japanese, so they played card games and giggled for a day or two before traveling to the orphanage, aptly named Glorious. The orphanage was a small elementary school with two open buildings next to Alice's house—the woman who'd started it a few years back. In the beginning, she'd used her home to teach kids who had deceased or struggling single parents, and she provided basic school supplies, occasionally clothed them, and would send them home with full bellies.

Her future goal was to build residential housing at the school for students in need. Grace admired the families and the community who welcomed these children into their lives, giving them more of a sense of home and family.

A month into her stay, she unexpectedly became the headteacher in the "baby class." Swahili was their native language but Alice wanted them to learn English, so Grace taught the four-to-six-year-old basic English and math. She was nervous at first but found it invigorating once she had the hang of it, grateful for the opportunity.

After school on Thanksgiving, she took the extra donation money from the market and bought enough food for four Glorious families to eat for a month. She went with another volunteer and Alice to a tiny shop where they bought rice, beans, cooking oil, cornflour, and a bar of soap for washing. Not realizing until after buying everything that they would have to carry it on foot to each home.

All three women held two heavy, stuffed garbage bags, trekking down dry dirt roads in the heat as they wove their way through cinder block, stick, and mud huts for miles. They passed piles of burning trash that drew bugs, street dogs, and chickens to their scraps.

Alice carried most of the load with two bags in each hand and one perfectly balanced on top of her head, propelling herself with flimsy orange flip-flops. She was wrapped in bright African fabric. Grace was impressed with her skills and would never forget the image of her carrying her load under the hot African sun.

On their next excursion, Grace and another Glorious volunteer, Kate, had planned and organized a field trip for all 40-50 students to go to the Snake Park on her birthday, two days before Christmas. Before leaving, they handed out new school uniforms, socks, and shoes that she and other volunteers raised money for. Kate had two skirts made that matched the girls' uniforms, one for Grace and one for Alice, who shared the same birthday. Although Alice was younger than her, she seemed older and more mature, having taken on so much responsibility in comparison to herself. That impacted her in a way she didn't fully understand, but she admired Alice for all she'd done and continued to do.

After all the students were dressed in their new clothes, everyone posed for photos before loading up two dola dola vans to the Snake Park. There were no seat belt rules, just pack everyone in. The day was full of fun and abundance, then they headed back to Glorious just before the sun went down. The day couldn't have been more incredible. All the work fundraising, planning and organizing was well worth it. She had a fantastic 26th birthday, and the best part was passing out new uniforms and celebrating with Alice.

After their Christmas and New Year's break, they made visits to every child's home on foot with Alice and Kate. It took two days. She met the guardians that cared for each child and a photo was taken of them for the website, newly created to raise money for the orphanage. It was also a great way to provide the opportunity for sponsoring a child.

She would never forget the last visit, where they entered an empty stick and mud hut. It was similar in size to a walk-in closet, squeezed within a crowded neighborhood. They gathered inside, standing near a hot simmering pot on the ground, while Alice explained Wazeri's living situation with his grandmother and nine cousins. Grace immediately glanced at the worn-out bed they must've shared since there was nowhere else to sleep but the ground, which continued in from outside. She imagined the rains bringing in a muddy mess and possibly roaming animals. Then her eyes went to the overflowing dresser and back to the thin sheet, dangling from the doorway they'd just walked through. She wondered if it helped keep trouble out—it certainly didn't stop *them* from walking in while no one was home.

The situation was humbling, considering how locals had limited opportunities for home and car loans, credit cards, or even clean drinking water, let alone a toilet and shower. She'd never seen a fridge anywhere, even in the volunteer house. There she stood, covered in soot, grateful for the day's trek, for the insight into each child's life, and a deeper appreciation for what she had back home.

Thankfully, they took public transportation—a dola dola ride back to Glorious, where she invited each teacher to pick out clothes from a pile she'd brought in that morning. It was thrilling to see their excitement, like they were on a shopping spree! A celebratory way of ending her time there.

Then, a round of goodbye hugs began. Grace cried tears of joy, sad to leave the experience and beautiful people behind. The moment was so powerful; it was hard and tender, yet emotionally expansive. Her intention on visiting Africa was to "give" and explore another part of the world. She'd fulfilled those desires, but in the end, she received more than she'd anticipated. Her heart opened wide to these people, to a simpler way of life, and she was completely enveloped by love.

The sensation was better than gold—like nothing she'd experienced. Her spirit expanded from her heart, out into reality—creating a highly sensitive moment. She was proud of getting herself there, grateful to all who supported her in doing so, for being strong while traveling alone, and for reaching out to another part of the world, to show "I love and care about you."

After flying back to the states, she was overwhelmed with emptiness, even though she was ready to be home. At first, she thought she was dealing with reverse culture shock, coming back to the reality of her life, unable to cope with change. That was part of it, but she wanted her focus to be on service back home.

* * *

Grace and Matt were all set up and ready for their first day of market. She was overjoyed with all the customers and market vendors who were curious about her trip. They were proud of her and happy to see her and welcomed her back like she knew they would. The people and spirit of the event energized her with comforting summertime vibes she needed to heal despite her hint of loss at the surface. She tried to push it aside and carry on, but it continued to linger. Her emotional equilibrium was slow to find balance, and she wasn't sure what direction to take, even though the market grounded her. She noticed the way she related to others and her environment had changed, but what hadn't changed was the ability to brighten someone's day with a positive compliment, being kind or receiving a smile—that's what she'd focus on for now.

Her friend Cray interrupted her focus, saying, "The display is beautiful," as he walked past the side of the table, to stand next to her.

Cray was a close friend of eight years who came down from northern Idaho for a camping trip. A few days prior, she'd accepted his invitation to join him and would meet up after market, on his way to Stanley.

"Hey, thanks," she smiled with a giddy shrug. "Did you just get into town?"

"I went on a hike nearby and found some camping grub for our dinner tonight," he said, holding up the bag of food. "Can we add your veggies to our market meal?"

"Yes, please. Pick out whatever you'd like and I'll put it all in a cooler until we leave."

"Perfect. What time can I help you guys pack up?" he asked.

"That's nice of you! Market ends..."—she glanced at their clock—"in 15 minutes," she said, ringing up another customer while he filled the bag.

"...Can I get started on something now?" he asked, handing her the bag of food.

Haze hurried over to him, "Here, I'll help you while

Grace rings up customers," he said, apparently appreciating the extra hand and a possible early departure.

When they were done, Matt closed up the trailer and said, "Have a great time camping you two," then hugged Grace. "Be safe," he said, patting her back.

"We will. Drive safe," she said, walking away with Cray.

"Matt seems like a good guy," Cray said after he'd already pulled away.

"He is. He's like a father figure, or maybe a young grandpa, to me and his family is very supportive. I'm lucky to have such a *home-like* work environment."

"I'd say!" he said, as they got into his car and drove to Stanley while they caught up. He asked all about her Africa trip before they found the perfect hilltop to sleep out under the stars, looking over the extraordinary Sawtooth mountains, beautifully capped with pristine glaciers. Cray pulled out his bouldering crash pad and put it amongst the sagebrush, ants, and mosquitoes to serve as a bed and a seat near the fire. They cooked a hearty steak and veggie meal in a cast-iron skillet over the flames, giving their food a hint of smoke and dirt. Flavors that spoke to their primal taste buds.

"So, Grace. I enjoyed hearing all about your adventure, but I picked up on some sorrow… Why the weight on your shoulders?" he asked, softly investigating as he tended to the fire.

"Am I that obvious?" She asked, swirling a bite of steak in the juices on her plate.

"Yeah," he admitted.

"Where do I start?" she asked.

"How about with the emotions that are still raw... Come on..." He nudged his shoulder into hers.

She took a deep breath and said, "It's hard to describe what I went through emotionally, other than it was amazing and wonderful." She paused to chew another bite and finished it before continuing. "It felt like my heart opened to a vulnerable space and when I left, it seemed I left something there too. I can't go backward. I know I'm meant to be here..." Her voice cracked not knowing if she was making sense and looked bashfully at her plate. "I just want to experience that same fulfillment here. I want to make an impact, but what do you do for others when they have everything in comparison to those in a third world country? Lives here seem—more opportunistic, smooth, and convenient. Providing a month's supply of corn flour to a family wouldn't be that helpful to most people here and I can't afford to give much more than that. I know no matter where you are, everyone's striving to be and do better in life and there's always a way to help out. But how? What can I do that will matter? How do I give something of *value* that's appreciated, something **I** find value in giving, and how to do it sustainably?" Grace nervously continued talking as if she'd make sense of her emotions, but it didn't fully satisfy her.

He nodded in understanding. "I'd keep doing what you're doing. Keep searching for ways to serve that feed you. See where you are guided and needed."

"Yeah," she said, drawing in the dirt with a stick. A tad impatient with her own process.

"When I get all bottled up in an emotion or can't express it, I let it out somehow." He looked at her for a quiet moment, wondering how to help her through this. "Try yelling your emotions out to nature."

"Yelling them?" she asked shyly, tucking her hair behind her ear. "Right now?"

"Yeah!" He scooted closer, putting a supportive arm around her, quietly faking a yell while extending his free arm then he looked back at her. "Like that."

She snickered, thinking, *Why not?* And she opened up— yelled, wailed, diving into her emotions.

"aaaAAAAAAAAAAHHHHHHhhh!" She pushed out all the confusing disconnected emotions until she was completely out of breath, and at that exact moment, a big elk called back to her. They quickly turned south to watch as tears streamed down her face in relief and to nature's response.

"Whoa, you summoned your spirit animal," Cray said, full of enthusiasm. "The elk heard your call and responded to your soul, Grace!"

They sat astonished, and she chuckled through her tears, watching the striking animal eat from a tree and wander off into the woods. She adored the elk for hearing her inner call and for his response, but the idea that she was the elk didn't resonate with her. It seemed it was her soulmate's spirit animal. One day they'd hear her call and respond, just like that.

# 2

## Close to Africa

2011, 2012, 2013

The following week, Matt hired Grace on as, "full-time" market manager" with a nice raise. She channeled her focus into her new position, her loved ones, gardening, yoga and nurturing herself. Healing was taking place, knowing it would take time to find emotional balance and a sturdy direction. She kept her head up, looking for ways to help others, and to celebrate her experience abroad. Instead of sitting at her computer—moping over photos of Glorious students.

The day was exceptionally warm and she intentionally wore a dress that reminded her of Africa. It was by no means Tanzanian, but the pattern on the kimono brought her close to Africa. It was the best mix of salmon and pumpkin with Paisley patterns running down the slinky, light fabric. It reached her knees with wide sleeves to the elbows and a mid scoop in the chest. She beamed within it as she set up the market.

"Hey, heart breaker." A woman's voice suddenly broke her routine.

She turned sideways as the gal walked close, too close

and she recognized her from childhood.

"Heart breaker?" Grace asked, confident that she was mistaken.

"Cray—" she said as though Grace should already know, "you broke his heart." she added, picking through a box of potatoes.

"Cray? We've always been friends. We just went camping together." She said in a defensive tone and stance, unusual for her. "I've never heard anything about breaking his heart." Confused, she couldn't remember ever breaking a heart, especially when she hadn't dated until her first year or high school and the guys she wanted wouldn't date her because she was too shy or skinny.

"Whatever, lovely." The gal said, raising her hand then waved it down as to bat the silliness out of Grace. "Where did you get that beautiful gown? I want one!" She said, picking up a few veggies from the copious piles on the tables.

Grace broke the market rules of *no cash transactions before 2:00,* in order to get her moving along.

"Thanks, Veggie Princess." she said, walking backwards, "Come up sometime and play with me and my friends-ies. We'll have a blast."

"Okay," Grace said, knowing that wouldn't happen.

"See you later, heart breaker." she said, playfully then spun a dancer's spin and walked out of the market.

Grace squinted her eyes in the gals direction—uneasy, wondering if she'd seen something in her that Grace couldn't see? Did others think that about her? Did Cray? Just then a vendor friend approached.

"Looking good in your African motif, Grace." he said, smiling.

"Thank you." she said, allowing his complement to balance out her previous interaction. The attractiveness was emanating from the tangible threads of Africa, wrapped around her. That's what made her shine, emanating reminiscent vibes that carried her through her day—which swept away as the market had been bustling. It was already time to organize empty boxes for a quick pick up. When she bent down she sensed a shift in energy as a familiar person walked behind. She stood to see more clearly and butterflies instantly tickled within.

*Piper?*

Her first kiss! He hadn't seemed to see her, which was an opportunity lost since she'd always wondered where his life led him after high school. *He must be married, living here in Sun Valley.* She thought, *Maybe he has a little family?* The "heart breaker" encounter from the beginning of the day interrupted her thought, *This heart breaker didn't break that heart… He shared my first intimate moment which was simply swept away with life. Too bad he wasn't close enough to catch his attention.* She watched him walk down the sidewalk and out of the market while she stacked boxes of potatoes. *He's just walking through…*

Then an older gentleman, who was new to the market, walked up to her tall stack and grabbed a few boxes.

"Where do I take these?" he asked.

"Are you sure?" she asked, surprised.

"Yeah," he said, carrying them towards the trailer.

She followed and hopped inside to stack and keep the trailer organized. *How convenient*—she thought, *not five minutes ago, I was thinking it'd go a lot quicker with more hands.*

Usually, Haze had a very considerate habit of helping vendors, especially the solo women and she'd follow his lead but to have someone help *them* was something new.

"Stay here, we'll bring the boxes to you." he directed.

"Alright." she said, while he and Matt brought her load after load. She broke a sweat, rushing to keep up.

"Last few," he said, handing her the last two.

"Thank you!" she said, relieved. "It's so nice of you to help us," she said with a thankful smile, hopping out of the full horse trailer. "I'm Grace." she said, taking her leather glove off to shake his firm grip. "You are?"

"River. And you are so welcome! I was already done packing up and saw you guys could use the help."

"River?" she repeated, using her forearm to wipe her forehead dry.

"Yeah, like the Snake River, or a long body of water." He said confidently.

"Okay, River," she said with a thankful smile. "Is this your first market?"

"Yep... I retired last year and dove into pottery making." He quickly shrugged his shoulders, "I figured I'd try selling it rather than letting it collect dust in my studio."

"Nice. I'll check out your creations next time. Thank you for your help, it's good meeting you. Welcome to the market!"

"Sure thing. Nice meeting you, Grace…" he tipped his hat in Matt's direction, Haze."

Matt returned a grateful wave, then jumped in the truck while Grace took one last scope, making sure there were no signs they'd been there. Then she bounced into the cab—ready to count the till and head home with engaging conversations until he dropped her off in the Barnes and Noble parking lot, two hours later. He'd wait til she got her car going then they'd wave goodnight. This is where she could finally unwind.

\* \* \*

River offered a helping hand many times over the summer; he always looked ready to go or take off in a sprint in his tennis shoes—seeming like a spry young guy in a long-lived body. Maybe that's part of what made him so relatable to her? He mentioned his twin sons who were a year younger than her and lived in Arizona as river guides. His parents lived near the Ketchum market and occasionally joined him in the evenings. She'd share produce with them and keep their friendly chats short, so as to not interfere with customers. If there wasn't time to catch up, they'd wave from their booths, across the way and when the cold weather rolled in, harvest season was nearing its end.

River sauntered up, "What are your plans this winter, Grace?"

She bounced her bundled self a few happy steps towards him and said, "I got Rosetta Stone and I'll be practicing Spanish."

"That's a good idea, sharpen your language skills," he said.

"What about you, what will you do this winter? Will you be coming back next year?" she asked.

"I'll be up there skiing'." He nudged his head in the direction of the main ski slope. "And yes, I'll be back. You?"

"Yep!" She said brightly, handing him a full bag of winter squash with her gloved hands, huddled in winter clothes.

"Well, good, we'll see you next year," he said, walking away. "Oh—thanks for the squash, Grace!" he turned back for a quick wave, "Adios."

"Have a great winter, River!" she waved and watched him walk away in his down-jacket and clay spattered Carhartts. He wore one of his many baseball caps—showing a bit of silver hair. *I wonder if he's missing some since it never comes off?* She thought, locking up the trailer. *Either way, he needs a good woman in his life*—previously sensing his desire for companionship.

The pressure rolled off her shoulders as she entered the cab of Haze's truck, grateful for an incredible end to the season. She rolled down the window, waved, then blew a kiss to the few still conversing or wrapping up. They waved and returned smiles, yelling, "Bye Grace, bye Matt!"—who were both ready to be done with long cold days, working at the farm and market. It was time to wind down even though she knew she'd be aching to get back to it all, come spring—she hadn't had one week off when Cray called with an offer.

"Hey, I was invited to house sit for Local Sprouts. I'll be staying in their hurt, caring for the greenhouses near Matt's place, want to join me? There's a nice wage involved."

"That sounds great. How long?" she asked.

"Three months." he said and Grace's eyes perked up to the cushy opportunity. "We'll watch over the property and greenhouses all winter," he added.

The idea of staying warm and working in the soil all winter was a hands down, 'yes!' for her.

"I'm sold!" she said, ready to go. "But, I won't take a dime. This will be my winter 'service project.'"

"Perfect." Cray said, "it'll be mine too."

"She loved spending her winter planting, warm and barefoot, playing with nature—soaking in the natural, cedar hot tub every night, even on the coldest days. She and Cray were joined at the hip, getting pretty close and intimate. He'd blown her away by proposing to her on her birthday, while on a hike in the South Hills. They were up at Ross Falls, where he pretended to slip on the waterfalls' frozen plunge pool, dropping to one knee—he pulled out a sparkly, one-carat diamond on a thin, white gold band.

"Grace, would you be my beautiful bride?" His eyes were staring intently into hers.

"Her heart was shocked and her first response was an unsure, *"Nooo…"*—then a quick, "Yes." He *was* a great option for a partner, *so, why not?*

He hugged and picked her up with excitement then told her how he'd planned the surprise as they walked back to the car. During a quiet moment on their drive back to the yurt, she adjusted the ring, thinking, *I assumed we'd date but get married? Am I ready for that?* Though headed on her new path, she didn't want to rush into wedding plans yet—and they didn't.

The following February, after their hurt stay, Cray moved with her in Twin and it was already time to prepare Matt's garden. Even though she had little time in between gardening gigs, she was ready to get going, and the months flew by as the market came upon them. She looked forward to sharing her engagement with her market pals. Vendors and customers came up one by one for hugs and hello's as always.

Matt would interrupt, saying, "—Look at her new rock!"

They'd glance and she'd show her ring as they continued with; "Congratulations, when's the wedding?" and "beautiful ring…" "How did he pop the question?"

She'd answer happily and the attention stayed steady, not dying down throughout the day. When River crossed the road towards her, the excitement built rapidly. She was ready to burst.

"¡Hola, amiga!" he said with a confident smile.

"¡Hola, amigo!" Her nerves flushed throughout her

body, anxious to show him her ring.

"You learn Spanish like you wanted?" he asked.

"Yes, I did my Rosetta Stone," she responded, able to cross it off her "To Do List," "but I didn't become fluent like I'd hoped. I was busy working in a greenhouse most of the winter with Cray." she said with a big grin, slowly bringing her left hand up—when his enthusiasm completely dissipated.

Confused, he looked as if he were thinking, *What am I looking at?* Then paused, realizing what it was and took a noticeable swallow, shocked rather than excited.

"When's the date?" he asked, trying to sound cheerful.

Not knowing how to react, she sheepishly put the last bunch of radishes in the display basket while her stomach turned.

"We don't have a date yet…" she said, thinking, *did I hit a soft spot? A wound that aches badly, or was it something he'd wanted for himself?* She affectionately asked, "What did *you* do this winter…?" Knowing what his reply would be.

"Skied 100 days," he said, changing his mood.

"Awesome! How are your boys and your parents? Her voice grew perkier.

"He replied with a short, "All good, Grace." As though he'd wanted to get away quickly.

"Did you make any new pottery creations?" she asked, trying to distract him from the awkwardness.

"Come see when you have a minute," he said before turning away.

"Will do." she said.

"Congratulations, Grace!" he said as he walked off. "Wow, big new adventures."

"Thanks, River… have a great market." she said, continuing her chores while her stomach squeezed harder as he entered his booth—curious as to why he'd responded that way.

Grace decided to respect his space the rest of the season, smiling and waving from afar. She noticed one day, he was barefoot too and thought it was cute and odd for an older man but she didn't allow it to strike up a conversation, letting him be. They even went without a *goodbye* on the last day of the season.

* * *

The following summer, Grace worked her last market mid way through the season. She and Cray wanted to focus on riding bikes, climbing, and working towards common goals, together. They peddled 450 miles around Eastern Idaho, along the Teton Mountain Range, down to Lava Hot Springs and back up. She put 1,000 miles on her bike that summer which is something she had always wanted to do—ride her bike for miles, exploring Idaho's countryside via two wheels in the fresh air with all the time in the world. That's exactly what they did. The ride enhanced her love for her beautiful, Idaho home.

# 3

# Moon Shadow

2014

Though it'd been nearly two years since their yurt stay and proposal, Grace and Cray stayed connected with the community near Local Sprouts. They'd bonded and made close friends with those who'd helped in the greenhouses. They were often invited to communal dinners and asked to join in on neighborhood projects. Gretchen, a widowed woman from Australia had befriended Grace and asked them if they'd be interested in building a yurt on her property, along the river. They would watch over her place while Gretchen was in New Mexico half the year and would have the opportunity to grow whatever they wanted in their own garden.

They thought it over for a couple weeks and decided to go for it, despite there being no geothermal water to keep them warm, they would have to get a wood-burning stove instead. They thought that would work and picked out a beautiful spot on the hillside, overlooking the river. Grace was in love with the breathtaking view, impatient for the following summer when they planned to level the ground for their 400 square-foot yurt.

It had glass windows, arranged to observe the spectacular Snake River and the surrounding nature scene. Most of their year was spent preparing for their move that fall.

While pouring the foundation, Grace received word that her grandfather, who lived in Twin Falls, was passing.

Her grandparents' place was her home during Jr. High and a family hub where 26 cousins, aunts and uncles gathered periodically. Grandpa built the two-story, country style house, using his bare hands and reclaimed materials with the help of his three young sons and never took out a loan on the place.

Her grandma passed 5 years prior, right after her grandfather suffered a stroke, leaving his stomach half-paralyzed—his body didn't process food well anymore and the tough ol' bugger quit eating... and he had been a hearty eater! She remembered visiting him in his garden with her dad when he pulled an onion from the ground. He wiped it on his blue, full-body coveralls and took a bite out of it—raw, like an apple. He was a legendary man from her perspective as a young teen, watching sulfur juices drip from his wrinkly chin as he leaned on his trusty shovel.

Now, he was ready to shut down his system, wanting to be with his bride, once again.

* * *

Grace thought of all their memories as she drove home and down their long lane, passing through the trees—giving welcome shade on the hot, fall evening—She parked next to his rose garden, grabbed the tiny bottles of rose, frankincense and myrrh oil, knowing he'd enjoy the scent of the rose especially, hoping to relax and aid in his transformation. She walked to his room at the far end of the house, passing the double glass doors leading to the back deck, giving view to his beautifully pampered acreage, wondering, *will this be the last time I walk through their home?*

As she entered his room her aunts got up and said, "We'll give you some one-on-one time, Gracie. Take your time. He can't speak anymore but he can hear you just fine."

She nodded and lay behind him on the bed, pulled her oils out and put a few drops of rose gently on his temples. Then reached down to pull the covers from his feet for a rub. She was taken aback from his pale skin hanging from the bones of his legs.

She rubbed the oils on the bottoms of his feet then moved up to give him a leg rub when he attempted to pull the covers down, as he must've been chilled. She rubbed the oils on quickly then covered him up and leaned in to spoon him, holding her hand to the side of his face and whispered what came to her.

"The earth is grateful for your every step on her surface. For the legacy you've created and all you've done for the people within your life. You cared for her land, for your family..." She paused as her eyes teared up. "I am grateful for all you have taught me about gardening, for showing me that being available to family makes for a strong character... and how to be tenacious. I love you with all my heart." Her voice cracked, allowing tears to run off her face, "Thank you for my family! Tell Grandma hi for me."

He reached over his head and squeezed her hand, holding on as Grace let out muffled whimpers. Her face swelled with dampened emotions.

She sat next to him every day, alongside the rotating relatives and one quiet night, she put on his worn dress boots —5 sizes too big. They immediately grounded her in comfort, sitting next to him alone. Her sparkly engagement ring flickered center stage in the dim room. She twisted it back and forth on her finger, wondering if Cray was the one she'd be next to when she passed?

*I can't see him,* she thought, envisioning herself passing and squeezed her grandfather's limp hand, "I hope to see *you* again, gramps."

Even though his body held strong, she'd grown exhausted, spending every night with him that week. She'd rested her head next to his and played, "Always" by Patsy Cline on her iPod. It was the song he sang to Grandma at her funeral.

As soon as Patsy sang, he said, "Mama... mamma" with a scruffy dry voice. The moment touched her heart, tearing up, knowing he'd be leaving soon and held his hand until 11 PM, depleted.

A dream of her grandfather's face woke her in the middle of the night. He was pale, hovering in the darkness with his mouth wide open and let out a long, loud exhale, rousing her from a deep sleep.

*That was his last breath,* she thought, knowing he'd move on. Tears welled in her eyes as she whispered, "I love you, Grandpa." from her bed then snuggled closer into Cray.

When she woke, there was a text from her dad who'd been with Grandpa all night.

*Pops took his last breath at 1 AM.*

Cray could tell what the text had said by her reaction and embraced her as she let out her emotions in the crook of his neck.

* * *

Big transitions were in the air as she looked forward to their new beginning along the canyon's edge. The continuous sounds of the waterfall from the opposing cliff, calmed her grief-filled emotions as she released into the river, gazing at its forever flow.

Fall was in full swing and there was a slight invasion of spiders inside that worsened as the trees lost their leaves. The outside temperature dropped below freezing and they weren't able to get the yurt above 40-45 degrees with the wood burning stove, but Cray had been working out a plan to get geothermal water runoff from the neighbors—once Gretchen came home.

Having hot water flow through the pipes inside the floor would help raise the temperatures into the high 50s.

Despite the cooling weather, Grace relished harmonizing with the rhythms of nature; she'd developed an ability to decipher between the sounds of ducks and geese as they constantly flew over the yurt. She missed them after they migrated south for winter and while the nights grew colder, the owls drew closer into the trees above, their light hooting often helped her drift to sleep.

Every night, she observed the changing phases of the moon, peeking over the canyon rim—even coming across a surprise lunar eclipse one night while unable to sleep. Nature was her world as she walked along the canyon, down the road, and sat near the river bank. She took canoe rides with friends and participated in outdoor get-togethers while sharing meals around the fire.

The following spring, her friend and Matt's field manager, came down and plowed a space for a beautiful garden on the hillside, in front of the yurt. She hand-pulled all the tall grass out of the dirt and put up a wire fence to keep the deer and neighborhood dogs from running through. It was an enjoyable task, shaping all the vegetable rows and laying bark for walkways. When the weather was warmer, she planted an array of seeds and didn't mind the tedious job of weeding by hand; it was therapeutic. The task nurtured her spirit, methodically plucking each weed. Whatever chore the garden craved, she loved satiating that need. Her heart was at peace being in that uplifting space, basking in the sun, listening to the sounds of the water's flow, and spotting the wildlife coming out around her. The most delightful scene was the swans with their graceful white appearance, slowly floating on the water for hours—without a care in the world. She thought, *that's exactly what I'd be doing if I were a swan… floating freely in the cool waters.*

Their like-minded friends in the area made a point to celebrate nature together. The men gathered on the full moon, and the women met every new moon. Grace looked forward to these get-togethers every month. One woman would start by sharing the current astrological state of the moon and what that meant. She found it fascinating how well it resonated with her mental and emotional state. It was usually a good conversation starter for the group, and incorporating the heavenly energies was enchanting.

During one new moon function, Gretchen brought out a self-help book called *The Dark Side of the Light Chasers.* After giving a brief description of the book, she suggested they all read it, planning to gather and discuss it that coming fall. Grace listened to it on audio book and was immediately captivated. She honored the process of diving deep into her inner world, to find meaning and believed it was healthy.

She engaged in all the guided exercises, giving her significant insights into her soul's desires. It also showed some areas that needed tending to.

In one exercise, she was directed to find her trigger word—a word that made her uncomfortable, as the author read a list of descriptive words. She found the word that caused tension in her upper body: "ugly." After finding this word, she paused and glanced down at herself, lying on the bed on her favorite teal, floral blanket—relishing the simple, beautiful life that was everything she and Cray had planned. She gratefully noticed how grounded and content she was—as to check herself, making sure she was ready for this... "soul work." Her body vibrated in anticipation. A sign to continue.

Her desire to submerge herself, deep within, was a step in the right direction. She tiptoed into the dark waters of her innermost self, open to trusting whatever was luring her. She gazed out the window to the budding tree branches that coddled their yurt, when the mood softly shifted, catching her attention as a well-intentioned invitation urged her into a sacred space. It was apparent she'd tapped into a dynamic vortex that would aid in evolving her spirit. This was possibly the reason she'd desired closeness to nature in the first place.

*Did she want to be nearer to earth's magnet, having perceived this on the horizon?* Earth grounded her in its energy before this natural metamorphosis—as a caterpillar prepares its cocoon.

*The time for soul growth is now,* she thought. The sentiment was... significant.

As she focused on her inner "ugly," her mind brought a visualized figure of herself into the room. She was gray, but the environment of the yurt stayed sunny, comfortable, and safe. This 'self' was: afraid, alone, skinny with damp looking skin, thin patches of long, oily hair fell in her face as she was pushed along the wall of the yurt, frightened and fragile. This soul part had been unloved, abandoned, even hated, and left in darkness. She was surprised by this image and had much compassion for her as she required Grace's attention. She was determined to find a way to heal this unforgettable—unpleasant wound.

The meaning of the word, "ugly" was irrelevant when the natural question of vanity came up. The word was simply used as a guide in conjuring this vastly, disabled part of herself. A manifestation rising from constant: "self-judgment, low self-esteem, the persistent putting "self" down, the belief in others' insults and the feeling of not being... "good enough." It was apparent she'd been rough on herself, which created this 'dark' side.

Just then, opposing thoughts arose of; how proud she was of her life's accomplished dreams and goals. Her mind's eye flash flickered these successes, while this tattered self was a forgotten—hushed whisper, coming straight from within. It wanted Grace to attend to her and she sensed a helping hand from spirit—encouraging her to incorporate her, moving forward. Grateful for the image, she promised to keep this "self" at the surface of her heart and a spark of intentional healing opened her up.

Standing with confidence, glancing at her reflection in the window... her established self, vowed to integrate this shadow that'd expressed herself so bravely.

"Yes! No matter what," she said aloud, "I will pursue this desire to heal myself—I'll trust this pull from within and consider my shadow often." She was empowered by her willingness to accept whatever unfolded, without trying to change or control the outcome.

The universe listened and from that moment, life changed. Spirit began to unfold an important path and what had been securely stable, crumbled… piece by piece.

# 4

# A Necessary Storm

2015

Grace was inspired by a little story that came to her often while sitting in her garden. She had a deep desire to write it out even though she'd never written a story before. It kept returning to her and she decided to put pen to paper—to bring it into the physical world. She dove into it, as it was ready and waiting for her. She'd get lost in the story with the boy;

It was about a woman who lived in a tiny shack on Ritter Island, (an actual island that Grace had visited. It was a good eight miles downstream from the yurt, past the blue waters of Box Canyon, another place she and Cray had gone on adventures—The water came out a striking blue, as though someone had dumped blue food coloring in the water.) The woman character was ill and slept a lot due to her illness. During these *long periods of sleep,* she lived another life, a life that was hers. One with no illness, no physical roadblocks, and one where she could be anywhere with anyone at any time.

She experienced exactly what her heart wanted, without disapproval or physical weakness, sorrows, or having to work for a paycheck.

It was a beautiful world she found in these dreams. They naturally added their spark to her moments of rest. When awake and alone, she wrote her dreams in a yellow spiral notebook and hoped to compose a story, integrating her dreams.

Her eleven-year-old son loved her dearly and took care of her. He always looked forward to when she woke, she'd often have a red balloon blown up, waiting for him when he came home.

He always snuck the notebooks from her nightstand to read. He used her dreams as a baseline for imaginative play outside, making him closer to her as she slept. He narrated the story, taking the reader on his adventures along the river and on the magical island with his mom. His best friend was a little owl that lived on the ridge beam at the highest point in the old, two-story barn. The island once raised dairy cows, and the old dairy buildings were still there, a perfect playground.

This story was so easy to tap into, like it was a life she'd already lived. Images would come so freely and often. She wanted to spend all her time in the story. It had a life of its own and would flow into her mind as a complete scene, like a movie. She enjoyed that life and immersed herself in her writing, taking her notebook out to her garden, allowing nature to inspire her. Her pain seemed to lessen while she wrote, which she was grateful for—indicating she was focusing on the right thing, but she kept getting interrupted by images that tampered with her story's flow—pictures of herself dancing, draped in elk hide, holding short antlers in her hands that she would raise to her head while spinning to the music.

What was this elk she was so curious about? It got to the point where every time she went to write, the elk wouldn't leave the landscape of her imagination.

This image of the dance kept urging her to bring it into reality. She couldn't ignore the desire any longer and wanted to see what would happen in the universe if she performed it. Consumed by the idea, she shared the dance with the women at their next new moon gathering. She was surprised to see Gretchen there—she must have come back that day.

When Grace presented the idea, saying they could all choose their animal and dance together, she wanted it to be free spirited and primal, but many women did not support the idea. Gretchen seemed to speak for the rest of them in a way that seemed a more fierce side of her. Grace hadn't witnessed this inside of her before.

"They don't want to dance in front of others, Grace. Dancing, covered in animal hide? It's risqué!"

Grace explained she had no ill intentions with the dance; it was more of an experiment to see how they bonded together, embracing or calling upon spirit animals to see what happened.

One woman disagreed with Gretchen and liked the idea, but she didn't encourage it—seeing that it wasn't going anywhere with the group. All Grace wanted was to summon the energy together, perform a spiritual and earthy dance for themselves like all creative manifestations.

Gretchen's response made her feel dumb for even bringing it up. There was something odd going on between the two of them but she didn't know what.

Grace had her animal dance outfit all created in her mind and the music figured out, but it was a no go. Suddenly, her supportive community seemed not so supportive and she had the sense she'd raised her hand in class, thinking she had the right answer to a creative question, but was laughed at as though she were immature—her ideas were unwelcome. She strived to be loved and accepted for who she was and what she wanted to express. She wished for the women's respect and thought it would be deeply connecting, hoping for that type of bond with a soul group. But she decided to forget the dance and focus on goals that wouldn't cause a ruckus, like her garden and writing.

When she gave up on the dance, the pain in her leg came back—full force. She didn't know what was going on, but she hadn't done anything physical to aggravate it.

Grace told Cray about the elk dance. He thought it was a great idea and what a bummer she'd been turned down.

She then told him about her "ugly" soul part that

wanted her attention and he encouraged her to explore that deeper. Then he talked to her about a conversation he'd had with Gretchen. She'd told them to look for hot water runoff while she was away, and now that Cray found the perfect opportunity, Gretchen didn't want to have it piped across her property. He asked Grace to casually bring it up with her. She said she would when the time was right.

The following day, she saw Gretchen and tried to find the right moment to bring up the geothermal water connection. But Gretchen was upset about her personal life, so she decided to listen to her problems and try to help. They were in front of her house talking, facing the yurt, and a friendly neighbor pulled up in his truck. He was catching up with both of them as usual, being a supportive pal who helped everyone in the neighborhood.

They were all having a friendly chat when Gretchen started talking about Grace and Cray like Grace wasn't even there.

Out of nowhere, Gretchen said, "They never leave!" she held her palm out towards the yurt and glanced over to it. "You would think they would have somewhere to go..." as she held an annoyed and nearly disgusted look on her face.

The neighbor glanced at Grace, not saying anything but giving her a sideways look as to say, "Is she talking about you guys in front of you?" Grace met his look and returned the confused glance. Then Gretchen looked straight at Grace.

"Don't you ever want to go on vacation and get away?"

she asked with an agitated tone, "You're always here!"

Grace just looked at Gretchen's unattractive expression, stunned. Wondering why it mattered to her anyway and stood there, knowing that she didn't have to defend herself about this. Although she was confused as to why Gretchen was so triggered by them spending most of their time at home. She glanced back at their friend who did a shoulder shrug like, "I don't know what's going on" as he shook his head and looked down. He didn't engage, just laughed it off.

Grace thought, *Okay, I'll have to talk with her later. She's probably having a hard day.* And they all moved on with brief communications on other topics.

On another occasion, she attempted to speak with Gretchen but the fundraiser for a community school up in Buhl they'd been working on, came up. The neighborhood had been participating and supporting it in any way they could. Grace made bright, catchy signs to inform the town of the fundraiser and asked Matt Haze to donate dry beans and meat for chili they would make for everyone. Of course, he donated.

But when she brought it up with Gretchen, she said in an annoyed tone and furrowed brow, "I've done all the work for this fundraiser, anyway… It's a lot of work!"

Grace thought of all the hands involved in the fundraising event as she looked at Gretchen's grumpy face and couldn't talk or swallow. She stood there watching Gretchen blow out her inner flame and was completely still in silence while the smoke blew away slowly. Gretchen continued on about the hard work while Grace did what she could to escape the moment internally as she stood there. She didn't know how to help her friend. Maybe she had regretted inviting them to build a yurt on her property? They had both been respectful, helpful, and clean, and they paid her rent on time.

Again, Grace finished their less-than-enjoyable conversation and walked back to the yurt with tender emotions. Her leg throbbed in pain that worsened. She kept trying to help Gretchen as often as she could, bringing in her groceries, helping her with yard work, and being there for her. She would do anything to try and lift the weight off her friends shoulders, but she couldn't help her—feeling she had to give all of herself for the friendship. It made her see that she'd put Gretchen on a pedestal, and rightfully so. She looked up to her and loved their friendship, but recognized the pedestal was unhealthy for their bond.

Grace had been sitting on a scale, and every time she showed up for her friend she found a way to lower herself on the scales for Gretchen to know she loved her, but she realized that wasn't love. Every time Gretchen could find a way to put herself on top, she did. Grace allowed it in the beginning, but now she noticed that during conversations she would open up, be kind and vulnerable to be supportive of Gretchen. It was as though Gretchen noticed Grace's lack of boundaries and would take advantage of her kindness. Grace imagined that flame burning inside her chest, and Gretchen would blow it out every time with the simplest of comments.

When the summer was coming to an end, Grace remembered how the cold made her body tense all last winter. Having this pain, she knew she had to ask Gretchen about getting hot water piped into the yurt like Cray had asked—it had been Gretchen's initial intention. So, she summoned the courage for the conversation.

After the new moon gathering at Gretchen's house, while there was still one other woman there—who also knew the plan of getting hot water to their yurt… Grace decided this would be the perfect time to bring it up with her; the neighbor might even buffer the conversation.

"Hey, Cray told me the neighbor to the south would happily allow us to pipe into their geothermal runoff for the yurt." Grace said, "He said, 'It's just going into the river, why not get more use from it first?'"

Gretchen gave a slight, deep laugh then said, "Why would I need hot water? I have a hot tub, and it's not that expensive to heat." She looked at her coldly and directly.

"Didn't you have intentions to allow us to pipe runoff to the yurt?" Grace asked as she shuddered with nerves. "We'd be able to keep the yurt warmer during the winter and be able to have running water in the kitchen!" She tried to positively remind her.

The neighbor walked off to the bathroom, likely to avoid getting involved and Gretchen looked at her again.

"I don't need hot water!" she said firmly and turned to Grace then finished with, "Oh, I hired Dane." A man Grace had opened up to Gretchen about, telling her how he'd assaulted her. "He will be helping me with yard and house work during the week."

Grace took a deep breath, knowing that was the last straw. The other straws didn't matter; it was the fact there were too many straws... and to *keep water from them?* Grace slipped out after saying goodnight to the two ladies and walked to the yurt, crying instead of sticking up for herself on the spot. She had that inner "ugly" creep up, and her leg pain intensified.

She thought, *no more keeping the peace just to keep the peace.* She couldn't tip the scales in her friend's favor anymore—she mattered to herself enough to stop it and knew she had to take Gretchen down from the pedestal that she had put her on. It wasn't doing either of them any good and she knocked her down by promising to herself to no longer keep being the *nice* girl or "turning the other cheek" with Gretchen.

Cray came home that night and told Grace that Gretchen discussed his hourly wage with his boss, telling him that he shouldn't start him off on such a high amount. Grace remembered telling Gretchen that Cray's new boss had been *so* generous to start him at such a respectful rate. Gretchen, who knew his boss, told him that it was *unfair* to his other workers that Cray started at such a high wage. His boss told Gretchen that it was none of her business.

This news made Grace even more frustrated. *Why would she care what Cray made, and why would she talk to his boss and try to get him to lower his wages? How ridiculous.* Her pain turned into aggression and anger. This wasn't like her.

She discontinued being helpful to Gretchen—not offering any kind of service or attention. She would notice when Gretchen came home from the store with a load of groceries and would not offer assistance, she would ignore the urge to help out when Gretchen was out raking leaves, and she stopped taking her garbage can to the end of the lane for her.

She wanted to stand up for herself and stop this rudeness. She wrote an angry note to her but threw it away and made a toned-down version. This *standing up* for herself was something new to her, and she did it the best way she could. She sent her a message telling her how her actions and her choice of words within their conversations made Grace feel and how she made Cray feel small too. She used words like "power-hungry," and "controlling." Heavy words that would tip the scales back quickly.

Well, it was quick—fully out of character—and it spiraled their community into drama.

Grace knew very well what this type of message would do and the domino effect it would set in motion. She decided to stand her ground, regardless. She also imagined holding up an invisible shield in front of her so that she wouldn't be so vulnerable when she had to face Gretchen for being brutally honest in her note. Everything went downhill, but she somehow knew to hold strong through this growth. Her soul said, "'*Kay, here we go!*" as the tower came crashing down. She knew it had to ignite this journey.

The community was taking a step back, not knowing what was going on with Gretchen and them. Grace asked Cray to have a productive conversation with her out in the garden. She was planting a fall sowing of spinach seeds and he gladly joined her.

She needed to express the amped-up energy within her. She thought back to her desire for soul growth and mentioned all that had happened since her promise to herself to heal her dark, "ugly" side.

"Cray, I'm going on a spiritual journey," she said with a very serious look in her eyes. "Do you want to go on that journey with me?" she asked him, thinking he'd say yes.

"No," Cray said firmly, looking at her like he knew it was a deeper question about their relationship. And he walked into the yurt.

There was an intense understanding in the short, concise pow wow. She knew, they knew it was ending and he wasn't coming along on her journey. She was full of conviction, willing to change course—yet not ready. Something was pulling her in a different direction, alone, calling her, summoning her, even though she'd just seemed to land at home.

Cray had always been supportive of all Grace brought to his attention. Not this time. And Grace knew Gretchen, the community, and Cray's desire to not join her new journey were roadblocks and stop signs, a way for spirit to guide her in a new direction. Nothing else needed to be said for now; she knew the energy between them was somewhat mutual. He knew that she was meant to move forward with this soul journey. She had the strength and didn't know where fate was taking her, but she knew it was worth following. There was an intensity beginning to boil within her.

Cray and Grace decided to take a break from it all: the community, yurt living, and each other. Grace went to California to stay with her mom and stepdad for November, and Cray stayed in Twin Falls to continue working. It was good for her to find refuge somewhere safe.

Her mom lived in a small logging town in Northern California on the Spanish Creek off Feather River. She spent a lot of time at the creek, all bundled up in the cold winter temperatures. She loved the cleansing qualities water had and how it was forever moving and changing, slowly taking what wasn't needed away. Grace allowed herself space to detox her soul and spirit. Cray came to visit for Thanksgiving. They talked a lot, and Grace was honest with him.

Their conversation ended with her saying, "Cray, I feel that life is taking me on a new journey and I'm going to go alone. I have thought a lot about us, and when I do, I see a planet coming by, picking me up, and taking me to another planet, alone." With a brave breath in, she continued by saying, "I'm choosing to move on."

Sitting across from her, Cray said, "I understand, but I still want to be with you, Grace."

She knew what he was saying was his truth, but she couldn't explain why she felt a strong magnetic pull towards something she couldn't quite see.

.

# 5

# Elk Trail

Late winter, early spring 2016

Cray went back to Twin Falls and Grace followed a week later. They were both disheartened after their split, but she knew to listen to her heart—which was hinting to move forward, and she gave back the beautiful ring Cray had given her. He was supportive, and she had a hunch that he was to embark on a journey of his own. Whether or not he wanted to see it as beginning a new path or not was up to him.

Her father's family invited her to live at the homestead. She took them up on their offer and moved into the basement of her grandparents' home. After gramps passed, renters had moved in upstairs. The downstairs was separate from the rest of the house. When she moved in it was full of her grandparents' belongings, so she put her energy into cleaning it out. It was healthier for her to be actively doing something rather than sitting in self-pity. Her uncle and cousins came to haul most of the furniture out and delivered it to donation centers. They also put the kitchen from the yurt into the utility room so that she could have a kitchen. She was so grateful for their help.

Grace stayed to herself mostly, full-on hermit mode, not wanting to talk with others about the sudden life changes. She was worn out with repetitive emotions that weren't so helpful, and it was good for her to invest her time in creating a clean space for her to begin again. She put her story away and turned to a daily journal to help her cleanse and process all the changes. A majority of her time was spent being quiet, close to the earth. It was emotionally healing for her to go on walks, all bundled up, down at Auger Falls. Which was her favorite part of the Snake River, just a couple miles west of the Perrine Bridge where there was a walk or bike trail and a closed-to-traffic road. She was safe to roam and venture into the wide-open canyon in the thick of the sagebrush, dry grass, and boulders.

One day she made it to the edge of the river and watched its treacherous, boiling rapids below and peered around to see if anyone was there. When the coast was clear, she loudly asked the water, "*Where's my story?*"—Okay, maybe she *demanded* her story. She paused to wait for some type of response. Nothing came. "*What's my mission… Where are you taking me?*" she asked, not caring if anyone had heard or seen her.

She experienced an opening sensation. It seemed as though the spirit of the place had all eyes on her. She knew to trust and keep trusting even when she found it difficult to do so through the intense adjustments. She thought, *The universe is wise.* She had no doubts in trusting it, and her heart that was connected with it, even when she felt tattered by change and often wondered if she'd handled everything back at the yurt and Cray in the best way, but she felt forgiven by this greater spirit she looked up to; it was her that needed to forgive herself.

Though her walks were emotionally strengthening, they weren't physically comfortable, and she found it hard to walk far.

After a while, she changed things up and started walking at Rock Creek Park. This was another nature escape she'd found herself frequenting since she was in high school. This park allowed her to drive right next to the creek so she didn't have to bear the pain of walking so much. She watched the current flow while she communed with it, and the water listened, as always. This time, she was filled with sorrow, focused on the immense emotions caused by her decision to *follow her soul.* This was a time when her trust in the universe was wavering. She spent her nights and days alone, wondering what the future would bring, knowing that one day she'd understand what this was all for and to be grateful to the universe for changing her course. But for now, it was hard to see the reason for it all. She noticed how the outer world mirrored her gloomy inner world with its gray, cold sky and dead foliage.

She naturally strayed off the path, through the Russian olive trees and the snow-toppled long grass, towards the creek. She kept her eyes down, watching her every step as she neared the stream. When she glanced up to see where she was going, her eyes fell upon a beautiful doe standing still, across the creek. This deer encounter immediately nudged at the idea of the elk dance.

Grace stopped in her tracks and was in awe of the stunning creature that stood before her. The doe was looking at her, making sure she was not a threat. Grace held her stance and soaked in the way those striking black eyes were gazing in her direction. Such long, lush eyelashes and tall, wide ears topped with black hair that pointed upward. Grace followed her sturdy neck and torso down to her thin nimble legs that held her up so stoically. She was enveloped with true beauty, causing tears to swell in her eyes. She knew then that she wanted the doe as her spirit animal, the deer that looked into her soul without judgment, something she missed about how she looked at herself and how the world looked at her. The spirit of this elegant creature warmed her heart and made the outer environment reverent.

She whispered, "Thank you, thank you" to the doe as she watched her chew grass and slowly move her way through the trees.

*This deer… and the elk…* Grace thought. *Again, why?* Whatever the reason was, Grace thought she would plan to do the dance herself one day and see what would come of it. For now, she wanted to do something different for herself, get out of her rut, get out of town, and do something other than walking alone in nature and journaling. She wanted to stop wondering if she'd made the right choices—her heart kept saying she had.

One day Matt Haze called her out of the blue, inviting her to take his place in a meeting in Hailey. There would be a guest speaker for a handful of select market vendors followed by a public talk, and he couldn't go. She thought that was a perfect way to brighten her days and be socially proactive—she jumped at the chance. In the meantime, she decided to have her half-acre garden the coming spring and planned on selling all the veggies at the Twin Falls farmers market. She more than enjoyed connecting to the earth, and the market was home to her. The moment she started her first plants in little containers, her energy changed for the better.

When the market meeting came around, Grace offered to drive two farmer friends that lived near Matt who were also going. Grace was light and airy with excitement for the special outing. When they got there, it was a small, private meeting with the guest speaker for a select group of market vendors. She loved the enthusiasm and how knowledgeable the speaker was. He mentioned that market gardeners should be at home tending to their gardens and not out at the farmers markets, they should have an "on-farm sale day" or every day where the customer comes to them. That would be the ultimate route Grace would shoot for one day; she could imagine herself with her sale booth in the side yard. It made sense to her to work on her garden in between sales, maybe next year?

She was looking forward to having her garden and was

pumped to encourage the local organic food movement.

The public talk was in Ketchum, off the Main Street. As she drove in she could feel the excitement that she always got when she and Matt were preparing for the Ketchum market —home away from home.

They had a few hours to spare before the main talk, so they shared a bite of food and great conversations at a local restaurant. She loved being up there with the people, the place, the energy—she cherished it. Grace sensed a fresh breath of life, getting back up to Sun Valley.

Grace and her buddies left the restaurant and got in line for the talk. They stood outside, and it was very cold. She saw many market friends and was full of joy. It was nice to have a smile on her face again. She spotted a tall man with white hair under a cap.

"River!" she shouted as he walked by.

She stopped him and gave him a hug.

"River, this is Mark and Keegan," Grace said, but he seemed very cold and standoffish, almost rude to her acquaintances.

He barely acknowledged them when he said, "Hi," without looking at them. She thought that wasn't like him. He looked older and a bit chubbier than he had last time she saw him, three summers ago.

He quickly said, "Good seeing you, Grace." Then he walked off in an agitated hurry.

She quickly apologized to her friends for him as the line

finally started moving. Once they made it inside to find seats, she passed River as they went to sit down. She felt like he was wanting her attention, but from the way he was short with her outside, she decided to leave him be.

The talk was inspiring and epic as expected, and when it was over, she walked behind the slow-moving crowd. But before she walked out, she noticed River looking in her direction. She thought if he wanted to talk he would come to talk with her, so she continued walking out and left—meeting her friends outside. They drove back to Buhl and said good night. She waited in the driveway until they were inside. As they waved her goodnight, she received a text message. Grace grabbed her phone before driving home.

It said, *Hey, Grace, missed being able to chat and catch up with you tonight. Wasn't the guest speaker amazing? He should become president.*

*Yes, it was very inspirational!*
-send-
*Sorry, forgive me. I'm not sure who I'm talking with.*

*River here,* he responded.

*Oh River, how's it going? How did you get my number?* she asked.

*From the market manager. She gave it to me a couple of summers back and said you wanted to bring Kai up to see my horses. Remember, I offered you guys horse rides?* he said.

*Oh, yeah. We wanted to... How are the horses?* she asked.

*No horses now, they're all down south for the winter. There's too much snow for them now. But there's this guy, hanging out in the barn eating my horse hay.* He replied.

Up popped a photo of a striking elk bull, walking through the snow towards the barn. Grace nearly dropped her phone, still sitting in her buddies' driveway. A huge smirk streaked across her face. *River Billings just texted me a photo of an elk? This is too much of a coincidence,* she thought. Her stomach was suddenly warm and elated, but she wasn't about to tell him of her elk. She took a minute to respond, though.

Grace smiled and typed, *How beautiful and majestic! My goodness, there's so much snow up there right now.*

*Yeah. Well, I'd invite you up to see the horses, but maybe in the summer. How's life down south?* he asked.

*It's good.* She said, *I'm going to have a market garden. Half an acre, lots of veggies to sell at the Twin Falls farmers market, this summer.*

*I always knew you'd do that one day. Good for you, Grace! Well, keep in touch. It was good to see you tonight,* River said.

*Hey, you too,* she responded cheerfully.

The next day, Grace focused on organizing her seed packets. She planned out where all the seeds were to be planted and when, then she started her artichokes, onions, and leeks in tiny pots next to the double sliding glass window. She had a new, upbeat attitude and was determined that things would turn around for her. She got a job at her favorite juice shop, next to her favorite local health food shop. She was a magnet for veggies; where there were veggies there she was, consuming them.

River checked in on her a few weeks later and asked how the vegetable starts were going.

*Hey River, veggies are doing good! Artichokes are nearly 2 inches tall and I bought some biodegradable black mulch to put on the beds when the time comes,* she said.

They had a mini conversation back and forth until he finally asked, *Would you mind if we talk over the phone? I can't text that fast!*

*Sure,* she texted, snickering.

They talked for a bit, and she ended up telling him about Cray and the yurt and that she was now living at her grandparents'. He told her he had no idea, and then he asked if she'd like to come up and go for a walk someday. She said yes, thinking it would be nice to have some good company.

"Really?" he asked.

"Yes." She didn't want to say she hadn't been out and about with friends lately, or that she'd been a "hermit" as she was focused on herself and getting better.

She went up the following weekend for a walk in the sun and snow. He lived past Ketchum, about 45 minutes west, into the Stanley hills. He directed her to a local park in town, told her she could park there and he'd be waiting in his truck. After driving nearly three hours, she made it to the park around 1 PM, not a cloud in the sky with about 4 feet of snow everywhere but the roads. As she was pulling up to the park the sun was so bright over the mountain ridge, its rays were magically shining straight down onto River.

She thought, *come on! Really?* He was sitting tall on the flatbed truck with his recognizable straight posture, his blue puffy coat, and his cap.

She pulled up next to him, hopped out—thrilled to hang out with him, and gave him a quick hug before they jumped into his truck to head to his place, where he said a groomed trail-head started. They were making small talk when they came up to a turn into his neighborhood with a bronze sculpture of an elk standing tall at the entrance of the road. As they turned she peered over to the street sign that read, *Elk Trail Rd.* She had that sensation that she'd had down at Auger Falls, the one where all eyes were on her. A feeling that she was inside her own story or movie, and the world moved in such an orchestrated way with her.

She made a note of all the elk hints. Every step... first the elk photo, then the elk statue at the entrance of Elk Trail Rd. It was as though something was trying to make a statement to her.

There were a few houses in the area with lots of pastures in a quaint valley surrounded by tall hills. They made their way to his house, out on its own, buried by snow, a two-story, rustic, simple house with a barn and corral on the east side of the property. Grace adored it.

He parked the truck, and they both went inside for a warm cup of yerba mate tea.

"Is it okay if we take the dogs?" River asked.

"Of course," she said.

Then they headed out for a walk down the driveway and east into the hills. They talked about what had happened between her and Cray, about River's twin sons in Arizona, her garden, her future, his past, and the speaker from the talk, and they talked about the market and other ways of selling her harvests. It was good to have productive, adult conversations again.

She noticed on their walk that her left leg was feeling better. Maybe talking a few things out relieved some stress?

Whatever it was, it was nice to have some relief.

"We don't have to walk to Boise... let's get back," he said.

Grace was fine with that.

When they made it back to his place and went inside, he made soup and got out a healthy piece of bread. She enjoyed the meal as they talked about so many things. It was all intellectually stimulating, light, and helpful.

He received a phone call and went over to the other end of the room to answer it. He was talking with his hands, and the way he moved them made her feel weak in the knees. There was no hiding it from herself.

He got off the phone, plugged it into the stereo, and played the Americana station. She didn't listen to that sort of music but was enjoying it anyway.

"Well, after we put these dishes away, we should get you back to your car so you can head home before too late."

"Yes, that's probably a good idea."

They cleaned up, and she couldn't help but look around at all the pottery and plants growing up the side of the big windows, which let in the light from the setting sun. They talked while they cleaned 'till the sun went down.

"Okay, I better get you out of here! I'll go out and warm up the truck. Be right back," he said.

She grabbed her things, and soon he came back in, then they walked out the door together, facing the barn that was several yards away.

"There he is!" he said as he motioned ahead.

Grace looked towards the open barn and saw the upper body of a majestic elk with a large rack of antlers. He was magical looking in the moon's light, and the cold air seemed to glisten off of him as she watched his breath in the frigid air. She acknowledged him as if *he* were calling her. Her elk, guiding her to River. She whispered a quiet *thank you* to him from within her heart. Magic fluttered through her as they stood there admiring him. She noticed their breath in the cold air, twirling and mingling together above. River started walking to his truck, and Grace followed quietly and hopped in. It was nice and warm inside.

They didn't say much at first, and the radio was on low. He turned, passing the barn, and she watched the striking elk stand with such strength. The lights from the truck hit the snow just right, causing sparkles all around the snowscape. White magic glistened all around the moment while a quiet smile stretched across her face—realizing she *was* in a storybook.

They chatted lightly until they arrived at the parking lot where her car was waiting. He pulled next to it to say good night and hugged her. It lingered warmly and she was nervous. She wanted to ask him for a kiss—which was unlike her.

"Can I kiss you?" Grace asked kindly. She was surprised by herself, but she did.

He said, "Grace, I'm too old for you."

"Your age doesn't matter to me." Then she whispered

again, "Can I have a kiss?"

He looked straight ahead and nodded stubbornly. She sat up enough to reach up and over the center consul to kiss him and *oh, dear...* the instant heat that began to radiate inside was moving.

Her body lifted towards his side of the truck as her mouth uncontrollably responded with a pant of warm air through the kiss. He quickly pulled away, back into the back window, and faced his window in the opposite direction. She sat back slowly, thinking, *We didn't even get started. I must've been too pushy. Or I'm a bad kisser? Or he didn't like my panting? I couldn't control that.* She sat and looked at him, confused. He continued starting out his window.

She waited for a minute and asked for another kiss. He nodded, again looking ahead with a straight face. She went up, melting like butter internally as she kissed him, but he pulled back *again*. He couldn't do it. She slowly sat back in her seat.

"Okay... Thank you for the lovely walk and food! We should try for a walk again someday." she said.

"Yeah, thank you, Grace. It's been a pleasure," he said, looking at her.

She got out of the truck and into her car with an odd feeling. A feeling like she had done something wrong.

He rolled down his window and said, "Goodnight Grace, drive safe. I'll wait 'til your car warms up."

The way he looked at her was so interesting; he looked so deeply sad yet opened up.

"Okay," she said with confidence, even though she wasn't confident, feeling the rejection.

She got into her red Jetta and waited for a couple of minutes then pulled back and waved before she headed home. It was late, around 10 PM, and she had at least two and a half hours home. She was aroused. Somewhat in disbelief about it, but she was. There was no denying it.

While she drove away, she wondered what had happened… had she done something to make him feel uncomfortable?

She was almost through Ketchum when she received a text saying, *Are you okay with how we left things? Don't respond while driving, please!*

Grace pulled over when the speed limit went down 25 MPH and responded, *I guess. I don't know why you were pulling away. Was I doing something you didn't like?*

*No! You were doing all the things I DO like,* he replied.

*Oh, okay. Well, thank you and goodnight*, Grace said, somewhat confused.

*Goodnight. Let me know that you made it home,* River texted.

*I will.* And she got back on the road, headed home.

She made it home safely and hopped into bed after she let him know she made it with a short message of *Goodnight.*

*Night, Grace.*

# 6

## A Raspberry Kiss

Spring 2016

Grace was so excited but didn't know what to do. A week later, River texted, *What steps are you taking to prepare for the garden, the market, and all that?*

She replied, *Still nurturing the baby plants. About to prepare the garden space.*

*Brilliant,* he said.

Grace asked, *Would you like to meet or hang out soon?*

He said, *Yes, I'd go on a walk with you, down at Auger Falls. That's your favorite stroll down in your neck of the woods, right?*

*Yes. Let's plan on it,* she said.

He came down a month later and she bought them

roast beef sandwiches on sourdough from a local bakery to eat before their walk. She also got fresh raspberries to save for later. He thanked her after eating the sandwiches, and they went on a nice walk in the breezy spring weather.

She said, "River, I don't know if we will become a thing or not, but I want to tell you that I've always admired you and your strength. You are independent, kind, and caring, and you are grounded in yourself. You worked hard for your money and now you enjoy it. I want to be like that. Like you."

River stood taller and chuckled as he said, "I will do what I can to help guide you in that direction. I appreciate that."

Even though it was a bit chilly out, they had the goal of making it to the water's edge. She found a nice big rock and sat to soak in the sun, facing him. He stood directly in front of her, not quite leaning into her and the rock. She wanted to snuggle him, be close, feel close, and feel his warmth, but she sat back.

A middle-aged guy and his younger friend came riding by on their bikes, and the older guy said, "That's what you get to be with down here? All I've got is this dude." He continued riding, followed by a guy Grace's age.

River seemed to like that comment, but Grace felt a little embarrassed, mostly by how the man referred to her as an object.

Grace thought she might as well ask a bit of an embarrassing question while they were at it.

"Why did you react the way you did when I told you

that I was engaged years ago?" She wondered if he'd even remember what she was talking about.

"Grace, I remember it being difficult. I was shocked and I didn't realize that I'd even react that way. I thought that our friendship would change, once you were engaged," he said. "I'm sure that's why I pulled away so much."

He moved forward to be a bit closer, and she naturally leaned her head onto his chest, holding each other, basking in the sun while the wind blew around them.

After their embrace, they made it to the water's edge, to Grace's favorite spot, right at the first rapid of Auger Falls. A nice flat body of rock welcomed them to sit near the rapid. This area was where the water roared. Grace always saw this area as the heart of Twin Falls, a perfect place to sit and express her heart as she had done with herself many times.

A bit nervous, she decided to come right out and say what was making her anxious.

"I'm not opposed to dating an older man." she told River, "I'm drawn to your maturity, your confidence, and you seem to care about me in ways that men my age don't. I like that you've lived twice the life I have. That's something I'm drawn to… your wisdom."

They were sharing what was left of the raspberries as she spoke. She put a few in her mouth, and River lightly cradled her face in his big, warm hand and leaned in to kiss a wild raspberry, kiss. She couldn't help but melt into the moment, highly grateful that he ended her opening up to him with warm intimacy.

"Grace, I hear you. It's very nice to be thought of and looked at that way. Appreciated, you know. I wonder, though, is this not another Africa venture? Helping someone out in need?"

She looked up at him, curious. "I hadn't thought about it like that. Do you feel you're in need?"

He didn't answer; he just shrugged his shoulders.

She continued, "Let's just keep hanging out and see where we go?"

"Deal," River said.

# 7

## Moving Water

Spring 2016

Grace was thrilled that it was time to get the ground ready for planting. She braided her hair in a long side braid, put on her thick brown and teal plaid jacket, her baggy salmon corduroys—two sizes too big, and cowgirl boots, and she grabbed Gramps' yellow working gloves as she slid the glass door open and went out into the crisp, chilled air.

Out in the crisp air, she marked out half an acre in front of the house, beyond the front lawn and along the lane where the mature walnut, cherry, and peach trees stood. Knowing these would shade out her garden in full summer, she smartly planned to plant her shade-loving veggies below them. Next to them, she would have a mixed flower bed for fresh bouquets to display on her market tables or to simply enjoy while in the garden.

Ready to go, she walked back to the side shop, pushed the sliding door open, took her yellow leather gloves, and dusted off her grandfather's tractor. It was a little red diesel Massy Ferguson from the '80s. The sound of igniting the engine brought forth her grandfather's presence strongly. She backed it out, remembering all the rides as a little girl, sitting on the rear, side-wheel fenders. The smell of diesel exhaust, grease, and dirt enhanced the vividness of her fond memories. Putting the machine in gear, she drove it to the front of the field, all while flashes of her kid memories followed her—dangling little legs to the side of the tractor, bursts of summer sunlight glistened through the trees, a flash image of Gramps turning around to check on her and her little brother with a smile—and lit up her heart with warm feelings.

She worked the bare dirt, disking rows lining north-south for the ditch water to make its way down each row to quench the garden plants.

She loved being out in the soil, under the sun again, despite the windy, Idaho spring weather. She jumped off the parked tractor, pulling her gloves off to pick up a handful of loosened earth. She massaged it into her cold, bare hand while she gazed across the freshly worked field. She was excited for the season of nurturing her field full of garden veggies, knowing the work that lay ahead of her.

After her tractor work, she picked up a rake and groomed the garden rows flat in preparation for her seeds to make their new home for the rest of their days. As she groomed the level beds, her mind drifted off to River's raspberry kisses and sounds of the water roaring as they delved into an intimate connection between their lips. When she replayed their conversations, it seemed as though she was thinking of a bottle of red wine: aged, full of wisdom, strong inside, giving off hints of warm, sedated feelings.

He was full of experience. She liked how she could see herself surrendering and opening to him, embracing what they shared. She had premature plans of writing her book in his extra bedroom, upstairs. She could picture him down in his studio making pots, out capturing a beautiful Stanley landscape, or cooking some breakfast while she wrote next to the second-story window. The simple life. She imagined it and hoped for it.

Grace enjoyed spending all her free time out preparing the earth for her sprouted seedlings and seeds; she'd be ready when the time came to sow. Throughout the day she informed River about what she was up to, and he'd positively encourage her. It was nice not to feel alone in her big project, alone in general.

She came up with a farm name to refer to while at the market, "Our Roots," representing the roots of her family and her soon-to-be root vegetables.

She loved working in the garden, even after the sun went down. She was looking forward to the day she could be barefoot in the soil. She took a break to lay on the earth and talk with the moon, spilling her soul while she snacked on whole apples.

When she couldn't stand to be out in the cold garden, she went in and made creative, colorful signs for each veggie with space to chalk in a price and display on her market table. She ordered crates and boxes to organize her produce, a market pop-up tent, tables, burlap table cloths, a scale for weighing her produce, and a money box. She was all prepared for the market, well ahead of the game.

She was trying to be independent, strong, and solid in herself while nurturing her entrepreneurial spirit. It was good for her to be self-motivated and focused. That being said—she imagined River would come to help her at the market one day. They always stayed connected throughout their days, never going a day without saying goodnight around 10 PM. He was always such a great support and cheerleader for Grace. She needed that.

After a productive full day of work, Grace happily plopped on her bed, about to fall asleep fully clothed in garden gear when she received a text from River saying, *I'm out doing chores, changing the water for my horses. You're gonna help me with them tomorrow night.*

Grace said, *Will do! I'm getting excited about our dinner tomorrow night.*

*I am too,* he said.

*Night River,* she texted, ready to fall asleep.

*Night Grace, see you mañana!*

Before she shut her eyes, one more message: *Can't wait to see you,* she sent as she whispered out loud to herself, "My Elk."

Grace drove up after a lazy morning of sleeping in. She figured they might have a late night. She arrived mid-afternoon for a beautiful smoked salmon meal. River greeted her at the front door dressed in a light denim button-up shirt, nice Carhartt pants… and no baseball cap? She had never seen him without one. Baring his white hair and bald top. She saw that as a good sign, one that showed he was getting comfortable with her. She liked that he was trying to be himself, knowing she won't hurt his feelings or be bothered by his lack of hair.

River had a nice infrared BBQ that he used to cook the salmon. They made wild rice and veggies together in the bright kitchen while he checked on the grill now and then.

They had nice conversations as usual; she enjoyed how comfortable she was with him. She felt beautiful around him no matter what, and she valued that. He always seemed so solid, physically and inwardly. That was attractive.

"I better head back," Grace said while she washed her dish. Even though she was hoping he'd invite her to stay longer, she knew he was taking baby steps with her, and that was okay.

"Alright, Grace." He seemed hesitant to let her go. He kissed her on the cheek before he walked her out to her car.

*A peck?* Grace thought. *I'll take it.* He closed the door to her car, and she rolled down the window.

Grace's expression must have shouted "More, *please!*" because he looked at her and said, "I know we've got something here…" He paused to look around and back at her. "We don't want to jump too quickly into this. Let's take it slow, see if it's the right fit."

Grace nodded silently in agreement even though she felt slightly needy, wanting to go back to his comfy couch, snuggle into him and rest.

He said, "See ya soon" with more hesitation. She could tell he didn't want her to go, but neither of them pushed the idea of her staying any further.

She drove home, thinking about how she wanted River to be her lover and partner, but she knew to wait until it was time. She also wanted to be sturdy on her own and sit with her emotions a little longer. She had dampened her self-trust, the way she left the yurt community and left all that wake behind her.

But she couldn't go back and she didn't want to go back, so she thought of what direction she did want to go and she immediately thought of tending her garden seedlings, growing in the basement window in potted trays. Those seedlings were just begging her for attention. She loved caring for them and watching them grow. She had onions, leeks, and artichoke hearts, and soon the tomatoes would be up too. She couldn't wait to plant them and the seeds in the soil. Her body was itching for the warm spring and summer days when she could soak up the sun on her skin and be barefoot, grounding herself to the earth. What she loved most.

Once home, she focused on creating a beautiful space for herself downstairs in her grandparents' home, working at the juice shop, and preparing for her farmer's market season. Getting done all that needed to be done by the busy spring season.

When springtime came, she could feel her body shift

into mating season inside. She texted to ask River if they could meet and for an intimate evening one night.

He said, *NO*.

Taken aback, she said, *Ok*. And nervously added, *I'm going to focus on preparing my garden. You're welcome to come to see me at the market here in Twin when it's up and going in June.* She felt that she might pull him off the fishing hook and let him swim free.

A couple of days later, she received a text saying, *I think I'd like to explore our intimate side a little.* Grace read the text and smiled a mile wide, giddy feelings filling her body. Happy, surprised. They made a date at his place the following Saturday.

The weekend came rapidly. She dressed in her favorite skinny jeans and a tight white t-shirt that showed off her upper body, and over that she wore a teal plaid shirt. She put on her favorite tall leather boots and let her hair down long. She enjoyed the drive as she listened to her favorite music and watched the beautiful scenery.

She pulled up to his house and was flushed with butterflies. She loved how remote, rustic, and romantic his place was. Together they made dinner with enjoyable music playing in the background while they chatted and sipped red wine. She couldn't help but notice how handsome he looked in his flannel button-up shirt while he was busy chatting with her.

After they finished their lovely meal, Grace stood to clear her plate from the table. He stood abruptly, stopping Grace in her tracks.

He reached his hands up and over to her to gently cradle her chin and kissed her willfully.

She drew herself closer to him. What a kiss. She let herself go, and the feeling from their first kiss in his truck weeks ago came flooding back. Grace giggled lightly with a smile after that. It left her feeling light, loved, and giddy, like a little girl. It also warmed her up. She took off her long sleeve plaid shirt and went to do dishes. It was dark outside, so the window worked as a mirror, showing him looking at her as he walked into the kitchen after her. She started cleaning dishes and noticed how tall and strong he looked. She watched him stand back in hesitation, then he grabbed around her waist, quickly pulled her body in close, and kissed her from the side. Grace's hands were all sudsy with soap bubbles, but she embraced him regardless.

They moved into each other firmly. Grace could feel the fire from within. She welcomed it, but it stopped abruptly as he reached down, took her hand, and led her into the garage, his pottery studio. He went over to sit at his pottery wheel as she walked forward, standing out front to be his audience.

In a matter of minutes, a tall, slender porcelain vase was forming on the wheel. Her eyes moved up his arms, across his flannel shirt and chest, then to his slight grin. His body was attracting her, and there was a softening, warming feeling filling the studio. She loved watching him and couldn't stop smiling.

Looking over to her, he said, "What?" warmly with a slight grin.

"I'm enjoying watching you create."

He smiled, clearly knowing she was adoring it. "This is to display your flowers at the market." He said.

"Aw, that's sweet," she said, watching his hands firmly mold the slippery clay, imagining the bright gladiolus and lilies bursting with color out of the vase. Seeing that there was extra room on the back of his chair, she moved slowly behind him, like in the movie *Ghost*. She gradually grasped the backs of his shoulders, taking one leg at a time to sit down. Spooning him, straddled to the chair. She leaned into his back, resting her head on his shoulder blade, her hair down and covering her back. She sunk into him as close as possible, snuggling into him as her comfort pillow.

A very satisfied grin bloomed from ear to ear. She could tell it was a bit close for him, but he was allowing it. She wrapped her arms one by one around his waist slowly. Not to startle him. To her surprise, he took her hands with his to cradle the rotating pot. It was wet and slippery. He silently and firmly held her hands to morph the clay. The Americana music slowed and seemed to grow louder with their energy, fitting the mood, permeating the moment. She adjusted to fit deeper into his back. Grace had her eyes closed, simply focused on the feeling of beautifully molding the wet earth in her hands. She didn't have to do any work, just feel through her senses for a moment. He moved her hands up and down the tall vase, putting her into an expansive, warm, relaxed state. Gliding with the moment.

After a good five minutes, he let go and turned around. She felt her pinkie finger slightly drift over the top of the rotating vase. She was so relaxed, and suddenly his slippery clay hand came up and lightly clutched under her chin and cheek. He pulled her close for a soft kiss. She felt it coming and welcomed the affection. There was a bitty flame that was being fed by their chemistry, melding nicely.

He stood, supporting her as he brought her along, kissing the whole way up. She gently touched his chin with her slippery hands, and he playfully swept her up. She yelped from the fast sweep of her body into him. He moved her long legs, one at a time, to latch around his waist. He continued the kiss, but now the pace quickened. He began to walk them to the doorway and out of the studio. She looked through the corner of her eye, catching a glance at their rotating vase. Happy for the slight imperfection they created on the lip. She smiled through the kiss, knowing she'd remember this night every time she saw that beautifully captured moment in clay.

He took her up the stairs, one sturdy step at a time, stopping here and there for focused, affectionate kissing, then he made it to his room. The music seemed to blanket the entire house, adding to their chemistry. They undressed, lips connecting and disconnecting, helping one another get bare. He grabbed her waist, then supported the back of her head, and laid her down. She felt her body, along with his, performing a slow and intimate dance throughout their fiery lovemaking. Her hair was sweeping all over everywhere. She merged into the space that was enveloped by the music. It moved her as though it were a part of her, and it was so thick, she was happily drowning in it and him.

After their lovely dance, she leaned in and over to kiss his bald head to show him she loved that too. She knew she had a love for him, but she didn't need to say it yet; she simply enjoyed how she felt. She wanted him to feel that love—she knew he was receptive to it. She'd let it take its course and its time, believing that if she gave real love then she'd receive it in return. They lay there, bare chest to bare chest, and talked about everything.

Grace draped over him, resting her chin on her clasped hands, looking straight into his eyes. He raised his hand to play with a long lock of hair as he told her his stories, shared his perspective, his heart, and the way he saw life. She opened up and shared her feelings too.

Their conversation got serious, and she decided to lighten the mood by lifting her head quickly and asking, "Where do you come from?"

He said, "Where do I come from? The real question is, where do *you come* from?

She immediately said, "Venus!" in a seductive voice as she brought her head and long hair up to face him.

He could see the strength in her conviction, and he held

his head up to say, "Really, why'd you say it with such assurance?"

"I don't know, it just came out that way." She did feel Venetian in that moment, youthful and naked with her hair draped all over them.

They talked through the night until she woke up with her hands clasped with his. They must have held hands all night. That made her smile. She could tell that he was stirring and ready to get up. He placed a soft hand on her cheek and gave her a sturdy good morning kiss before he climbed outta bed and she hopped out too. They dressed and made a yerba mate and a little breakfast. Even though it was a bit chilly, they sat out at the table on the front deck. Huddled in wool blankets across from each other. Grace looked over at River and couldn't help but imagine them together.

They enjoyed their morning meal under the bright sun, then she made her trip south to the family homestead.

When she wasn't working at the juice shop or adventuring down at Auger Falls, she was passing time lounging in the sun in her garden space. She'd talk with the sun or moon as long as she could stand the cold wind. Doing this made her feel connected with the heavens and earth.

Grace asked River if he'd come down the following weekend. He replied with a surprising *Yes!* That made her excited because she was going to have them plant Red Ace beet seeds. She'd waited to plant them since they were his favorite vegetable and she thought it would be nice to plant her first seeds together.

When he came, they even went to the store to get some compost. It was their first public outing together. It went well. Nobody knew their story and gawked at them. It gave them both a more positive outlook concerning their "comfort level" as a pair. They went back to Grace's and sat on the west side yard to converse, snuggle, and nibble on treats.

In the still-windy spring weather, they lay on a blanket under a tree, listening to Gregory Alan Isakov out loud on her iPod. They shared some red grapes and some smoked cheddar cheese. They talked about the family homestead, its story, the possible future of it, and his old family ranch they'd sold the year before Grace met him. He told her about his days playing polo and explained the rules. She found that fascinating; she could imagine him riding a fast horse while trying to hit a ball on the ground and how attractive he'd look doing it with those tight pants. They ended up snuggling with the blanket covering them through a cat nap. Afterward, River headed home to care for his dogs and horses.

The days following his visit, she planted her cooler weather plants; sugar snap peas, more beets, spinach, and some flower bulbs. She had to wait a while on a few of her other seeds and seedlings to be planted in a warmer soil temperature. They were still too delicate for the cold nights that would be with her for another few months yet.

The first day she got water from the canal was so exciting. She loved thinking about the water traveling from the mountain tops down south, making its way into the canal, to her ditch, and into the pipes where it would evenly disperse into the garden rows. The head gate a mile up the road needed to be cleared out from winter debris. She cleaned it and every ditch from there to Our Roots on her own. They had to be cleaned out to prevent flooding of roadways, backyards, or fields. If flooding did occur, the canal company would shut her water off.

It was her most hefty project for the garden. She had to make sure all the pipes on the homestead were properly lined up with the corrugates (narrow ditches in the dirt that the tractor made for the water to come from the pipes along the garden beds) to water the seeded soil garden beds. She loved walking down the neighborhood with messy jeans, her plaid jacket, boots, and leather working gloves, carrying her teal painted shovel, which found balance on her shoulder. She felt tough, independent, strong, and attractive—mostly because she felt good.

Grace had to change the water's direction down the road and in a neighbor's backyard. This was all something her grandfather did. He even helped put it in place and was the one who would always do the work to get it going each season; even though it was everyone in the neighborhood's job to maintain the ditches, he did it to be helpful.

When she pulled up the lever in the neighbor's backyard, she grabbed her shovel and ran back down to the dry, open field next to the pipe where the water would change directions. She beat the water there. It was a big, open connection pipe, she could hear the water coming through it and got all giddy.

It filled up with water and she pushed down one of the three levers to fill it up then pulled up the lever to her acreage pipe, visualizing what Gramps would do. She walked her long-booted legs proudly down the pipe, beating the water to the end, near the lane to the homestead. She listened to the water trickling through the pipe, waiting until it filled up, then, one by one, opened the little plastic doors that lined up with the corrugated ditches to let the water burst out. Grace jumped up and down, purely excited.

She sat on the steel pipe, basking in the sun. It was now warm enough to take her jacket off, maybe due to the running and excitement. She was humbled by the arrival of such a magnificent element.

She watched it meet her groomed soil, the water glistening like it carried magical powers. Grace felt she was witnessing the initial connection of nature's spark. One that would trigger the gentle sprouting process for her seeds below and later quench their thirst and encourage growth. She was grateful to the water for its presence.

She played with the moving water for some time. She dammed up the narrow ditches with loose soil, encouraging the water to stick around in one spot to moisten that area fully. In some cases, she had to move mud from the ditch to allow a free flow of water to pass through. This, more than anything, reminded her of her grandpa. She used to watch him flood irrigate the yard with his shovel, which he would have propped on a shoulder, or it'd be in the dirt while he'd be leanin' on it. She felt like she was following in his footsteps, feeling like a little kid watching an adult do a chore. When a kid tries, they say, "Look, I can do it too!"

"Look, Gramps, I'm doing it," she said out loud. She loved working her grandfather's ground. Something told her he shared in all her joy that day too.

While she was out moving the water, a young man on his bike rode up the lane. He was wearing a bright blue t-shirt with khaki shorts. She thought it was still too chilly out for that outfit. She figured he was selling something or needed drinking water or to pump his bike tire? She walked over to him as he took off his helmet and placed it on the ground. He held his hand out to shake hers while the other held his bike. She thought he was smart looking as he introduced himself. He said he was from Estonia, here to sell children's educational books in the States for the summer to earn money for next year's college tuition. She said she didn't need any books, but he insisted on telling her about them. She politely listened. He used broken English as he spoke, and in the end, he said he and two other students were looking for a host family to house them for three weeks. She thought of her solo trip to Africa and knew she would hope someone nice would do the same for her... if she were in his shoes.

She said, "Yeah. I'll ask the renters upstairs if they are

willing to share an empty room for a few weeks."

He couldn't believe it. As though his luck turned around that instant. They exchanged numbers after a long, "Thank you!"

He was very grateful. Grace watched him ride off down the homestead lane in her muddy boots, all her weight leaning on her shovel.

# 8

## Elk Dance

April 2016

It was already mid-April and Grace knew River's birthday was coming up on the first of May. He was heading down to Arizona for a month to spend time with his boys. He looked forward to mountain biking and enjoying family time in warmer weather. He was leaving a few days before May, so Grace had planned a surprise for him the night before he left. She'd worked on it for several weeks now and sent him a close-up photo of part of his present. She knew he'd have an idea of what it was—it was one of her chairs, which was painted white and had a dainty design carved in the upper shoulder rest area.

The next week, when he came down, she made him a healthy avocado chicken salad. Then, she took him to her room for the first time. She'd been preparing it ever since she moved in. Now, she had it all ready for him to see. She painted it a soft yellow with a mandala tapestry cut down the middle and attached to the curtain rod as drapes to open and close to the double bed area, set in the wall. They plopped on the bed.

She said, "Are you ready for your present?"

"Sure," he said.

"I'll be a minute, okay?"

"Okay..." he replied curiously.

Grace went into the empty room next door to her and put on a short, flouncy mini skirt, cream color with little light purple and peach flowers on it. It had layers to fluff it out, like a bohemian tutu. She put on her unpolished tall leather boots that were his favorite, a black lace bra, and a blue plaid button-up shirt with snap buttons and put her straight strawberry blonde hair up in two long pigtail braids on top of her head. She pulled the black eyeliner out and gave her eyes a sleek, bolder shape. It reminded her of the doe encounter. She walked into her room where River was still lying on her bed, she quickly pulled open the curtains to the bed, finding him half dozed off.

She jumped on the bed playfully and leaned in close to his face. He looked at her with surprise at the new look. He grinned, and she smiled, sitting up raising her hand to present her pigtails.

"Like my antlers?" she asked.

He sat up, ready to engage. "Yeah."

She hopped off the bed eminently playful and walked over to the white chair sitting solo against the bare wall. She pulled it forward.

"Does this look familiar?" she asked.

He looked a little confused at first.

"Oh, it's the photo you sent me. A close-up of the

chair. You made me a chair!" he said.

"Nope…" She set the chair in the center of the room in front of a 4-foot-wide by 5-foot-tall mirror on the wall. It was directly across the room from the bed.

"Have a seat!" she said as she held her hand out, welcoming him over.

He looked at her shocked, she could practically see him asking the world if this was really going where he thought it was going?

He sat down and started getting jittery—he kind of started blabbering. It made Grace giggle confidently. She turned around, picked up her big elk antler she had found in the shop, and put it on the floor along the wall, below the mirror. She had told him all about the elk dance idea of hers. This was going to be a mini, intimate version, just for him.

She turned her iPod on to the song she'd been practicing with, "Jackie and Wilson" by Hozier. It started with drum sticks tapping on the metal edge of the drum, then the guitar came in and Grace ripped through the buttons on her plaid shirt, facing River. He was so excited he couldn't sit still or stop nervously babbling. Grace held up her finger to her mouth to say, "Shhh…" He stopped mumbling but his smile never left his face as she danced her slow dance around him.

Sliding down the side of his chair then turning to put one leg, tiptoe in her boot, on his thigh. Leaning down her leg slowly, walking back behind him. Running her fingers through his hair on the back of his head, following the words to the song. She walked slowly behind him, around to the front, did several dance moves, facing herself in the mirror, and sat down on the edge of his knee right when the singer suggested. *So on point,* she thought as she smiled at how exact she was.

After gently caressing his face, she stood back up with her hands behind her head. One tiptoe out with the leg, the other tiptoe out with the leg, she stood up with sturdy stems wide and bent forward, allowing the short skirt to tease. Down to the floor she went for a slow back arch and up again to twirl her moves around, facing him when she shook her head "no," along with the song, hair dangling back and forth across his face. She lifted a leg up and over, then the other, ending the song straddling him in the chair for a kiss.

It didn't take long before she was picked up.

As she clutched him, he carried them over to the bed where they ever so quickly made love. He lay down next to her, and she laughed in relief that she was able to do what she'd always feared: being seductive… she realized it was harmlessly playful rather than scary.

She snuggled into him and he couldn't stop saying, "Whoa, whoa, I've NEVER experienced anything like that."

She laughed and asked, "Did you have any idea I was going to do that?"

"Not until you moved the chair to the center of the room."

"What was your favorite part?" she asked curiously.

He thought for a minute and said, "The mirror. I could

see you well… the mirror amplified it."

Grace laughed, mostly proud of having the guts to do her dance. She thought about the elk dance idea she came up with within her community last year. She could see how they wouldn't want that, but she didn't plan for that dance to be *seductive*. It was going to be *creative*. That was what she'd hoped for.

Grace's favorite part was the mirror too; she could also see herself and recalled seeing confidence reflecting back at her and thinking, *I see the confidence and I feel confident so I must be, even though I'm nervous.* At that moment she wondered if this exercise would help heal her inner "ugly," or maybe partly? She thought it was more of the judging of herself that imprisoned and beat up that part of her curious self?

River spoke, interrupting her train of thought. Grace paused, getting back to the moment.

"Did you have to practice?" he asked.

"Yes. Couple times a day for a few days…" she said honestly.

"Really?" he asked.

"I'm not a dancer. I like to do yoga… but I loved that dance. It was just for YOU!" she said.

He grabbed her like a kid, grabbed his favorite teddy bear and brought her close... "Thank you! Best 60th birthday EVER!"

She giggled and squeezed him tighter, and out slipped "I love you" without her realizing it. She didn't take it back or apologize for it because that was obviously how she felt at that moment, thinking about how she loved that she didn't hold back with him.

"Thank you!" He said, "It's good to know that you love someone enough to say it."

She knew it would take him a while to say it back, and she was okay with that. She wouldn't force it. In order to change the subject, she took her pigtails out and started braiding a side braid.

"Your hair looks like long strands of wheat." he said, seeming to enjoy watching her.

She smiled thankfully then turned on a romance movie from the bed then fell asleep in each other's arms, when they woke, his truck was already packed and ready to go, so he headed out from there for his vacation south.

He texted her on his trip down. He said *I heard that Hozier song on the radio. I couldn't help but smile the entire song. Remembering your dance.*

She laughed and texted back, *The gift that keeps on giving.*

*Ain't that the truth.*

She said, *Drive safe and let me know when you've arrived.*

*Will do. Have a great month and time in your garden,* he said.

A few days later, on River's Birthday, first thing upon waking she texted him *Happy Birthday!*

And when Grace was out planting heirloom carrot seeds by hand she got a text saying, *Thanks! It's been a great birthday. For sure, such a lucky guy. An elk dance from my stunning woman and this beautiful rug to hang on my wall from my parents. You must see this.* He sent a photo of a cream-colored rug with a woven red petroglyph male elk, a female elk, and little elk.

*What?* she responded. She couldn't believe it.

*I know. I can't believe it either. It's not like I collect anything elk. It's just a magical year for me and the Elk.*

Grace was baffled by the coincidence as he sent her several texts telling her how he was so lucky to have her and how great it was to have her in his life. She returned his text with the same vibe, grateful for their experience too.

She spent her month without their get-togethers focusing on getting her market garden planted and thriving. She loved grounding to the earth and spending time under the sun and moon. If she wasn't at work, she was in her garden or roaming down at the river, near Auger Falls.

\* \* \*

She heard from the Estonians who were in the states selling educational kids books. The time in their current room they were crashing in was ending, so they needed a room quickly. Grace talked to the renters who lived upstairs about them staying in an extra room. She had asked the first time right after she talked with the Estonian that day on the lane. They had agreed to it until they showed up to look at the room and changed their minds. Grace felt bad, so she offered to let them stay in one of the back rooms downstairs. They were ok with that. The extra bedroom already had a set of bunk beds, a double bed, and a mattress on the floor from all of her grandparents' rooms upstairs.

Of course, she came up with some rules. They could never go into her room and only shower at night so that she could shower in the mornings before work. They agreed to keep the kitchen clean, and, the best part, they had to help her with yard work on their day off. Every Sunday, three hours each. Minimum. That helped lift a heavy load off of her shoulders. Plus, she didn't feel so alone with them there. Even though they were gone all day, consistently until 10 PM, six days a week. She also got to talk about Estonia, learn a little about the people, and imagine what it looked like. They called her "Village girl." That's what country farm girls are called in Estonia, and she liked that name.

When River was headed back, he stopped on his way through and wanted to see her garden's progress. The seeds were starting to bud out of the bare dirt and it was warm enough that she could transplant all her seedlings: tomatoes, leeks, artichokes, onions, summer and winter squash, and okra. River helped her transplant a few pots into the garden beds then they started another bunch of seeds in trays. That was very helpful. She was getting busier and the market was around the corner, a couple of weeks away. She asked him if he'd like to help her at the market one day.

"Grace, I'm not ready for anyone to know about us yet. Especially Matt," he said.

"Okay. I get it," she said. She kept it simple and changed the subject. "Hey, I grew this wheatgrass tray for you while you were away." She handed him the tray of thick green grass as he was ready to head home. "Take my juicer with you and juice every day. It's good for your heart."

"You are good for my heart," he said as he took the tray. "You take great care of me." He smiled before he kissed her and left.

* * *

The market started, and Grace popped up her tent at the Saturday Twin Falls location. She was down the row from her old boss, Matt Haze. Her dear friend and veggie guru. She was so at home here. It wasn't Ketchum, but she still enjoyed being at the market.

# 9

# Valley of Fireworks

June-July 4, 2016

One day in mid-June River texted Grace, *Come up for the weekend!*

She was happy about that request and went up, dressed all nice. He wanted to plant some flowers with her for Father's Day like she'd asked for his help with planting beets. She brought up the first harvest of their beets and roasted them with dinner.

She was dressed in a fitted gray t-shirt dress and her favorite boots. She wore her hair in a ponytail, long and straight. She got out of her car, felt that early summer warm air, and simply soaked it in as she walked across the yard. River was waiting for her at the raised flower bed. He glanced at her and whistled.

"You look good, Grace. Let me look at you for a minute."

She let him watch her as she tried to walk proudly over to him and the large tin flower pot. She couldn't help but smile bashfully.

Together they planted the vibrant flowers, filling up his metal feeding trough that lay near the edge of his property, where the yard turned from lawn into sagebrush wilderness at the base of the hills.

They finished planting and she carried her bag of stuff in for the night from the car. She made it into the doorway, and he came walking up to her after turning on the music, looking all tall and white-haired, a romantic gentleman. She noticed, as always, his sporting good posture as he came close to grab her waist. Simultaneously, their favorite song, "Rivers and Roads," came on the stereo. She loved the way he snatched her while that song played.

He took her bag from her gently and set it down on the bench as he leaned in for a kiss. Grace felt so tall, so beautiful, so… *her*. She was so sturdy inside herself. He gave her a big squeeze, slightly lifting her off the floor while he leaned back a bit and gently put her feet back on the floor. He started to get a little rowdy, and Grace welcomed it. They were kissing with such power, it was heating up quickly. She was lost in the warm summer temperatures, the warm juicy feelings, and the music that always enhanced her senses.

He instantly picked her up, legs straddled around him, and they performed an intimate dance in the doorway. She glanced at the front door with glass, seeing his reflection entangled into hers, and she took pleasure in what she saw. Swept from her glance, he took her up to his bedroom. She clung to him as they made it up each stair. Nearly undressed, he went to assist in taking her boots off as she leaned back onto the bed.

He said, "Actually, let's leave them on."

She smiled, feeling her boots dangling near the floor. Soon, they were up in the air where her long skinny legs danced in them above his head. They enjoyed lying comfortably still on the bed, him next to Grace's long, lean, nude body. One worn-out leg crossed over River's legs while he lay there to rest. She leaned into his head near his ear and softly said, "I finally found you."

His reaction wasn't what she foresaw. She watched him pause, then he awkwardly kissed her a bunch with a slight strange feeling creeping itself into the warm, intimate moment. Hinting that the feeling was not mutual.

He said, "Grace," as he breathed in and out heavily. "My heart is like Fort Knox. It has a lot of walls up around it."

"Ok…" She proceeded lightly, "Is there a chance these walls will ever come down to let me in?"

"There is a possibility." With slight hesitation. "I've only ever loved one woman. I've loved her for nearly 10 years."

"Where is she?" Grace asked with compassion.

"We both decided we were going to move here. I invested in moving here, and she didn't end up coming as she fell ill."

"What was she sick with?" she asked with concern.

"I don't want to get into much detail, but I want you to know that I've waited *so long* for her, I can't give up on her now."

She gave a slight head nod.

"I offered to move closer to be with her, but with her illness, she won't let me close… won't allow it."

"Why not?" Grace asked.

"She says she doesn't want to be a burden. She wants me to move on, even though there's a chance she can get better. I won't leave her. Even if she doesn't want me near her while she's sick. I can't."

"I see."

He added, "She had a baby when I met her. Her husband left them, and their son is nearly 11 now. Great kid, he helps a lot while she's sick and resting."

Grace gave a caring, "Aw," pausing before she continued. "So, you don't think there's any chance between *us?*" thinking she may *have* moved too fast.

He sighed as he took a minute then said, "I'm saying… It'll take a lot of work to get these walls down for me to consider it."

"OK, well. Let's see where we can take us," she said. "River?"

"Yeah?"

"I want you to always follow your heart, okay?"

"Okay." He gently caressed her neck with the back of

his index finger, making it to the edge of her chin then lightly pinching it. He whispered, "You're beautiful."

"Thank you," she whispered as she leaned in for a kiss on the lips then reached up like she always did and kissed the top of his head before they passed out, wrapped in each other's arms, like his dogs who slept spooned together at the foot of the bed.

They woke in the morning with the sun shining right into their eyes, peeking up over the mountains to the east. Grace loved his quiet home. She adored the modest size and how it was nestled in the open valley, surrounded by mountains. She felt like she was in a Western movie. She welcomed that feeling every time it came around.

She grabbed his white robe three times her size and opened the balcony door, walking out onto the deck for a good yoga stretch and a few deep inhales of fresh air. She noticed a little twin bed over in the corner of the deck and wanted to sleep there the next time; maybe it'd be warm enough at night by then.

River called loudly from the kitchen, "Join me for breakfast."

Grace smiled a giggly smile as if he were surprising her with a gift. She went down and said, "Hey, I see a little bed out there. Can we snuggle on it next time?"

"You bet!" he said as he handed her a plate with eggs, bacon, sausage. and fresh avocado on it. "Let's eat on the patio?"

"Let's!" She smiled on their way out.

"Grace, you lovely doll… if you could pick any actor to go on a date with, who would it be?"

"Oh, okay… hmmm, well… that's an interesting question. I know who I've always liked. There are some that I've found attractive, but who would I be proud to sit and have a wholesome chat with?'

"Yeah," he said.

"Okay, Sam Elliot," she answered.

"I should have guessed!" he said. "But why Sam Elliot specifically?"

"Well, he's a wholesome kind of guy. A gentleman. Of course, I don't know him, but based on his character and what I know… he seems solid, and he's been faithful to his wife. I also LOVE his voice, so deep… and his smile."

"All good things, Grace!" Quickly changing the subject, he said, "Hey, how's the market garden?"

"Great! The season is in full swing. You should come down soon," Grace said, and he looked at her like" *That's not happening.*

"I'm getting ready to go see the boys again." he said, "Next week. I'll only be there a week."

"Okay…" Grace thought, *thwarted again.*

"I'll be home by the Fourth of July. We should watch fireworks together," he said, walking behind her and wrapping his arms around her as she stood up. She snuggled into him tightly, wanting more time with him rather than less, but it was his life and his family. She didn't want to complain about their time apart.

It was hard to not text him all day while he was away in Arizona, but Grace kept busy while he was gone, and he was back before she knew it.

When the Fourth came around, he drove to Twin to spend the night with her. They went out to dinner. She dressed in a white and paisley skirt romper, dainty flip flops, and a ponytail.

They met in a parking lot and drove her car all around town looking for a place to eat. She wanted to take him to a nice local restaurant, but the only thing open was Chili's. She was not afraid to be seen with him, not at all, and was ready for whatever came their way. It was a success. She could tell that River was a little nervous with the young male waiter who came to take their order. Grace tried to show him that it was okay, that she wasn't going to hit on the waiter or check him out… mission accomplished.

"Well, Grace. Tell me what's new since our last chat?"

"I took a new job with a physical therapist."

"As if you had more time to add another job into your week?"

"Well, my leg and back don't seem to be getting any better. Working out in the garden is hard on my body, and the pain is so intense up and down my leg into my foot. I figured I could learn something new and get worked on as well."

"Good for you." he said, "Such a self-reliant way of

thinking. Is there anything you can't do?" Grace laughed. "Well, how's it going?"

"Great. I help in the back as an assistant. I write down what the two doctors do for the patient. They work on muscles. It's very interesting but hard to remember each muscle and what it does. There's a book of 600 muscles, and I flip to the specific muscle the therapist will work on and help them work on it. It can get a little stressful, especially when we are so busy. But I've seen so many people get better, which is great!"

"Well, that's wonderful, Grace. Keep up the good work."

"I will," she said in a matter-of-fact tone.

"Let's head up the hill for those fireworks, shall we?"

They finished up their meal and drove up to the south hills, 20 minutes south of town. They drove up the first hill and turned the car to face the entire Magic Valley to see the fireworks all around. They turned on Gregory Alan Isakov, and she moved over to the driver's seat. She straddled River and leaned his seat back, telling him how she felt about him and that he was an angel, that she was so grateful for him being in her life.

He teared up and just allowed her to spill her heart to him as the sun set behind her. She kissed him sweetly, then the fireworks started, and she moved back to the passenger's seat to watch the valley of fireworks.

"Whoa, what a view, Grace." he said, "Great spot. I'm surprised only one other car had the same idea."

"Me too," Grace agreed.

When the fireworks ended, they climbed into the back after putting the seats down and made out.

They spooned as they heard the booms of fireworks across the sky and he spoke up a bit while she was facing toward the side door, looking out the window at the night sky.

"Hey…"

"Yes…?" she said.

"I love you too," he said.

She smiled so big and nestled closer into his curved body.

He said, "I don't know what will happen with us. but it's been very interesting, and there's such a deep feeling I have when I'm with you. It feels like a movie. Our movie," he said. "Have you seen *Roots*?"

"No," she said apologetically.

"Yeah, it came out before your time," he said before asking, "Have you seen *Shawshank Redemption*?"

"Yeah, a long time ago," she said, still looking out at the star-covered sky.

"Those two movies keep popping up in my head when we are together. It's not that we are in any way connected to them—it's the feeling of those movies."

"I don't know those movies well, but I can relate. I feel like our love and our romance is… unique and beautiful, *our movie, our romance*. Made for the screen of *our* hearts." Grace giggled, turned, and kissed him, thanking him for opening to her. She snuggled deeper into him then looked back up to the stars and said *thank you* inside with a smile before she drifted off in River's arms.

They woke after a good nap and headed down the hillside, back to the parking lot where they parked to meet.

They both got out to hug each other and kissed, then he held her out in front of him, looked at her, and said, "60 years, Grace, it's taken 60 years to find you!"

She smirked, giddy as he pulled her in for another big hug, wondering if he'd turned a new leaf.

"Okay," he said, "I gotta get back and let out Maggie and Max."

"Travel safe," she said as she walked back to her car door.

"You too," he said, walking backward too.

Grace was happy. She didn't realize that they wouldn't see each other for another month and a half. She was busy working hard at her new job, the garden, the farmer's market, and the juice shop. River went on a camping adventure down in Arizona for two weeks with his boys. They talked via text every day until he went south, and she didn't hear from him much while he was floating with the boys.

While at the market one day, she heard that Gregory Alan Isakov was playing in Sun Valley. Then one night, during her downtime, she bought herself a ticket for mid-September, about a month away. She thought of having River go too, to spend some good, quality time together when he got home.

Grace got a text from him the next morning: *Hey Grace. I'm about to head home. Missin' you.*

His text woke her up; Sunday was her only day to sleep in. The sun was shining brightly through the little bedroom window, down on her. She was just waking from a dream about him. As she opened her eyes, she realized her behind was slightly raised in the air, and the heat was all residue from a dream. That didn't cause her rear to change positions though. Grace reached for her phone, one eye open, the other smashed to her pillow.

She read his message then decided to reply in a frisky, playful way: *Miss you too. Woke from a steamy dream about you. My bum was slightly lifted in the air all warm, thinking you were close.*

*Oh...?* he replied.

*Yep, I'm still in bed. Lounging my Sunday away,* she said.

*Me too,* he replied.

She thought she would practice not holding back, being playful, and proceeded to tell him about her dream. Her body was warm. Continuing to replay her dream, she touched herself, her warm body releasing like a blossom made of butter, moving into a warm liquid release.

*I just released thinking of you.*

*So did I,* he said.

Grace laughed and thought, *How Fun! We just shared a lovely moment from far away.*

She turned her face to soak in the warm summer sunbeams coming through the only basement window in her room as she drifted back to sleep with a smile on her face.

\* \* \*

River made it home at the end of August. He headed straight home without stopping, and he wasn't responding to her texts during the drive. She thought, *Ugh, we need to spend some quality time together!*

# 10

# Downpour

*I miss you!* Grace texted River. *It would be so nice to spend more time with you when you get home.* She was yearning to share her exciting news and make plans with him. *Hey! Isakov is playing next month in Sun Valley. I went ahead and bought a ticket. Would you care to join me?*

*Grace, I'm not quite ready to be seen together locally.* He replied.

*Okay*, she said, deciding to respect that. She wasn't going to push him into feeling uncomfortable, knowing that he'd wanted to take things slow, although her hopes were deflated.

He added, *We do need to spend some quality time together, though. Why don't you come up the day before the concert, we can meet at the Ketchum Market and head to my place for a couple of nights?*

*Sounds like a great plan!* she replied, seeing the positive side of the compromise.

When the anticipated week arrived, she took Wednesday off, already having no work on Tuesday, and drove up that morning. She was so excited to get away from all responsibilities and spend a couple of good days with her guy.

Once she made it to the Ketchum market, she walked around talking to everyone, catching up with all the market vendors and old customer friends; she could easily spend all four market hours chatting. She bought potatoes from Haze, a steak from Full Bull Organics, some fresh salad greens, a yummy lemon custard yogurt for breakfast, and of course some fresh raspberries.

She slowly approached River's booth to test the waters, seeing if it was alright to walk up and engage with him while he was helping customers. She wasn't too worried since everyone knew they were good buddies. Nobody would know they were a "thing" unless they made it obvious.

He welcomed her presence and she opened her bag to show him all the goodies she bought for their meals.

He said, "You got some good stuff there. Looking forward to enjoying it with you. You look so *graceful* floating around the market."

She blushed. This was good. He was being supportive and not scared of them as a couple, at least in that moment. It was an encouraging sign for her.

Only minutes before the market closed, she offered to help River take his booth down.

"I've got this, Grace. Simple system. It'll take less than 15 minutes."

"Okay, I'm going to go help Matt take his booth down," she said as she walked out of his booth with her groceries. "See you in a bit."

She helped Haze and his crew take down their booth. It was done in no time. She said goodbye as they loaded up to head south to Buhl. She helped another elderly woman vendor load her van then walked back to River. They were some of the last ones to leave the market and walked through the area together, towards their vehicles that were parked near the same spot. She thought, *Walking out of the market together, in broad daylight? Yes… baby steps.* It was good progress. He walked her to her car, then she followed him up to his house in Stanley.

"So, how did your trip with your boys go?" she asked while they prepared to cook.

"So good! There was such a good group of people. There's this gal, Lacy… she's been the boys' friend for a few years. She's mentoring them out on the water. Such a pro, major pro. We hung out a bit—she's 40." Grace knew in her gut that that was a stab to her confidence, a jab poked into her gut with jealousy poison at the end of it.

She could see there was something to this little comment. *Sounded like the highlight of his trip?* She swallowed and tried to let it go then changed the subject, saying "Maggie doesn't look so good."

"Yeah, Grace, she's nearly 15, and she's gone downhill since I left for Arizona. It won't be much longer for her." Maggie was skinny. Her ribs were showing, and she wasn't moving much. "Hey! I think we should take the horses out for a ride in the morning, what do you say?" he said, changing the subject.

"Sounds great! Are you sure? It's been 20 years since I've been on a horse. I had always dreamed of having horses when I was a little girl."

"Yeah, you'll do fine. Look how quickly you've picked up all the muscle stuff at work," he said.

"Yeah, my boss says I'm understanding it pretty well. I worked hard at it," she said as he looked at her, nodding his head affirmatively. "It's nice too that my back, leg, and foot are doing much better after getting treatment myself."

"Way to make things work for you," he said. "How great, Grace."

Their food was ready, so they took it out to the back porch to chat and share grub. Once they finished eating, he came over and gave her a quick, romantic kiss with a raspberry that was hiding in his mouth. He started moving down.

"*Whoa...*" Grace said, nervously giggling. "No, no..." she added playfully, but it was happening anyway. He then picked her up and carried her to the bedroom.

After they made love, he said, "You sure know how to make an old man feel young again." She laughed, kissed the top of his bald head, and snuggled into him.

"Tomorrow night is a full moon," she said. "It's a Super Moon. Full moons bring endings, climaxes, and beginnings. A Super Full Moon can bring all those times three."

"Really?" he asked.

"Yeah," she said, feeling that there was something in the undertone of that *Really?*

"Well, it sure is a beautiful sight, isn't it?" he said as he gazed out the bedroom window at the bright, nearly full moon.

"I LOVE the moon. My first memory ever was of me as an infant inside the moon with my whole family, meeting me for the first time, coddled in a Christmas stocking."

"How adorable. You are adorable, Grace," he said as they drifted into sleep holding each other.

First thing in the morning they made a quick breakfast and had it with tea out on the patio. As they made their way to the horse stalls, she glanced all around. *Sigh...* She longed to reside there with him—his home was simple, wholesome, and there was such a honey sort of filter over the whole place.

They went into a mini cabin that was very tidy inside. It looked like a display room of collectibles, rather than a gear shed. He grabbed a couple saddles and harnesses.

"Can you grab those brushes on the table, Grace?" She grabbed them on their way out. He put everything down in a neat pile and she offered the brushes. "Thank you," he said, and he started grooming Luna.

"Which horse will I be riding?" she asked.

"This gal," he said as he patted Luna with the brush. "She does very well teaching little kids to ride. I trust her with you. I'll ride Tahoe, he's younger and easily agitated."

She couldn't help but soak in how handsome he looked in his modest western attire and white cowboy hat. She'd never seen him in anything like it. She thought it was romantic, and he was so sturdy brushing the horse. Her midsection was warmed with butterflies and the smell of horses and hay brought a strong hint of nostalgia from her childhood.

"Grace, come take a turn," he said.

She took the brush and started to stroke Luna. She could tell River felt the romantic vibe. He turned her around, slightly lifted his hat, and swooped in for a knee-weakening kiss. He grabbed her waist and pulled her in close. Grace just relaxed her arms and weight into his grasp, fully enjoying the wonderful moment. She even sensed the horse picking up on the incredible energy.

"Mmmmm," River said as he leaned back, looking relaxed. "I better get these horses going." She helped gear them up then he led her and the horses to the open corral. As they walked past the high stack of hay, she noticed a chain link fence caged around it.

"That's new," she commented.

"Yeah, got that done before winter so our elk can't get in," he said.

*Closing off the elk?* She thought, *Hmmm… putting up more walls?* Her heart began brewing nervously, but she let that go for their time with the horses.

He opened the gate to the corral, directing her first then walked towards the training arena. Once inside, he helped her up onto Luna. He taught her how to direct the horse left and to the right, how to get her to stop and go. It was so fun, and she liked how he was with her: patient, firm, and confident, not to mention good lookin' in his cowboy hat. She was seeing a different side of him.

"Alright Grace, it's time we go out and exercise these horses."

River hopped onto Tahoe and they rode side by side out to the paved road, and once they got to the narrow trail through the sagebrush, she followed behind River. They moved slowly for a good hour until they made it to a dirt road where River said, "Now for the fun part." He explained how to trot, gallop, and canter.

She tried, getting Luna into the canter, and *so* enjoyed that motion. She could see River to her side, watching to make sure she was good. She liked how he was there with her, teaching her. Trying to keep up as he said, "Faster!"

She took his advice and nudged her feet with a quick kick to Luna's belly. They moved into a gallop, holding on tight, and she threw her head back, unable to control the laughter escaping her abdomen. Happy, free feelings exploded throughout her as if she were always meant to have that sensation, even smell the dust and soak in the sunshine. She was running out of a straight road so she slowed and turned to

~112~

River to say, "I love it!" She tipped her head back again, giggling.

"See, I knew you'd pick it up quick!" he said, panting.

They slowed to chat, making it up the hills and back down, and the horses took them through the sagebrush. When they made it to the road, just before the house, she got Luna up to a canter then galloped again until they made it to the driveway of the house. She was so *free* on that horse, moving in that motion, at that speed.

They walked the horses to the same place where they combed them and took all the horse attire off, put it all away in the little riding cabin, and brushed the horses' sweaty backs. Then they took them to the pasture to feed, gave them fresh water, and let them roam until evening. They went into the house, knowing they'd have some free time until she went to her concert later.

"Are you sure you don't want to go to the concert? You can take your truck. Sit on your own?" she sorta pleaded.

"No," he said firmly.

"Okay. Well, I'm going to get my swimsuit on and lay out for a bit, okay?" She wanted to give him a break to think about things instead of irritating him more.

She got her paisley bikini on and grabbed a towel, laying it out near the table on the patio, and got her iPod to listen to some tunes.

She wasn't there for 20 minutes when River came up, leaned over her, next to their breakfast table, and said in a firmly disappointed way, "If you're going to lay here all day, I'm gonna go on a mountain bike ride with my buddy."

"Oh, okay... I wasn't going to lay here long. I have no plans, and I didn't think you'd wanna go out to lunch in town," she said, hoping to change his desire to leave.

"Well, Pete wants to ride. I'm going," he said sternly.

"Okay..." she said, somewhat apologetically. She didn't understand how sunbathing made him upset. She got up and grabbed the wide-brimmed hat he had given her for gardening. "I think I'm gonna go for a walk. You wanna go?" she asked softly.

"I'm already ready for my ride," he said, gruffly.

"Okay..." she said, not wanting it to go that way.

She got her tennis shoes on and started to walk down the road in just her bikini and hat. The neighbors drove by, they waved and she waved back in a not-so-friendly way. They both looked at her oddly, and she kept walking, thinking, *I don't care what you think of me.* Soon after, River pulled up next to her, rolled down the window, and said, "Looking good, Grace..." *He's trying to be chipper.* She just kept walking.

"The neighbors stop and say anything?" he asked.

"No, they just waved," she said, continuing to look straight ahead.

"Oh, well... enjoy your walk and the concert," he said.

"'K." She continued to look ahead, and he drove off.

She walked up the paved road in the hot sun, onto the dirt road that went south into the brush-filled hills. She stopped to lie down on the ground and looked up to the sun, who she often counseled with. *What happened?* she thought to herself as the puffy clouds were starting to roll in. She watched them change as one cloud moved into what looked like River's grumpy face. *Strange…* she thought, *or the devil's face.* She couldn't comprehend what was going on between them and decided she would just suck it all up. Be strong and carry on. She stood up and walked five minutes before she made it back to the paved road and it started to lightly rain.

She was alone and in no rush to get back to River's, but the light rain turned into a straight-on downpour—what she loved was that the sun was breaking through the clouds amazingly to the west, near the house. The house looked like the farmhouse on *The Wizard of Oz.*

She began to run towards it as bright rays of sunshine beamed directly onto his house. She held her hat to her head, turned up Imagine Dragons' "Gold", to top volume and ran as fast as she could with squinted eyes through the pouring rain. The raindrops stung when they hit her skin as she ran into it. The music helped her speed up, hold her speed, and let out the tense emotions she was experiencing. She thought, *How appropriate that I'm in my swimsuit.*

When she made it back to the house the rain slowed, and she didn't want to go inside because the bright sun was beaming so radiantly through the dark clouds. It was a spectacular sight. So she went to the southwest end of the yard, tearing up and exhausted from her sprint home.

"God, I tried. I tried!" she cried out as she looked up at the heavenly sky, and seemed to be listening to her. "What else can I do? I can't make River love me…"

Just then her hat blew off and she let it. The rain was getting her entire body and it bled into her tears down her face. She got an answer from the sky and inside herself, simultaneously. One that she'd gotten many times while with him… *keep loving him the way you want to be loved.* She recognized this as if she remembered a promise to herself or as if it were part of her purpose. This centered her and brought her back to focus, so she went inside, up to the bathroom to take a shower.

She hopped in, turned the water as warm as she could stand, washed, and got out. She turned on some upbeat music then dried her hair. She got all dressed up with the perfect outfit for her outing: a halter dress that was light gray paisley print with a hint of pink and a dot of teal here and there. She put on a wide leather belt that narrowed in the back, making her waist look itty bitty. She zipped up her tall leather boots and kept her hair down and straight

When it was time, she drove east to Sun Valley. Once there, she grabbed her blanket and walked into the outside pavilion. She noticed she was getting looks. She found an empty spot in the grass and sat her blanket down up front and happened to sit next to a woman she recognized from the farmers market in Ketchum. They talked for a while, then the music started.

She was highly enjoying the performance!

She saw Hilary Swank as she was heading backstage after the concert. She looked right at Grace and smiled a warm smile. Grace thought, *Only in Sun Valley would I see fame.*

After the concert, she got up, said goodbye to the lady she knew, and started to walk out to her car. On the way, she noticed several guys eyeing her again, one following her nearly to her car. She knew she was of value, but why did River not see it? Why did he resist her and her open arms?

She drove back to his house with an odd, empty feeling. His truck was there when she pulled up. She went inside and walked past sleeping Maggie and Max who were spooning in the entryway. She made it upstairs to his office where he was watching the Summer Olympics. There was only one single chair in front of the TV, so she stood on the step of the doorway to the room.

He saw her and said, "Hey! How was it? You look stunning! Perfect attire for Gregory Alan."

"It was good." Her voice lacked enthusiasm, and she didn't feel his complement made up for encouraging her to go to the concert alone.

She walked over to him, moved his arms to make room for her to sit on his lap, and leaned back into his chest, wrapping his arms around the front of her.

"Tell me about it," he said.

"I sat next to a lady market customer. That was nice… and they never played 'Idaho.'"

"Really? You'd think they would!" he said.

"The crowd begged them to, but they didn't," she said, noticing how small she felt, even though she knew she shouldn't. She reached back behind his neck and clasped her gentle hand around it to hold on.

She knew he wanted to see the band play live, and that made her cranky deep inside like a little sore was being irritated, and she wanted it to feel better. She looked around at the small TV and computer room, thinking, *He'd rather sit here alone in his single chair being grumpy instead of enjoying lovely music with the person he says he's grateful for?... This must be hard for him.*

They sat and watched the Olympics for a minute. Grace had never owned a TV. Never wanted one. Didn't have the patience for it—which was the case here.

"What *did* they play?" he asked, breaking the silence. "Were there a lot of people there?"

She named the songs and then said, "It wasn't full, but I did see Hillary Swank!" She said enthusiastically.

"Hilary Swank?"

"Yeah. Funny, Cray said he didn't like her sharp features. He never talked like that about anyone, so I found it odd for him to say something like that, and when I was in Costa Rica, a lady said I looked like her. I was flattered to resemble her, personally," she said, bummed that Cray wasn't attracted to her.

"You're prettier than Hillary Swank." As he said this, Grace felt it was just his way of apologizing for the way he was earlier.

"Oh, really?" she said playfully, breaking the tension a bit. She reached up and started kissing him softly. He welcomed it. Then he interrupted the kiss by asking, "Do I remind you of anyone famous?"

"Actually, one time I remember watching you help someone pack up at the market and I thought of Brad Pitt in his movie *Across the Tracks*—something about your posture, tall white socks and tennis shoes. You always looked like you were ready for a sprint at the market."

"I don't look anything like Brad..." he said and changed the subject. "You wanna sleep out on the back deck tonight, like you've always wanted to? Watch the moon?"

"Yes!" she said.

They walked into the bedroom and took the bedding out to the little twin bed in the corner of the bare, second-story porch. Grace loved sleeping outside and was getting excited about it.

Even though the house sheltered them from the western wind, the branches of the aspen trees beyond the balcony blew in the wind, adding movement, gentle sounds and life into the moment. The bright full moon was coming up over the mountains in a clear, darkening blue sky.

River took the spot closest to the wall, spooning her from behind. They snuggled in with the puffy duvet.

"Grace?" he said. "I think we should take a break."

She took a deep inhale and let it out slowly as she kept her focus on the beautiful full moon in front of them.

"So, this is the end… The full moon *did* bring an end…" she said. "I was afraid of that," she added in a whisper.

He choked down a swallow and said, "I guess."

They lay there in the twin bed, spooned together silently. Grace watched the bright moon come up into the dark blue sky as the wind continued to blow around the house. She felt as if she were Dorothy from *The Wizard of OZ* and she was getting ready to leave Kansas. Knowing that there was nothing to hold on to. She knew there wasn't anything to do but to let go and let her course change itself again.

She gently drifted into sleep, wrapped in River's arms, as the moon moved overhead. In the morning she grabbed her things and petted the dogs on her way out—

"Stay for breakfast," River said.

"'K," she responded.

They made granola with lemon custard yogurt and their yerba mate tea.

"Grace…" River said as she sat across from him at the table outside, thinking to herself, *He looks so attractive in his teal jacket against the contrast of his white hair and sturdy posture.*

He chipped in with a slight, nervous head bobble, "I'm not what you want. I'm too old for you."

"Well, I disagree," Grace calmly said. "I can tell you how much I really love you and want you over and over, but you keep pushing me away, not listening." She paused. "River, I see love as an investment. I've been so *open, so loving, so accepting* with you and us, investing my love, always showing you that. It doesn't seem like I'm getting the same in return. Only when you feel like it. You pick me up just to drop me. I know it might take awhile for you to open up, but your lack of confidence has been painful. Last night was sad. Going to the concert *alone* because you don't want anyone to 'think' of us in a weird way." She got up from the table, trying not to tear up.

She knew to be grateful for all she'd already been given. She walked behind him as he sat in his chair and started massaging his neck but mostly to tell him what she wanted to say without having to look at him.

"I want you to know you've been an angel to me in many ways…" Just then, "I Can't Help Falling in Love." came on Pandora. She couldn't continue with what she was saying.

They both just listened while she massaged his neck. After the song she walked in front of him and straddled him on the chair, hugging him deeply. Not wanting to leave. But she knew it was time for their season to end.

She sat up, looked him straight in the eyes, and said, "I want you to know, I love you so much" as she spread her arms out wide. "I love you this much and more." Tears welled up and her voice cracked with the effort to keep them in. His eyes began to well up. "When we both get to a place…" she paused to swallow down her emotions. "Where we can get together, it would be great to come up and go for a walk with you as we did in the beginning."

"Yeah, Grace. I'd like that. My walking buddy…" His lips quivered. "It'll have to be after this winter's snowfall has melted," he said, indicating that he needed time to heal and the warm weather will have melted what it could from his heart.

She nodded, holding back tears. "Whenever it is, I look forward to it. I better go," she said.

"I'm glad we aren't angry with each other, telling each other to 'fuck off,'" he said kinda awkwardly.

"I'd never do that," she said.

"I know, Grace," he said.

She got up and went inside to grab her things. On her way down the stairs, she saw him leaning on the railing of the stairwell. She sat on the stairs, holding on to the railing, looking him straight in the eye.

"You know, we could make it, River? If we had rules and boundaries."

"Yeah? We could come up with our own rules." He said, suddenly sounding positive, seeming interested. Then he quickly added, "But I'm in high demand here in Stanley. Not many single guys my age."

Grace's stomach turned, and she was unable to take a breath. "Then why are you pursuing and being with me?" she asked straightforwardly.

He never answered; he just swayed his torso back and forth uncomfortably. His lack of response encouraged her to get up. She was now looking down on him, noticing the warm yellow sunshine bellowing into the entire downstairs. She loved the comfort it brought, despite the hard conversation. She took a deep breath in, let it out with her let-down emotions, and moved down one step.

She sighed, saying, "When I'm laying with you, talking with you, opening up and being intimate with you, my heart is giving out love and intentions of love. When you talk about your heart being Fort Knox and being in high demand, I don't feel like it's resonating at all with the feelings in my heart or yours.'" She grabbed her jacket off the stair rail. Again, no response from him. She walked down the stairs and out the front door to her car. He stood outside on the patio while she put her things in the car and walked back to hug him. She was a bit shaky and afraid to say anything for fear of tears.

"So, is this the last time we will be together?" he asked. She could tell he was sensitive.

"I don't know, River." she said, "This time hurts."

He swallowed hard like his strategy wasn't working. Grace knew she was better than to try and figure all this out when it was her that would end up in pieces. She got into her car, slowly backed up, took one look at his heavy expression, gave a sideways wave, and drove south. She cried the whole three hours home.

She got back around noon and got herself ready for her half a day of work. She tried not to seem at her emotional wits' end when she walked into work a bit early. The lights were out, but her boss was there.

"Grace! Come here…" He walked her into his office, and they both took a seat and jumped right in. "We need to downsize. You're the newest onboard, even though everyone here *loves* you, all the patients *love* you, and you have done such a great job here! You have... You picked up quickly, and you work well on your own too." He paused before he said, "sorry, I've gotta let you go."

She couldn't believe it and did her best to hold in her pain, trying not to cry.

"Okay." She was surprised her voice didn't shake. She didn't know what to say. "Do I leave now?" is all that came out.

"Yeah, go ahead and clean out your drawer. If things pick up, you'll be the first we call!" he said.

*Yeah, so you can pick me up, just to drop me... like River.* she thought.

She left without being able to say goodbye to her coworkers, her new friends. She drove straight home, flopped onto her bed, and cried. She let her heartbreak. Lying backward on her bed, her heart squeezed so painfully deep into her chest. Holding in her breath so long, to where her ribs reached their maximum flexibility. *Here it is,* she thought. *This is heartbreak—this is what it feels like.* Her head was dangling off the edge of the bed, full of pressure and intense, squelched facial expressions. Her face was covered in all types of facial drainage: tears, snot, saliva. Not such pretty emotions.

*Well there are two endings.* She thought, *there must be a third around the corner.* Every time she stopped crying, she'd think about River and it'd start all over again. Enveloped in sorrow, there was nothing else she could do but drown in it. She did her hermit thing, not leaving her room for a good while. She knew the Estonians in the room next door would wonder what was going on, but she didn't stop herself from processing the pains of a broken heart.

She didn't get out of bed until the next day when she went to the juice bar where she'd been working weekends and asked if she could pick up more hours during the week.

"Heck yes, Grace!" the owner said. "When do you wanna start?"

"Tomorrow?" Grace asked, as lively as possible.

The owner looked at the schedule. "Looks like I can get you in here on Monday. Will that work?"

"Yes. Thank you!" she said as she had to fake her smile, covering her tattered heart. She went back home to lie in her garden and ground her soul. She watched the sun move across the sky and then observed the moon coming up, thanking it— asking it to aid her in her healing process.

A few days later, she went to the grocery store for a few essentials. She was in the checkout line with an expressionless face when she looked over at the magazines all over the counter saying that Brad and Angelina had ended their marriage.

"Well, this was a very intense moon for sure!" she said aloud to herself. *That's a big ending… bummer. They did great humanitarian work together.*

With the added bad news, Grace grabbed her groceries and walked out of the store with little energy for life. She got into her car, and before pulling out she saw Cray with a cutie. He was smiling happily, reaching for the gals hand. She took it and swung it back and forth, full of love. He pulled her in and kissed the top of her head.

"Well, there's another ending…" she said aloud as her gut turned. *Probably my karma for initiating the break-up with Cray*, she thought.

She drove home and walked straight to her garden to hand weed her baby carrots. She was very meticulous, not letting one weed survive in her favorite root patch. Once she finished hand weeding, she looked around at all the dragonflies hovering above her. They looked magical, clean of emotion, living the simple life in nature. She wished her life would magically be free and simple, if not now then… someday.

She reached over to her 10-foot row of vibrant orange and yellow Calendula flowers. She pulled a small bouquet, inspected them closely, then smelled them. She enjoyed their happy color and scent—then picked a handful of petals off the flowers, into her hand. She laid on her back on the bare dirt and threw the petals up as high as she could, watching the orange against the strong contrast of the bright, clear blue-sky. They fluttered down, sprawled apart, falling all over her and the ground that supported her firmly. She felt as though the petals represented the best parts of her, and it was a good reminder that her flame hadn't fully gone out. She was content laying there as she counseled with the sun than the moon and sensed herself re-grounding to Mother Earth. She stayed out late then went inside to bed.

The next day, she went to Auger Falls for a walk, run, a

bit of stretching and sat next to the water, allowing it to clear her energy and wash her soul. She spent all day out there and when the moon came up—her trusty companion—was right there with her. She was there while Grace lay in River's arms for the last time, a witness of her inner sorrows and she was there to comfort her now.

She admired nature's connection. She cherished the sun and its life-giving rays just as much as the moon. She watched the water flow from the same spot that River gave her her first raspberry kiss. She'd never had this sort of heartbreak. It was deep. Maybe because she had been brave and courageous in this love but he couldn't take the relationship on even though he did have feelings for her?

When she got in her car, she started it and checked her phone. There was a message. It was River.

*How are you doing?* he asked.

Sigh.

*Heartbroken but picking myself up. You? How are Maggie and Max?* she asked.

*Buried Maggie out in the hills behind the house the day after you left,* he said.

*Ohhhh…!* she responded. Grace imagined him taking

her body out into the hills, digging a hole, and burying her alone. She couldn't hold back her tears. That must've been tough for him. She knew he'd never tell her how hard it had been.

*How was your drive home from my place? I'd hoped you'd let me know you made it back safely,* he texted.

*Drove home crying the entire way,* she said. *Went to work and my boss let me go that day.*

*What a tough one,* he said.

*Yep,* she texted as tears continued down her face.

*Just wasn't meant to be, Grace,* he replied.

Totally unhappy with that last message, Grace responded with, *K. Well, River you have a good night, okay? Take care.*

*You to Grace!*

# 11

# The Wedding

September 2016

Grace's blonde, blue-eyed, now very tan Estonian roommates were leaving the next morning, the first of September. Their three weeks turned into three months, she concluded that with the language barrier there was a bit of miscommunication. In their first conversation, Aron said their stay would last three weeks but he meant... three months.

She didn't mind having them there all summer. They were great house companions, and she didn't feel so alone with them around, even though they came home every night at 10 PM, Monday through Saturday. They were such a great help on those Sundays off. They mowed the lawn and helped water, which was a feat since there was about an acre of grass. They trimmed the hedges along the lane, weeded flower beds, trimmed trees, and swept off the big deck upstairs. She wondered what her neighbors had thought about her having three young, shirtless lads working in her yard every Sunday but she didn't mind because it was all the help she could get. And she needed it.

"Hey princess," the youngest Estonian liked to call her. "We'd like to take you to dinner tomorrow night, in gratitude for your generosity."

"…and for our new friendship." Said Edgar the Capricorn Estonian.

"Of course." she said, surprised.

"We are buying, so take us somewhere really nice!" said Marcus, "come straight home from work. We will make the date."

"I have the perfect place in mind!" she said, excited for tomorrow.

She only had a little bit of time to shower after work the next day, to be on time for their reservation. She pulled out the same outfit she wore to the concert in Sun Valley, knowing it was nice and wouldn't have to put any time or effort into it. Once she was dressed, they took photos of themselves together out in the yard, before heading to the restaurant.

Aron, the one that she met first on his bike, had to move to a different location a few weeks back.

So, it would be just the three of them going to Elevation 486. It was her favorite restaurant in town, right on the canyon edge. She brought everyone from out of town there to dine. It showed off the best of Twin Falls, in her opinion. The view of the striking canyon, the river, and the beautifully designed bridge with wide-open skies in the background.

She requested a patio table. They had a glass of wine each while sharing a lovely conversation about their time together, what they came to know about each other, keeping it positive and healthy with a few *suggestions for Grace.*

Marcus had to tell her, "not everything is about you."

"What do you mean?" She asked. Trying to be open with what was about to be said.

"Me talking about my hangnail toe doesn't have anything to do with you." Grace looked at him curiously. *"You* don't need to try and fix it," he said.

She nodded as she took it in. That was a good insight for her to think of. She thought about trying to explain why she wanted to help him with his toe but that would emphasize the point he tried to make. So, she told them about River, and they empathized then quickly moved on to other subjects. Edgar talked about being a military kid and Marcus about his parent's recent divorce and its impact on him. They all mentioned it would've been nice if Aron were with them celebrating as well.

The night was so enjoyable. She was connecting with these young men visiting from a faraway place. Relating to them, almost more than the people she saw locally, every day. She was bummed they were leaving, but that was part of why it was such a great moment—because it was fleeting.

Grace watched the moon start to peak up on the horizon.

"Look at the moon," she said. It was just a tiny sliver of a new moon. The boys stared for a bit, while Grace was pleased she was having a better experience as she watched this phase of the moon rise, compared to the full moon from two weeks ago, in Stanley.

Marcus nudged her gently. He directed her attention to a nicely dressed family at the next table.

He kept saying, "That mom keeps looking at you!"

Grace knew there was nothing she could do about that and said, "So what."

He said, "It's 'cause you look beautiful, my princess," with his Estonian accent, "and you are having a nice dinner with two younger, good looking men! She should stare." He said it confidently and loud.

Grace said, "Shhhh!" embarrassed.

The waiter brought the ticket and the boys both paid for her meal. They got up from the table, and as they started walking out, Marcus came right next to her. He looked back at the starring woman and said, "She's still looking!" loud enough for the woman to hear and he grabbed her hand. Grace thought it was a bit juvenile, but she tolerated it.

Then Edgar walked up to her other side and grabbed her other hand. All three of them giggled with an innocent playfulness. She could tell that would catch some attention as they walked through the patio tables, laughing and swinging their hands as they went. She couldn't help but smile freely, appreciating their kindness towards her in that way.

They drove home, and Grace got ready for bed. As she snuggled into her blankets both guys climbed in with her. She looked at them and thought, *no…* on second thought, *why not?*

They snuggled her all night, fully respecting her. She

was sandwiched between them throughout the night, while they both grasped for cuddles. She was loved and embraced by the world at that moment. She embraced it as a gift for being open and kind and offering her home.

The morning came quickly and they had to catch their flight. Grace stayed in bed, but they each came in, one by one after they put their bags in the car. They kissed her on the top of her head and told her "thank you" and "good luck." They told her that she was a successful woman and to believe in herself. Again, she felt so loved.

Marcus said, "My beautiful princess. You are my home away from home," and walked out. She smiled and rested her head down, flashing back to the way that doe had looked at her in the park that day. She felt the Estonians looked at her the same way and sighed a delighted sigh before falling back asleep.

When she got up, she noticed a Post-it note on the outside of her bedroom door that read, *you're a beautiful princess.* It was spelled wrong but she didn't mind. She decided to keep that note and put it in her medicine cabinet upstairs. After they left, she moved up into her grandparents' master bedroom since the renters upstairs had just moved out. Grace found new renters for the basement and was going to find two roommates to share the upstairs with her. She noticed the new moon brought a few *new* beginnings.

Her cousin, Sam invited her to dinner, after her long day of moving upstairs. He was getting married at the end of September. His Fiancé, Kaya, knew about her breakup with

River and wanted to hook Grace up with a friend of hers but Grace didn't want to meet anyone straight away. She was still heartbroken. Sam must have told Kaya about River, because right off the bat, Kaya said, "Dude, you need a younger man. You don't wanna be 50 taking care of an 80-year-old!"

"You're right," Grace said, "but I couldn't help falling so hard for him—That's not like me and I was with him for less than six months."

"You're too nice. You want everyone to feel loved and not left out. He's choosing to be single and has been for 30 years, Grace. There's no changing that man!" Kaya said as a matter of fact. "Plus, you gotta think of Kai."

Grace appreciated her perspective and giggled a bit. "Yeah, you're right about that but I don't wanna jump into another relationship right away with your buddy."

"Okay." And she left Grace alone.

The wedding came up quickly. It was out in an open valley in New Meadows, Idaho. Everyone camped in a five-yurt campsite. Grace stayed with her mom and stepdad in a house in town, since all the yurts were filled. The rental was big and grand, it had five bedrooms with a vaulted ceiling.

Grace thought, *Huh… I just lived in a yurt and now there's a wedding where everyone is staying in yurts, but I somehow ended up in this gorgeous big house!*

The wedding was casual, she wore a button-up plaid dress with her tall boots and hair down. She drove up to the camp spot with all the yurts, a couple of hours before the wedding. She helped her cousin pick all the little lint flakes off his pressed tux as he sat on the edge of the deck to the bride's yurt. She liked taking care of him, doing something simply for him on his wedding day. He seemed to appreciate that too.

He looked up at her and asked, "Grace, would you be my best man?"

"Seriously? Yes," she said with excitement.

"I mean, you have to ask Kaya if that's alright first," he said.

"Okay," she said and ran into the yurt to find her.

Grace was so delighted and quickly found beautiful Kaya in her stunning white sundress. She was being doted on by her female family members and friends.

"Kaya?" Grace whispered, "Sam asked me to be his best man, as long as it was okay with you?"

Kaya got the biggest smile on her face. Almost teary-eyed. it was something she'd wanted. "Really? That means my brother gets to be my Maid of Honor." She got all giddy. "Go tell my brother he's walking with you and will stand next to me," she directed, beaming.

Grace obeyed her request happily. This was thrilling and unexpected. It was time to start the ceremony, Grace and Kaya's brother were the first to walk out with hooked elbows, moving at the pace of the slow guitar song into the dry, grassy opening of the valley. The pine-filled mountains curled up around them. The rest of the wedding party followed and they had a nice, simple ceremony with Kaya's mom. Grace loved the way Kaya was looking at Sam. She watched her tear up and was sensitive to her emotions as she spoke. She couldn't hear what they were saying, but she thought it was lovely and she teared up with her.

After the ceremony, they played music and danced while everyone brought out a dish of food they'd made. Grace met Sky, Kaya's friend. He was a tall, stout, smiley guy with a thick, medium-length dark beard and short hair. Kinda looked like a lumberjack who was wearing Chaco sandals, a t-shirt, and shorts. He was two years younger than Grace, 29.

He came up to her and introduced himself while she was standing near the fire pit, surrounded by wedding guests. She wasn't feeling it, but she wanted to be nice and see what he was about. He got her a glass of red wine, she didn't feel like drinking it, so she politely held it. He talked to her about the wedding, and she asked him about playing his guitar. He had been the one playing during the ceremony and Sam and Kaya's first dance.

He walked away and she stayed at the fire pit with everyone else. She was chatting with a lady next to her, as she was getting up to leave, she heard a laugh from behind. It pierced her ears and it poked at something inside of her. She looked back, and it was Sky. She'd never heard a laugh like that and it stirred her. So familiar! She was unable to say goodbye to him or anyone else, since she left the wedding party with her ride who had to head back early the next morning—and goodbyes take too much explaining sometimes.

Sky texted her on the drive home the next day, *Hey, missed saying goodbye last night. Kaya gave me your number, hope that's alright. I was wondering if we could get together?*

*Maybe in a couple of weeks?* She replied.

*Sounds good, Grace. Nice to meet you. You're a good lookin' girl.*

*LOL,* she responded, thinking that wasn't very mature, but he was using his playful side and that's alright. She could see him worrying about that text once he'd sent it. *Thanks, Sky. I'll text you sometime next week, see what you're up to.*

*Great. Drive safe.* He texted before saying, *And I didn't mean you're just cute, you were fun to talk with too.*

Grace laughed and thought to herself, *Yep... I called that one.* It made her chuckle anyway, and she welcomed it.

A few weeks later, Sky came to visit her. She gave him a walking tour of the homestead and made a steak dinner with sauteed veggies from the garden. Then they watched a few music YouTube videos while they chatted. Grace thought he was nice and a good guy, but she couldn't quite move forward, after River. She didn't want to overlap her emotions but her curiosity drew her to Sky.

While they watched the videos, he laughed a few times, causing her to have flashes of a king in armor without a helmet on. A similar-looking guy with a beard. Jolly guy. Grace immediately whirled her head toward Sky when he laughed. She normally wasn't attracted by his body type: tall, broad shoulders, long beard, and a bit of a belly. But that laugh... she'd watch his cheery face, so happy with that chuckle. It kinda made her wanna snuggle into that torso and get lost in comfort, maybe make him chuckle.

He asked her a few questions about what she was striving for, her goals, dreams, and wishes. She told him all her big picture goals as well as her immediate goals and felt the need to mention River, and that it was a fresh wound and she still had feelings for him.

He listened.

He asked if she wanted kids and she said, "of course." He informed her that he didn't want kids and that he was leaving for Oregon to school, after Christmas until he finished his studies, two years from now. Grace thought, *Well, this won't work for a love relationship but maybe we could be friends*? He was close to Kaya's family and she was sure they would meet up again in his home town of Bliss. Sky didn't stay long and Grace was ready for bed. She was looking forward to spending the next day on an adventure, alone—delighted to spend her time in solitude when the opportunity presented itself. She knew that Jupiter would be aligning with the sun on this day, making it the luckiest day of the year, according to astrologers.

She charged her iPod, packed lunch, and spent all day in the canyon, out on the rocks, watching the waters flow, and lounged in nature. The outdoors were cleansing and healing for her. She didn't notice much "luck" on this day, but she did sense the sun seemed bigger, brighter, and warmer. That was all she needed.

She thought about how the market season was winding down. She looked forward to not having to spend all day Friday into the late-night harvesting, preparing, and loading up all her veggies into her crammed Jetta. She decided her last day of the market would be the first week of October.

When that day came around, she had several refugees come into her booth. They were haggling with her on prices, trying to get a 25-pound box of tomatoes for $15. She told them to come back after the market ended, and if she still had them she'd sell them for $15.

Nobody ended up buying them, and the couple came back. So she sold the $40 box of tomatoes for their requested price and gave them another box full of veggies, at no charge. She told all her vendor friends who didn't have veggies of their own to come and get whatever they wanted. She had plenty of leftovers in the garden.

There were several who took her up on the offer. It made her feel so good. She loved sharing the abundance of food. That gave her the idea to call the college's refugee office and invite anyone who wanted to come out and harvest whatever food was leftover before a heavy frost. There was more than she could eat or give away and told the neighbors to come to get what they wanted too.

The next day, a long van drove down her lane. Out of it appeared half a dozen or more refugees from many different countries. They were all so kind and grateful for the opportunity to harvest. Some tried to teach her about the plants and how they'd used different vegetables and plants in their home countries. Most of it was lost in translation. But she enjoyed the interaction, regardless.

They cleaned out the garden and she watched everyone pack all the overflowing boxes, then stuffed themselves in. A couple had to stand next to the door inside to fit in and they had to try several times to slam it shut. She watched the packed van drive away and felt that she got way more out of that moment of giving than she did all summer long, wondering how much she was going to make in a day at the market.

What she received in that was more than the feeling of money in her pocket. Plus, she didn't have to worry about wasting good food when the frost came, even though it would have made good compost for the soil—but there was plenty of plant matter left over for that.

When the frost did come, she felt bad that she neglected her overflowing apple tree in the backyard. It hadn't been pruned in years and was *full* of apples. She beat herself up about the waste. She did offer them over social media to whoever needed or wanted them. Her boss at the juice shop was the only one who wanted a box. She saved a little box for herself and took them to share at a pumpkin carving party that Sky invited her to, in Bliss.

He introduced her to all his friends as they carved pumpkins. She carved an overly happy Jack-o'-lantern. The guy who grew the pumpkins was the son of one of her farmer friends she knew from the Ketchum farmer's market. He was about eight years younger than Grace, but she'd remembered him from the market. Sawyer's dad was one of the Three Organic Musketeers. Matt was another, and the third one farmed in Shoshone.

Grace was excited to be a little more social—She talked with Sawyer about his upcoming trip to Costa Rica. She'd been there before, living, working, and volunteering on a permaculture farm off the Caribbean coast. While they were talking, Grace heard a coyote howl outside, even though several party people were talking and playing Ping-Pong in the garage.

"Coyotes. I heard when they cross your path, your life changes," she says.

"Let's go listen and howl back," Sawyer said.

They went out to the fence while Grace noticed her left leg and foot were hurting her again, badly. They howled together and the coyotes howled back.

He turned quickly to Grace, "I have animal cards in my van. I pulled the Lizard card, which is the dreamer." He said while he pulled up his shirt to show his lizard tattoo.

"Whoa," was all Grace said.

"Come pick a card," he said, all eager.

"Okay," she replied, quickly following him back to the garage.

"What do you think your spirit animal is?" he asked as they sat on the ping pong table that wasn't currently being used.

"Well, I'd love to earn the right to be the deer," she said, then proceeded to tell him about walking along the creek and suddenly meeting the gaze of the lovely doe face to face.

"Gentleness. The deer represents loving gentleness," he said from memory.

"Aww, that's sweet, I like that." Grace said as he handed her the box of animal cards.

She pulled the deck of cards out and the card facing up was the deer.

Sawyer said, "Whoa, that's never happened before," smiling with enthusiasm.

She shuffled and cut the deck, revealing a random card. The deer, again. There was one deer in the whole deck of 30 cards. It was the only animal she'd laid eyes on and it seemed to *want* to be the only one she saw.

"That's it. You are the deer, Grace." Sawyer said confidently.

Grace smiled so proudly and said, "I guess I am." She strongly sensed that something assisted in making that clear to her.

Sky came up and said, "I'm ready to head out with my buddies."

Grace said, "Thank you" to Sawyer for having her pull

an animal card.

"Thank *you*, Grace." he said, "It was a pleasure hanging out with you tonight."

"You too, Sawyer. goodbye." She said as she walked out of the garage with Sky.

Sky insisted that he give Grace a piggyback from the party to her car—without knowing of her pain—and they said good night before she drove 40 minutes back to Twin and thought how fun it was to have a good group of like-minded friends to hang out and have fun with. Life didn't always have to be about hard work, solo contemplation time, and heartbreak. She looked forward to another trip to Bliss.

The next day, she woke, and her leg and foot were so sore that the arch of her foot throbbed. She wished she still worked with the physical therapist; it seemed to have helped it get better.

When she got to the juice shop, she was limping around a bit. It was slow, and her co-workers made it easy for her. When she got home, she made dinner and washed her dishes. Then heard a knock on the door in the kitchen.

She thought, *it's odd to get a loud knock on the garage door— instead of the front door.* She opened the door and it was her old boss, the therapist.

He said, "Grace, I need you to come back to work..." He seemed desperate.

All she could think to say was, "Have a seat." as she ushered him to the kitchen table while drying off her hands.

"Amy quit." he said, "She was causing a lot of unnecessary drama in the office and told me, I had to choose between her and Lindsey. You know how everyone loves Lindsay and how great she is at her job. So, I let Amy go. Can you come back? You would take over her position. It's the hardest job in the office, so I'll have to train you for a while, but I know you can do it!" he said.

"When do you need me?" Grace asked, not knowing why she wouldn't say yes… but she did wonder if Amy could have been part of the reason she was asked to leave…? Either way, that was currently irrelevant.

"Can you start tomorrow?" he asked with a pleading face.

"I'll have to give my two weeks' notice at the juice shop. They brought me back when I needed work—immediately, no problem," she said. Then she asked, "What are the chances you let me go again?" She was starting to wonder…

"I won't need to. I appreciate you coming back, Grace!" he said as if she had already said yes to him.

She looked at him and said, "I'll come back, but I'm giving the juice shop a solid two weeks."

"Alright," he said, opening the door with an upbeat attitude before saying "goodnight."

She put in her two weeks at the juice shop again, and they were very understanding and supportive of her. They knew she'd be in to eat and get her juice.

When she went back in for work at the physical therapist's, they worked on her leg, and foot. That *did* help along with laying on the water beds on her lunch breaks. One day, she was on a water bed, listening to some organ music on her iPod, and looked up at the ceiling. In the little random texturing above, she could see the shape of Sky in his armor. His long beard and wide, big chest. She could hear his laugh and was taken into an image of him standing out in a grassy area next to a forest. He was standing in the center of several men on horses who were listening to him give guidance. He was a jolly king. It made her wonder more about Sky.

She couldn't tell if she liked him as a friend or if she could see more. *Better not, since he didn't want kids,* she thought. So, she left that subject alone. Just then a coworker of hers came and interrupted, asking if she wanted to take an astrology class with her. Grace decided that would be a great way to get out and do something fun!

* * *

The astrology teacher just happened to be her favorite yoga instructor while in college. She was introducing the basics of a star chart, which Grace had no idea how to read, but she wanted to learn. She honored the cycles of the moon and enjoyed reading about what zodiac sign the moon was in and what it represented for the lunation cycle.

She went to the class and had a good time changing it up and doing something different. She found out she was a Taurus rising; she was born with the sun in the sign of Capricorn and the constellation Taurus was coming up on the Eastern horizon. Her teacher said, "That means you show up and appear as a Taurus. You're supposed to become a Taurus this lifetime."

Her teacher explained every student's sun sign and its meaning and the meaning of the rising sign—first house. When she got to Grace, she said, "Taurus is ruled by Venus. Venus is the planet of love, food, abundance, money, art, projects, and beauty." She spoke with enthusiasm. "Taurus is an Earth sign— it's the gardener along with Capricorn, and it represents the house and food. It's the most stubborn sign in the zodiac, and it's also what we value. It represents a solid foundation. It rules money and its pleasures of all sensual kinds." She paused. "Grace, your North Node lies in this first house. Your soul is meant to go in the direction of these things, this lifetime," she said.

A lady sitting right next to her said, "You fit that description, by the way. Very earthy and grounded."

Grace had her hair up in a messy bun and wore earthy yoga clothes, and essential oils. She loved that she fit the Taurus, first house description, but what got her was that River was a Taurus.

She flashed back with deep feelings. Back to that day

she walked with him to Auger Falls, remembering herself saying, "I don't know if we will become a thing or not, but I want to tell you that I've always admired you and your strength. You are independent, kind, and caring, and you are grounded in yourself. You worked hard for your money and now you enjoy it. I want to be like that. Like you."

His reply was, "I will do what I can to help guide you in that direction. I appreciate that."

Maybe River came along to help her develop her Taurus rising? She was destined to go that way this lifetime. Was she destined to be with him? Her gut said no. She thought, *No, it's the first house. So… it's me. Not the other.* This was a good bit of information for her, and she loved learning about the heavens more.

She wanted to be a student of astrology one day—when she had time. In the meantime, she'd just watch her daily astrology video on her astrology app. She loved knowing what was happening in the heavens every day, whether she knew exactly what it all meant or not.

\* \* \*

Thanksgiving was around the corner, and she received a text message from River.

*Happy Thanksgiving Grace! Do you have any plans for the holiday?*

*Nope. Just work up to Thanksgiving. You?* She wondered why he was asking.

*Headed down to Arizona to see the boys. I was wondering if I could meet you on your lunch break to give you a few things?* he asked.

*Sure. How about meeting at the Twin Falls visitor's center? I'll text you when I'm about to leave for lunch,* she texted back.

*Okay. Looking forward to seeing you.* He said.

*You too, River,* she said and left it at that.

She pulled up to the visitor's center, on the edge of the canyon next to the bridge. He was already there with his horse trailer and horses to take them south for the winter.

He got out, walked over, and opened the door to her car. She got out and gave him a happy hug. They exchanged "Hellos," then he handed her two books on straw bale and adobe houses, then the vase they had made with the finger through the lip. Grace loved that little imperfection, forever saved in stone. He handed her a tiny loaf of banana bread too. Her hands were full, and she thanked him for the gifts, set them in the car, and said, "Shall we go for a walk?"

"Yeah," he said.

They walked along the canyon rim next to the Perrine

bridge. They didn't talk at first.

"You look good, Grace. Wearing makeup, even." he said.

"Yeah, I need to for work." She thought that was an unusual thing for him to notice and comment on.

"Well, it looks nice," he said.

"Thanks!" she said.

He pulled two old photos out of his plaid, button-up shirt and said, "I wanted to show you these." It was him with his boys in a raft that was sitting on a riverbank. The boys were young, River's hair was dark black, and he looked chubbier... odd, she thought he was more handsome now as an older man with white hair.

"A trip back in time," she said. "Thanks for showing me that."

"Yeah. So, how are you doing?" he asked.

"Good. Heartbroken, but ok." she said.

"You know there are no hard feelings, it's just our age difference. You are such a beautiful person." he said in a way to try and make her feel better, but it was more like he was irritating a healing wound than caring for it.

"Brrrr," she said, kinda ignoring what was said.

"Yeah, it's cold. Can we go sit in the car for a bit?" he asked.

"Yes, let's," she said, grateful for that suggestion.

They walked back to her car quickly, and she turned on the engine and heater to warm them up. Her music came on and added a spark to their little meeting.

"How long are you going down south?" she asked, hoping to maybe get closer to the reason why they were meeting.

"Till the snow melts!" he said. Grace knew he was referring to what he had said months ago about being walking buddies again, "after the snow melts." She glanced at her dashboard that just happened to have a small container of raspberries sitting there for her lunch.

"Gottcha," was all she said. "Look at the garbage can." She pointed to it and tried to change the subject to something a little lighter, "It's the shape of Idaho."

"Oh, yeah," he said. "Upside down."

"No, it's right side up. It's in a square, so it looks like a double Idaho. The black is the cutout," she explained.

"Oh, yeah. Wow, opposite perspectives,"

"Yeah…" she said, thinking that overlapped their current perspectives on their relationship.

"Grace, I want to say you are such a beautiful person! You love me unconditionally." He choked up and swallowed as he held back tears, looking out the window. "I've always thought of how… *pure* you are, even the moment I met you. More people should be like you."

"Well, thank you, River." *Was he apologizing?* She wondered.

He paused for a quiet moment then said, "I *asked* the universe for you and you came to me but I'm not brave enough to accept you."

Grace didn't know what to say, so she picked up the last raspberry, put it in her mouth, and started to chew. Unexpectedly, he leaned in and assertively landed a powerful, ever so perfect kiss on her as the song changed to her new favorite, "Darlin."

Grace naturally reciprocated. It was no work at all for them. Their tongues simply melted together. Dissolving the raspberry juice all over their mouths, feeling the seeds mix with their tongues.

She felt like a magical flower spiraling into a beautiful blossom, initiated by his charmed kiss. She soaked it all up into her being, soul, and heart. Grateful for that final kiss. Oh, so grateful for it. She knew to be strong and not get her hopes up but to embrace that beautiful moment.

River got out and said, "Goodbye." and walked around the front of his truck to his door.

"Bye." she said, "Text me to let me know you've made it to your landing zone, please!"

He nodded to her as she started her car and drove around the front of his truck and headed back to work.

* * *

It was no coincidence that that February had been their hardest winter with more snowfall since the year she was born in '84. Twin Falls had snow coming down for 3 days straight and the Stanley, Wood River valley had even more.

The wind drifted 3-foot snow drifts over the driveway and lane at the homestead. She couldn't get the tractor working but work was canceled and she was stuck inside. Everyone was inside. So, she cozied up in her room.

After spending two days and nights hanging out writing and listening to astrology videos, waiting for the snow to stop, she looked out the window to the bright white, illuminated night. She saw a few dark mounds under the tree and walked over to her pile of blankets and pillows that she'd made as a bed. She looked out the window and saw 20 head of deer, all bedded down in the snow, surrounding the corner of the house around her room.

She teared up, thanked them for their company, feeling not so alone anymore. Feeling loved by the deer, and fell asleep comfortably.

Grace woke up on that Saturday morning. She looked out the bedroom window for the deer and saw multiple nests in the snow where they'd slept through the night with her.

She called several plowing companies to plow the drive, everyone was booked until Monday. She would be stuck for a few more days. So, she went walking around the yard, through last year's garden patch, through the many deer nests in the snow, and followed their tracks to the apple tree... The one she felt so bad about wasting its apples. When she went underneath the branches, she noticed all the apples that had fallen in the fall were all gone. Not one was there. The deer stayed overnight and must have eaten them all! That made Grace feel so good about not getting to the apples.

She mentioned to her friend at work that she had 20 heads of deer sleeping outside her room and that they'd eaten the old apples.

They said, "Yeah. You bet they ate them. They said on the local news how this winter was hard on the deer. Finding them starved to death."

Grace felt so much better about how she neglected to find a way to use all the apples, but she helped many deer eat and survive during a hard season! There was a reason for leaving them on the tree and it ended up working out for the best.

* * *

Sam and his new wife moved up to Hailey after the wedding but now were moving to Glenns Ferry. She drove up to help them move, April 1 after the snow had melted. It caused major flooding, and when they drove through Fairfield to Glenns Ferry, the raised roads looked like bridges over lakes. Homes were sitting in the water with mini tides, a sight for sure.

She'd never experienced this intense flooding in her lifetime. It made her connect emotionally with the weight of her and River's agreement about meeting again after the snow had melted. And *oh*, was that interesting that it was their most significant snowfall since she was born. She had fed the struggling deer, and now the worst flooding from snow melt *ever* in the Valley? It fit too well for the weight of this heartache… as she witnessed flooding for miles, she wondered if they were ever going to get together for that walk?

* Darlin' by Ryan Bingham

# 12

## Yellow Chariot

Neptune retrogrades, June 16, 2017

Grace found herself unable to let go of River… still. She'd been watering the yard all morning, unable to think of anything other than him and why they weren't together. Her heart loved him and wouldn't let go, maybe she was expecting that they'd actually go on that walk in the spring. Either way, she knew it wasn't any good for her to obsess over him, how they were together, and what plans were swept away *prematurely*.

She *had* to lay him to rest and move on. Why was she addicted to him? Was it the toxic relationship she was addicted to? Was it an intimacy disorder? She loved him so deeply and unconditionally. She knew he loved her too, but they were just too different for him, embarrassing for him. She knew it wasn't healthy to still be so attached to this heartbreak.

Tense body, she took a break from watering. She could feel the fire roaring deep inside, beginning to boil the inner waters of her soul. She thrust the sprinkler stake into the grass and walked with rigid confidence across the lawn in her short cowgirl boots and up the front steps. She swung the front door to the house open, moved swiftly down the hall into her bedroom, and grabbed her green spiral notebook like she had a bone to pick with it.

Grace headed into the kitchen, snatched a chunk of dark chocolate, filled a mason jar full of water, threw a lemon slice in it, and headed to the bright living room. She flung the sliding screen door to the side with no intention of closing it behind her. She made it to the picnic table on the open deck and firmly plopped down in a sunny spot, facing the white brick house and the window to her bedroom. She flipped open her notebook, pen in hand, ready… *oh,* so ready to write River out of her head and heart for good.

She wrote how she loved him still; that didn't help—the fierce conviction, her full throttle, determined energy quickly transformed into a limp, wimp. She wrote how horrible he was to her, that didn't help. She wrote how she wanted to open her heart for a man who was worthy of her love, spirit, and attention. She started crying hunched over her open notebook, thinking about how pure her intentions were with him. *Why was he pushing me away? I was sure he loved me.* She paused, getting up to move a second sprinkler off the back deck behind her.

She was so grateful to switch her attention to something solid, real, and in the physical now. She focused on moving the sprinkler from one area of the yard to another. She looked around to enjoy the warming sun that she craved all winter long. She took a long, deep breath while she closed her eyes and gradually let it out, paying attention to the slowing of her heartbeat. Opening her eyes gently, she walked back to the deck and swiveled her bottom onto the picnic table. Grace looked down at her notebook and decided to help her anxiety by closing her eyes to meditate, despite all the pumped-up adrenaline, inner frustration, and anxiety from moments ago.

She focused on her breathing. Deep, long breaths, in… out, in… out. She began to relax. She made her intention… letting go. She heard cows mooing from across the field; she let them fade away, lawnmowers out from their sheds, eager to eat the neighborhood grasses, and the sound of sprinklers behind her…

Slowly

Fading

Away.

…she noticed the slight trickling of distant sprinklers.

Breath.

In and out.

Nothingness…

P E A C E.

She is finding calmness in the dark, yet her ears are still alert to the light sounds. She is out, in her lovely meditation, feeling peace and content until the sound of a lawnmower pulls her out of her meditation.

The noise starts in the distance, getting louder to the point where it is the only thing she can hear. It pulled her quickly out of her peaceful Zen state.

She looked around with a stunned face to see if her neighbor was mowing her lawn?

No lawnmower.

The sound got louder and quicker and closer. She gazed all around with a face full of curiosity. From the table, she looked up through the tree branches that are just starting to bud leaves. She saw a little yellow plane fly directly over her head. She smiled in euphoria and surprise. It is low, way too low, and right over her. She heard it start to slow down as if it were preparing to turn. Sure enough, she can hear it turn in the air. She looked around the house to the left, seeing it headed back in her direction now. The new farmer plowed the field perfectly flat last week, and she could tell that the plane was thinkin' about landin' on the fresh open, plowed runway.

He flew down low as if he were going to land, but at the last minute he pulled it up over the pasture full of cows, now running away in fright. She thought, *How Cool!* As she stood up to lean on the deck railing, watching with pleasure as the plane turned around, came back again, and gracefully landed in the field. She watched to see what the pilot did as the dust flew everywhere. He slowed the plane, turned, creeping slowly in her direction. Grace hopes they come over closer.

The plane approached slowly and parked near the corner of the front lawn, shaded by the old walnut tree. She watched in disbelief, blinking, to see if it would disappear. Still there. She waited for a while to see if anyone would come out. The plane sat for a bit, then the engine turned off.

She stands in waiting. Minutes later a man opens the door to this shiny yellow toy, and out steps a man in a baseball cap. River. Her breath catches deep, and her heart starts to beat so fast. Her whole body goes a little numb from the nerves flaring from 0 (meditation) to 110.

She backs up slowly, turning to walk off the deck, into the yard, and around the house, knowing that he doesn't know she's back here. She walks slowly and looks around like, Is this real? He closes the tiny door of the plane, slow and hesitant.

Grace is curious but also honestly ready to jump into his arms. She walked toward him. He's walking along the ditch to the yard when she says, "Hey!"

He doesn't hear her. He's adjusting his cap as he walks, lowering it in a nervous way over his head. She gets anxious and attempts to say it again. She starts a little jog in his direction. Eventually, she says, "Hey!" and he looks up quickly to see, and she surprises him.

"Oh, Hey!" He looks around, and they slowly walk

towards each other. "How's it going?"

"I'm good… You?" She slowed her walk towards him.

"So good Grace, yeah, so good." He's a bit apprehensive, she can tell. "I'm, uh, I just got this little beauty and a pilot's license." They both stop walking. "Thought I'd take her for a spin… ended up here." His voice cracks a bit, sounding unsure.

She said, "Oh. Well, that must be a great new hobby for you. She's beautiful." Trying to reassure him in his decision to fly here, "I was sitting on the back deck writing and you flew right over me. I couldn't believe it! Then the plane lands in my field and you come walking out of it. Now I know I'm dreaming." she said and he chuckles as he turns away and back again.

"What are you up to?" He asked.

"Just watering the lawn, writing, and enjoying our spring weather." She wasn't going to mention that she was about to write him outta her heart.

"Yes, isn't it nice?" He said, "Great weather, just great! Would you like to go for a ride? Take her for a spin with me?"

Grace jerked her head back in doubt. Looked at him sideways and said, "Really?" with a hint of skepticism.

"Really! The snow melted. *And boy has it melted!*" He said, referring to the flooding. "I figured this would be a fun adventure. It's not a walk…" he replied with a shrug of his shoulders and a bit of a shy twisting back and forth motion…

"Okay, let me go close the door and shut the water off."

"Alright. The place looks good, Grace. You're working hard."

"As always," she replied as she started walking to the house to put her notebook inside.

"Oh, grab that plaid jacket of yours." He added.

"Okay." she yelled back.

Then she ran to turn the water off and grabbed her jacket then back to him in the lawn. He checked things out and said a simple, "Hi."

"Hi." She said, beaming. She nudged him with her shoulder in a bit of a flirting way. He reached his arm out for hers. Once she allowed it, he pulled her in for a hug, a sweet hug, then said, "Let's be off, Grace." She walked up to the other side of the beautiful yellow plane, welcoming her so kindly, like a kid's toy.

"Wait." He said.

She stopped before her hand touched the door handle, and he came walking over to open it. He held his arm up in a direction like a chauffeur.

She said, "Why, thank you!" and curtsied.

"My pleasure!" He tipped his hat.

She watched him walk around the front of the plane, still skeptical of all this, and noticed he looked about the same as last time they were together. She got a bit anxious then reminded herself, River is here. He climbed into the plane. She can't help but hold a huge grin on her face. He looked around at the inside of the plane, inspecting it a bit, glanced over at

Grace, and stopped mid-glance to see her all smiles. He's got that look, that sturdy in himself look, that she remembered. He gave her a big smile back and her heart fluttered, she's a bit curious about all this but she's up for the adventure. River looked over at Grace and asked, "You ready?"

He handed her a set of earphones. She put them on, and he started the engine. They slowly moved back to the top of the field, then they went very fast. He pulled up on the handles. They take off, and she's so in awe. Nervous and feeling her body push back in the seat as they get into the air. Just when she was about to write him out of her life and heart completely, he showed up most uniquely.

They don't talk since it's so loud. He can probably tell that she's taking it all in as they turn and follow the Snake River, west. They fly above everything: above the past, above their lives, above their worries. She looked over at him, he looked back at her, and they both smiled. She mouths "How beautiful" and smiles so big. She looked back at him, and he tried to mouth something. Confused, she looked like, Huh? He held up one finger while keeping control of the plane with the other hand, telling her to wait... then he reached under his chair, pulled out a piece of paper, and held it out in front of her. Written in red marker she read, "Have you ever been kissed in midair before?" She looked at him and shook her head with a smile as she reached up and over to him for a kiss. She kisses him deeply and cups his chin in her hands, and her whole body is ecstatic to be in his presence again. She started to cry in the overwhelming feelings, slightly sobbing as he pulled back, unable to control herself. Knee controlling the wheel, he grabbed her shoulders, looking at her again.

They can't hear much with their earphones on, but they can feel the deep emotions shared by both. Again, he grabbed the papers in his lap and sifted through them, till he held up, "I'm sorry!"

She snickers through the tears and can't believe he planned this all ahead. She took a deep breath. Then she let it out slowly, grabbing the paper and holding it for him to read. She pointed to her chest with tears streaming down her face. He let out tears too. They hug again and kiss a sweet kiss that intermingles a tear into the corner of their mouths. Letting out the pent-up sorrows. They cry, the loud plane covering the sounds of deep emotion. She lets go and lets him fly while she leans into his side, laying her hand on his knee and tickling it like she used to do with his head and chest.

They flew for a good while. She couldn't believe she's in his arms and he's inviting her into his heart again. The energy penetrates her heart, adding so much joy, love, and happiness, knowing he's right next to her, holding her as if he heard her every thought over the last six months, and finally surrendering to the love that they both felt.

Here, flying above the earth, they are free from everything but themselves. He steadied the plane and he gave her a honey kiss. His heat is exactly a match for melting her honey, and they are two chemicals together causing a beautiful reaction. One she longed to experience, again. Her soul searched and searched for this bond, and now, thanks to following her heart, she gets to experience a wonderful connection with another human.

The yellow plane made her feel like she was in the warmest, safest place, perfectly meant to be. Flying above everyone's fears, doubts, and insecurities. She doesn't mind flying, but she does start wondering where they are going and how long they'll fly. About 30 minutes later, she looked out the window. He grabbed a piece of paper that said, "Almost there."

After another 15 minutes of flying, they came to a lush landscape full of trees. They must be in Oregon or Washington somewhere. There was a clearing that they started to lower into. Grace got a bit worried preparing to land. But they land slowly, solidly, and safely down. They slowed to a stop and River turned off the engine to the plane. Then he turned to Grace and held his pointer finger up to his mouth to say, "Shhh."

She held her pointer finger up in front of her mouth to copy him and smiled. They both took off their earphones, and River got out of the plane, walking slowly around the front to her door. He opened it, clasped her hand to help her out, it felt like they were in the middle of nowhere. She gazed around, knowing that she'll return one day to this heavenly, peaceful place in her mind for tranquil meditation.

She said, "It's beautiful!"

He nodded his head as he approached her climbing out of the plane and swept her up into his strong arms. She giggled, trying not to interrupt the gentle peace. He carried her through the trees and mist. He doesn't walk long, and they can't stop smiling at one another. Not saying anything. She realized he planned something more. They eventually came upon a tree house in the tallest tree in the area, which has a spiral staircase. The house is petite with flowing, transparent, white drapes swaying in the breeze. She looked at him with a big open mouth and large eyes and said, "River!" And he smiled.

He carried her up the steep, spiraling staircase built around the tree. She didn't mind holding on tight, continuing their closeness. As he carried her up the stairs, she glanced over his shoulder and saw the yellow plane down below. She clung a little harder from fear of heights and is reminded how grateful she is to be holding him again. She watched her hands gently grip tight, feeling his back while he took step by step, making it up the staircase. He stopped at the front door of the little raw wood, beautiful abode. He opened the windowed door, carried her inside to a single bed with a bug screen romantically draped over it. There were screens on each window with thin white curtains moving slowly and a few ambient lights. They stand in awe for a moment at their glowing nature getaway. So simple, divine, and perfect.

He walked them closer to the bed. She reached for his face, cupped his cheek and chin in her palm, and moved closer for an embrace she longed for. She moved gently, afraid to scare him away. She tried to show him that it was okay to let her in. The emotional pain was not a focus, there was an absence of bitter feelings, and an opening in what was once a wounded heart. A sensation of surrendering to love. No more battle or heavy armor needed anymore, for either of them.

The room was emanating that warm, honey light.

They embrace in wet kissing for a while. He took off his cap, and she reached up to kiss the top of his head. Heavy breathing began, a language they both understood.

They undress each other slowly, piece by piece, while they continue to kiss. The movement is unhurried, methodical, elegant, and strong yet tender. They stood next to the bed, and he pulled her in close. He gripped the back of her head gently. They pull away from their kiss to let out several pants from both their open mouths. He laid his forehead into hers and said, "It seems I've loved your lifetimes." Trembling in emotion, the urge to cry wells up inside Grace. Her body allowed it to transform into a smile. She cupped his jaw into her hands and said, "We've made it a long way. I'm so grateful we've made it right here. I love…"

— "I love you." He said, interrupting her.

He swept her up off her dainty feet and onto the bed. He laid next to her and grinned as she looked up at him. He put his big hand on her bitty hip. No more words are exchanged, just the sound of breathing getting deeper and the bellowing sensation of surrender.

Finally, she was getting a second chance. A second chance to be with this love. They make love that moves mountains and kiss each other's breath. She always knew she'd come across love like this. Now she is indulging in it until they drift into the night, bodies intertwined.

* * *

She woke to the bug net drifting back and forth on her bare leg. She opened her eyes enough to see the white sheets and blanket all messed up on the bed. River, asleep at her side. His legs tangled with hers. The room was a place of peace. She loved the feeling of being securely suspended above the ground. Grace watched the drapes blow gently in the breeze together with the bug net... River turned to her and whispered, "Mornin' beautiful."

"Mornin." She leaned in for a quick kiss.

"Hey, I know it's soon. But I feel like we had a good break and have had some time to think about things. I don't wanna waste anymore time without you by my side."

"Agreed," she said.

"What do you think about moving up to Stanley with me?"

"River, yes! I would love that. It's what I've wanted."

"Good, it's a deal then," he said.

* * *

They flew home after spending all day talking about their future and playing in bed together. River flew east into the evening, landing in the field just as the stars were peeking out.

He said, "I'll be down no later than two days to help pack you up and haul your things north."

She kissed him and said, "okay." feeling fortunate that they were finally solidifying their commitment to each other. *Finally*, She felt all their walls dissipate while a rising of the warmest light-flooded throughout her heart. She opened the door and whispered, "Goodnight, River."

He mutters back, "Goodnight, Grace. Take care—two days..." She winked and blew him a kiss before closing the door to the yellow chariot. She stood back, wrapped her plaid jacket around herself tight, and watched him turn the plane gradually, facing north. He gains speed and lifts off into the night sky. Beautiful feelings embrace her spirit.

The slight sliver of a crescent moon is out gleaming elegantly. Settled in a naked sky. Sprinkled with stars, all shining as if they've been watching their escapade the entire time. Grace acknowledged them, and instead of taking a bow for the brilliant audience, she grinned so big. Then jumped into the air with her arms up high. She howled a deep, primal howl as she watched the dark silhouette of River's plane grow smaller over the row of trees at the bottom of the property. She thrust her head back with her eyes closed, arms out, and palms up, allowing the happy tears to drip down into her ears as she chuckled out loud.

She laid down in the field of fresh dirt and looked up to the stars in deep gratitude for her journey—breathing deeply.

She is so appreciative to God for it.

She stood up after a while of basking under the night sky and walked inside the house with a lighthearted feeling. She hummed while she put her hair in a side braid and went to bed. She woke early and was full of ease. She had the energy that she hadn't had in months. She turned on her music, and started organizing her clothes into boxes. All other items were in boxes already from her move out of the house with Cray. It only took her half the day to be completely packed up and ready to tow it all to River's.

*Hey, I just crossed the bridge into town.* River texted.

So she went outside to wait. She started sweeping up fallen flowers from the chestnut tree in the driveway when River rolled down her lane. He was pulling his horse trailer and it was exactly two days after their venture. She saw his head sway back and forth in the truck, with a delighted expression beneath the baseball cap. She leaned the broom against the chestnut tree and skipped over the driveway to his side of the truck, which was slowing down to park. He got out, grabbed her, and said, "Hi," then kissed her real fast on the cheek. She was suddenly swept up onto the flatbed of his truck, with a big laugh and smile. River wiggled his way between her legs that were dangling off the edge. She appreciates the way he takes charge with her.

"You ready to pack up and go?" He asked her.

"Readier than ever." She said,He helped her get down as she wrapped her arms around him then stood to head inside. He smacked her butt as she huddled away and said, "Alright, let's load this baby!"

He followed, and they loaded up the boxes in a happy manner. It reminded her of when they first met, loading Haze's trailer at the market. They are quick, quicker than she thought, it was nearly effortless. She didn't need her bed, table, or couch, so they just kept them in the house for the renters to use. They grabbed her dresser and armoire, tucked them tidily into the trailer, and were off. Headed true north, together.

She couldn't stop smiling and felt like she drank a pot of green tea... buzzing on caffeine. They listened to all her new albums on her iPod, mostly Americana, the good vibes made her thankful for who she cherished in her life, the way everything had aligned for her, for them. Right here and now. The sun was so warm and yellow, as it began to set west of them. Filling the whole world and her range of sight with that warm honey light. She felt it all around her, just harmonized in sweetness.

Love like this does exist, and now she's enjoying it like a doe out in nature, knowing she's safe, fully fed, water nearby, baby by her side, and the bucks all surrounding her. Delighted with nothing to do but be in love. She held his right hand the whole way home, leaned over the console, to tickle his hand and arm. She felt confident, true, mature, loved, and ready to continue the dream they had started then let go of, and she decided it truly was worth all possible strife. Their fears of what people would think had hindered them so. They both knew that blows of judgment may come their way, but obviously, it's not enough to keep them apart.

Three months later, Grace was out helping River feed his horses and looked around the barnyard, she felt like she had been there a lifetime. She had looked forward to being there, home. The two of them flow together. Life flows. She made it over the rainbow. Everything she wanted and envisioned living there was coming true.

She was writing her book every day in her room, facing the west hills, the hills she was confronting after she ran in the rain. The spirit in the environment whispered to her that day, beckoning her to endure and to keep loving River. That day he was afraid of her spending so much time with him. She'd shouted, "I tried, I tried" in the pouring rain. "I'm doing my best." The universe wanted their union as much as she did. And here she was.

She always knew she'd be writing their love story, in this room at her desk, gazing out at the Sagebrush filled hills and blue skies, so right. Her place. Their place.

River brought her breakfast and their favorite tea. Grace took a break from her book to chat with him. He sat on the bed and she straddled his lap, soaking up warm love that energized her. They enjoyed the flow of their love all around the house. Doing dishes together was fun, cleaning, even laundry and horse chores didn't seem like tasks. When done together. Going out wasn't as hard as both thought it'd be. They just acted normal, and everyone would act normal with them. They saw River was happy by her side and she by his.

Grace bought herself her dream motorcycle. A vintage BMW boxer scrambler with thick treaded tires. She ventured into town when she wanted a change of pace, to go for a ride. She rode into Ketchum or Hailey for a longer ride, gliding freely through the scenery with no effort. Something about it gets her imagination running, propelling ideas for her book. The movement and flow brings inspiring new ideas, trailing more ideas. Grace loved seeing the lush mountain forests, the smells of fresh wildflowers, dirt, and the scent of a flowing creek, and pine wood. She inhaled deeply while gliding along the curving roads, and noticed the feeling of the tires working with the pavement, pushing her along methodically. She *was* that bike for the moment. She often ended her rides with a writing session at a coffee shop or breakfast house.

This visit to town, she overheard a group of older men talking about her and River. They didn't realize she was in the booth right behind them.

"Did you see that gal who got off the BMW?" said one man.

The two other gentlemen said, "uha!"

"That's River Billings' girl. She's such a darling. River is a lucky son of a gun. I was watching them at the live music pavilion the other night, and the way they are with each other is so attractive. I'm inspired. Even with their age difference."

Another guy said, "Well when you're that old and have a sweet young lady, who wouldn't treat her well?"

Grace sank down, aiming not to be seen. She would be embarrassed if they realized she was right there.

"I'm just saying, they're more than the average couple." He paused for a minute and said, "I'm genuinely happy for them. And... I'm proud of them."

That lit up her whole world. She whispered, "well done *us*, well done." As she nodded her head. Not that she needed outward acceptance of their relationship. They're being true to themselves and people see that. It's a gratifying feeling.

When Grace returned home, they got ready to go on a long horse ride in the southwest hills. River packed a romantic lunch with purple grapes, a few cheeses, red wine, and some salami. Grace put on a white summer dress, to enjoy before the fall weather came.

Grace was on Luna, behind River and Tahoe. River slowed, taking in the world. The sage smelled wonderful, the air was warm, and the beautiful sun was setting with brilliant mixes of orange, yellow, blue, purple, and white. She was so content. She inhaled the fresh air and got Luna into a gallop. She threw her head back and allowed the deep pleasure to burst out of her tummy through the movement and let out a happy chuckle with her smile, letting go of the reins to feel the freedom in the wind. She grabbed the rains again and looked forward to River looking back at her. He's happy that she's happy.

He sat and waited while Grace caught up, then said,

"Feelin' free?"

"Free, happy, and loved." She replied.

He says, "Me too. Me too."

They arrive in a grove of bushes and decide to stop for wine and dining. They hop off their horses and walk them to the creek for a drink, then they go back to pull out their wool blankets and lay them out one at a time, creating a gentle pad for their bodies. They lay down across from each other, huddled into a grove of bushes with their horses. They pick at the food while they chat about their day. Grace told River about her trip to the breakfast shop and hearing those guys talk about them. She expressed how she was proud of them and grateful for what they had.

"Yea, Grace, I'm feeling it too," he said, "The way everyone is reacting to us as a couple is such a blessing to me." Grace knelt next to him and tucked her feet under. He took her hand in his while he said, "As it is for you. I'm sure. But especially for me." He got choked up and his eyes began to water. He interrupted himself, asking, "Hey, why did you choose to wear that beautiful white dress tonight on a ride? Isn't it itchy on the horse?"

"Well, I wanted to enjoy one more beautiful summer dress, out in our lovely hills before fall is officially here. Is that okay? Doesn't it look nice?" Grace asked.

"Yes." He propped his head up with a bag full of stuff. He looked good with his cowboy hat on. "It's beautiful! I didn't mean anything negative by it, I simply think it's so conveniently appropriate."

"Oh, really?" she said while she sat up a little taller and shimmied her shoulders, raising her head. She added a bit of nose in the air funniness. "Why's it so appropriate?"

"Because it's a beautiful dress, on an elegant woman, on a lovely day, on a wonderful ride, with a stunning meadow, and I'm curious?" His voice got faster and his energy built as he sat up, face to face with her. "I'm curious whether this woman in her beautiful white dress would marry me and be by my side for the rest of my days?" Her head was in a bashful head tilt against her shoulder until he worked up to "Marry me!"

Her jaw dropped through the biggest smile, she threw her hands up and fell over straight into him, arms over his head.

She said, "YES! At the top of her lungs. Oh, my GOODNESS! Really?" She pulled away to look him in the eyes.

"Yes. Really!" He lifted a box from behind his back and opened it to a beautiful, antique, tarnished silver ring with an amber stone in the middle. It's beautiful. He took it out of the bitty box and put it on her ring finger. It was a precise fit.

"Perfect." She can't stop saying, "Oh, my gosh, oh, my gosh! It's beautiful, River." She cried out, "So BEAUTIFUL!"

"Like you are to me," he said proudly. She plowed into him again and smothered him with her giddy body. He said, "You gotta let me breathe, or we might not make it to the wedding... I'm an old man, remember?"

She pulled back, only enough to get a kiss. They kiss and kiss and kiss, smiling in between, messing up the kiss. They're back at it again until they lean back into full lovemaking. She'll never forget watching the stars gradually come up and out of the darkening sky while she climaxed and saw them watching them, again in such satisfaction that they're merging their souls. Afterward, they decide to bundle together and just camp out, wrapping the blankets around them.

River told her how he felt about her and how he's let down all his tall walls around his heart.

"If there is a God." he said, "He has listened to my heart, and guided it to your heart. You are a true gift to my life." He paused, "God has blessed my soul with great love, and I will care for you from that loving space, 'til the day I die."

Grace soaked it all into her soul, every word, every facial expression, feeling a great, expansive heart.

"I will love you from my heart until the day I die." she said and kissed him as they cuddled closer, looking up at the stars. She scratched his back, arms and head. They fell asleep in each other's arms, warmed by their bodies.

In the morning she woke to the sun just beginning to peek up over the hills. She looked around, and everything was all packed up, ready to go. Except the two wool blankets tucked around her. She stretched out, and he said, "Morning, lovely. Ready to hit the trail?"

"Yes, indeed, Mr. Billings!"

He walked over in his cowboy hat to help her onto

Luna. Before she hopped up, he asked, "Why don't you ride on the back with me, on Tahoe?"

"Sure."

They got onto Tahoe, said goodbye to their new memory in the meadow. She glanced back with a smile and thanked that spot, wishing it well as she hugged River tight. Knowing they'll be back one day. As they ride, she daydreams about their wedding and what they'll wear. It will be out in the sagebrush, and she'll have wildflowers in her hair. Small wedding. River looked back and asked, "What's on your mind?"

She bashfully responded, "Caught me thinkin' wedding." She shot him a look when he turned to look back.

"Didn't even need to ask. You pickin' a date?"

"How did you know?"

"Just a guess, tell me how it's going to go."

She proceeds to tell him.

He said, "Perfect. I like it."

She can't help but glance at the tarnished beauty that took place on its new home, her finger. Her hand looked elegant with it.

They made it home and walked the horses into the corral and released them from their horse attire and gave them food. River leads the wheelbarrow with hay. Grace followed behind, breaking it up with her hands. She looked over at River and he stopped pushing the wheelbarrow, eyes fixed straight ahead towards the mountaintop. She smiled and looked to see what he was looking at. He moved his arm up to his chest in a weird way. She stood up and swallowed hard. She started walking towards him and watched him collapse to the dirt in slow motion.

Grace started running, yelling, "River?! RIVER?!" Her voice got shaky, screeching.

She reached him, and he went limp with uneven, short breaths. He wished to say something. She is grabbing onto him, huddled over the ground, saying, "NO!"

He said, "'Til next time."

"No, no, no, not now!" she said, "Not yet, not yet!" Her voice raised. "Please don't leave me, tell me what to do! What should I do?" She got louder and louder as if it would bring him back. His eyes roll back a bit and close halfway. His body went limp.

"NO!"

"NO!"

"NOT YET, GOD."

"PLEASE NOT YET!!!!"

Grace began to whimper… then let him go, stood up, and ran as fast as she could to the house to call 911. As she ran, she started to lose her hearing. She ran through the corral, through the gate like her limbs were submerged underwater.

Legs heavy and arms were dragging through the air, aware of the fact that all she can hear is her panting breath… in and out. A fast heartbeat pounded in her chest and head as she continued to push her body to the house. Everything was in slow motion, and her body went completely numb. She finally made it to the door and can't get her hands to work to open it. She hears muffled buzzing and her heartbeat. She tried to take a deep breath and she turned into pure panic, like a dream where you have no control of your body.

Pounding.

Muffled hearing.

She eventually got the door to open, walked in, and looked in the hallway for her phone, knowing it wouldn't be there. She could tell she was talking out loud but couldn't tell what was being said. She's stumbling in her boots and white dress as she runs upstairs, shaking. She thinks, No. no. no and found her phone plugged in next to the bed. She grabbed it and dialed 911. Quickly, someone is on the other end, but she cannot tell what they're saying. She put her hand to her forehead and squeezed her eyes to try and make her ears work. She looked out to the corral and yelled, "My husband just had a heart attack, please come help him! 2479 Elk Horn drive."

She couldn't tell if she was even clear. She tried repeating it twice, but she didn't know if it made sense. She ran down the stairs as fast as she could without falling or dropping her phone. She jogged back to River with a half-functioning body. She was too shocked to cry. She ran as best she could, trying not to push too hard. Not wanting to pass out.

As she approached the corral gate, her guts cringed at the sight of him lying unmoved on the ground where she left him. She swung the gate, clenching onto it to steady her through. She swiveled with it, and her stomach thrust her adrenaline-filled body into a head jolt while puke lurched itself up her throat and through her mouth. Out and onto the ground below. She didn't have control over her boots getting hit.

She ran to him and looked at his face, starkly pale with purple lips. He's gone, but she doesn't want to acknowledge that. She slouched onto her knees next to his body… here came the moans, tears, and saliva dribbling down her face and all over his upper body. It took all her strength to lift his head and plop it into her lap. She could tell she'd gone a while without breathing while she sobbed deeply over his face. Her heartbeat got quicker and quicker. Finally taking a breath again. It hurt so good to not take a breath.

She eventually vacuumed the air inside and screamed as she looked up at the clear blue sky.

She cried out, "HELP ME.

"WHY, WHY?!"

"He wasn't supposed to leave yet."

"Why?"

"Why?"

While she brought her gaze back down to meet the horizon, flashing lights caught her attention. They were headed in her direction. She sobbed and lost control of her exploding emotions and a river of tears fell onto the dwindling essence of her lover.

# 13

## Neptune Retrograde

Neptune will Retrograde

June 16 — November 22, 2017

Grace sat beside River's horizontal body inside the ambulance. As they rode away, the thought that he was gone weighed heavily on her while holding his clammy hand, staring at his limp form. The cold metal rail bumped against her arm as they drove to town and the smell of medical mixtures and sterilized plastic permeated the ambulance, adding to her nausea as she glanced at the clear oxygen mask pressed into his cheeks—no condensation present.

Gazing around, she met the paramedic's eyes, and gave a shaky smile. The polite thing to do would be to strike up a conversation, but not here, not now. Instead, she looked at her beautiful ring—twisting it back and forth; the sorrow bellowing deep within her, creeping up to tug at her heart. She extended her palm gently to rest on River's chest while her weary eyes settled back on the ring. Just hours ago it symbolized their beautiful new beginning.

She breathed deep and rested her head on his chest.

Her tears dampened his shirt and she paused to listen inward—nothing. Closing her eyes, she imagined life after this and wished death would fill her body as well.

A kaleidoscope of color sauntered onto her eyelids, her ears rang, and her body shut down. Surrendering into darkness.

Grace opened her eyes to the sun's warm rays, and tears swelled realizing she was staring at the brick wall of the homestead. The lemon water and chocolate sat untouched as they watched her surrender a layer of self.

A gentle motion drew her attention to the wisping notebook, revealing its last entry: "I need to release River for good!" The breeze carried the paper back and forth, disclosing the blank sheets that followed. She realized her time with River was all a lovely daydream. Her subconscious granted her the second chance she'd wished for—to be with him until the end.

Staring at the bare pages with gratitude, she acknowledged the nudge towards stepping into future possibilities.

Her attention broke as the sound of the bright yellow plane started its engine; bringing back thoughts of the imagined motorcycle ride, engagement, and River's fatal end. The plane flew away with a pilot that looked nothing like River—loss and emptiness emerged... of true love that never was—echoing in her mind as she glanced at her bare finger.

She knew.

Her time with River was all in her imagination and the time with River had already ended and another layer of sorrow hit, further overwhelming her.

* * *

Grace drove to Auger Falls in the afternoon sun, her music loud. After parking, she grabbed her jacket, her favorite wine and iPod. She walked into the welcoming sunlight with the pumped-up, Imagine Dragons album blaring through her headphones. Her intentions were to purge the uncomfortable energies with a nature excursion. It was working as Grace sensed a beneficial release, power walking the dirt road. Without slowing her pace, she made it to the furthest part of the canyon's edge and found a lava rock with the best view. She sat and sipped her wine until it numbed her pain.

She allowed the warm light to enter her heart as she gazed downstream. The sun glistened off the water, causing her to squint and glare at the view as if it—personally—were to blame for all this.

After some time reflecting, she began to wander along the canyon's edge, back towards the falls.

Sauntering upstream, the sun warmed her back, stimulating a loving sensation throughout her body. She slowed to bask in it's healing rays before proceeding to the ridge, where she watched the waters move from a reverent calm to a rapid boil and back to calm.

This spot was where she asked the river once before, "Where's my story?" During the time she and Cray separated, and she left the yurt—when she had to split her time with Kai.

She knew the love of this place, of the flowing water. It had supported her in finding her story but not the one she'd expected. Now she begged the river's spirit to support her through this heartache and trusted it once more.

She sat, wondering if the day's astrology had any insights. *Maybe it will provide some comfort?* She wondered as she pulled out her iPod to check.

"Get comfortable with uncertainty as Neptune goes retrograde today." The astrologer explained, "Neptune blurs the lines of reality. These transits are for dreaming or allowing a beautiful vision to carry you through moments of harsh reality or a long journey of despair. So, get out of your tangible world and into your imagination. This is true with any Neptune transit: you're supposed to be dreaming."

*How fitting.* She thought.

The astrologer continued, "These are some energies we will deal with while Neptune appears to be moving backward: feelings of hurt love, vulnerability, and anything under the umbrella of escapist activity such as dreams, addiction, fantasy, and film."

"Great!" she said out loud, "I have to spend the next

five months with *this* energy?"

"On a more positive note," he said, "one may have stronger psychic intuitions or enjoy a more mystical side of life. This aspect also carries the energy of beggars, poor people, and even savior-like individuals. Look forward to when it moves direct; it'll bring more clarity."

* * *

Grace lounged the rest of the evening near the river's edge, where she felt her best. Nothing made her more grounded than soaking in the sun on a warm day. Soon the stars came out, and she lay back on a warm boulder to watch the beautiful heavens show themselves.

She was content until her music randomly switched to "I Can't Help Falling In Love." The vivid image of her massaging River's shoulders emerged in waves of sorrow—piercing deep. Instead of fighting against it, her body squeezed, pushing the air and emotions out. Her surroundings embraced her and together they wrung every last trace of River from her heart.

* Imagine Dragons, Smoke + Mirrors album
* I Can't Help Falling In Love by Haley Reinhart

# 14

# Queen Dream

July 2017

*Hey, Grace!* Sky texted out of the blue. *My birthday's coming up. I'll be back in Bliss and a bunch of us are going to the local winery then floating the river on the 4th. Come with us.*

*Aw, that sounds fun,* Grace replied. *I'd love a summer float.*

*I know everyone here would love to see you!*

She adored the slow pace of Bliss. It was such a small, sunny town. It had an enjoyable chill vibe with the salt-of-the-earth people, and everyone knew everybody.

When they met for Sky's birthday, after they all left the quaint winery, they went back to Sky's mom's and crashed in the front room. The next morning, Grace made tea while everyone woke one by one. A girl on the cushioned chair sat up and reminisced about the good ol' days. They all joined in happily.

"Jake, who was your first kiss?" the girl asked.

"Gabby... Who was yours?"

The girl bashfully mentioned a guy in the room, hinting

that she still had feelings for him, maybe the reason she brought it up in the first place. Then she asked everyone else in order to rid herself of embarrassment.

"Grace, who was your first kiss?"

Grace was caught off guard, surprised she was asked.

"A boy I went to school with. He stood next to me in PE class, we flirted a lot and found out we shared the same birthday—two days before Christmas. He invited me over on our last day, before school break and we kissed."

"Aw, that's *so* sweet. How old were you?"

"Sixteen," Grace replied. "We got together again on our birthday." She giggled along with the girls in the room.

"Oh, my goodness… that's such a *cute* first kiss story!" the girl said as she sat forward to dramatize her response, while most everyone else nodded.

She thought, *I never told anyone that story… It is cute!* She was proud her first kiss was at 16, thrilled to claim it as her story, and glad to be included in the round of questions.

\* \* \*

Once at the river bank Sky said, "Grace, you ride with me" as he carried the canoe with the help of another friend.

Everyone else filled a six-seater raft, a couple of kayaks, and a few paddleboards. Once they'd helped everyone onto the water, Grace and Sky hopped in the canoe, facing each other.

She thought, *This is such a fun way to spend the warm holiday. A handful of friendly people… gently floating down a cool river with a great view around every corner.* She was grateful for the invite and glad she'd accepted.

"Hey, thanks for inviting me to your birthday and

float," she said while he put the paddle inside the boat for a break.

He chuckled, "Of course, Grace. You're always welcome here with us."

She appreciated that and adored his deep laughter. It reminded her of someone from her past, but she couldn't put her finger on whom. She enjoyed hearing it as they spent most of the day together.

He invited her to stay another night with everyone since their float ended at dusk. She slept next to Sky in his bed. Exhausted, she drifted directly into a dream. It swept her away.


She appeared on the inside of a dark doorway, trapped behind layer upon layer of dense drapes. Struggling to make her way into the bedroom, she heard voices, then a flush of nerves flared within.

Finally, a view revealed: two nude figures aglow with hues of a tempered fire.

She recognized Sky, her husband—The King she wholeheartedly loved, leaned against their elegant couch, supporting a blonde mistress.

They'd just finished making love and were embracing face to face, sharing a glass of wine. The woman exuded victory and great triumph in seducing The King.

He chuckled at something the woman said. That laugh—she cherished and instantly recognized it in life. He followed it by inquiring about her chances of having a son.

The Queen's heart plummeted.

Grace, as his queen, was never able to bear a

child, and she carried that fact heavily.

She recognized the woman. A widowed mother of four boys. She had served them in their home after hearing of their hard times.

Her soul couldn't keep the anguish inside. Loud moaning and wailing came from the deepest part of Grace's soul. She did not hold it in as she lost *everything* in that moment.

The nude widow heard The Queen and scrambled, clearly knowing the depths of her heart's new debt. Grace watched the woman realize the impact of what she'd played a part in and set in motion.

The woman was uncomfortable. As if the wails themselves were pulling her soul into its next life with debts unknown. She couldn't hold still, her body flailing, looking like she feared for her spirit. Grace felt the woman's panic within her own core, adding to the intensity.

The King on the other hand… he had a love for his queen and was a good man. But he never moved. Her sorrow and heartbreak did not affect him. Not one bit.

He watched the exposed woman flail as he drank his wine. He looked at this as his obligation, his duty to create and pass on the next generation. If The Queen wouldn't carry his son, he would have someone else do it.

The moans summoned Queen Grace's soul into the untouchable death. There was no reason to live for him any longer, knowing her entire life was dedicated to him and their ruler-ship was just a "duty." She felt her affection for him morph from her heart down into metal shackles, binding to her wrists. Once full of devotion and sacrifice for her lover, now altered into a lifetime of enslaved emotions, broken love, and sorrow.

She had wanted love and found it in him, even though arranged. She thought he felt the same. He did not. Intimacy with another didn't faze him.

Grace's cousin Sam entered the room in a handsome, tightly fitted golden suit. He went to the mistress, wrapped her in white sheets, clenched them harshly, and yanked her to his face.

Fierce and unapologetic, he yelled, "Look at what you've done!" He forced her to look at the moaning, shackled queen. "Look at what you've done!" His purpose was to serve as a witness, overseeing how each soul's karma would divvy up.

The Queen went silent forevermore, alone in the south wing of the castle, and The King never conceived a son, nor a child. He never admitted it was him that was infertile. The kingdom had changed for the worse without his queen.


Grace's rapid heartbeat woke her. The moans persisted through the dream. She sat panting and parched then opened her eyes to Sky lying next to her, breathing calmly. He *was* The King with his long beard and laugh.

She whimpered in silence, staring at Sky—deep jealousy, pain, and heartache flooded her body and soul. She lived for him, made sacrifices for him, her king. It was not her time to live for him, this life.

She knew the former existence could have been purely

created by her subconscious. Even still, there were indicators, signs and deep insights showing she was meant to move on. The dream was a reminder to evolve her soul, in a direction of self-love, first. Even though the potential for love and pleasure was there. Her direction was clear. She had to move on. This would be her last time visiting Sky.

Grace drove home after heartfelt goodbyes, knowing she'd made the right choice. When she got home, the new renters now occupying the extra two rooms upstairs said the two sinks in their bathroom were plugged.

She called a plumber and set up an appointment to meet the following Monday on her lunch break.

When she met the plumber and explained everything, he said, "Aw, this is an easy job," followed by, "Hey, do you own or manage a rental on Washington St.?"

"Yes. It's my dad's," she answered.

"Yeah, I replaced a pump in the basement apartment a year ago. No wonder you were saved in my phone," he said.

"Yeah, you were in my contacts too," she said, thinking he was a happy-go-lucky guy.

"This might sound nosy... I was wondering, are you single?" he asked. "It seemed like you were single then. It's a shame to be all alone."

Grace made it obvious when she gazed at his wedding ring.

"My little brother... he's single. Nice. A bit older than you probably, but he's had a motorbike accident and drove through a barbed-wire fence. He cut his face from chin to ear —" He drew a line across his face. "Made a really bad scar. He's embarrassed about it. Would you consider going on a date?"

"Aw, you're a nice brother," she said, adding, "I don't

judge features like that. You can send me his number and I'll think about it." Grace thought, *Knowing my luck lately, maybe a friend would be enough for now.*

"Ok. I'll text you his number."

Grace received his number that day and forgot about it and their conversation. The plumber texted her a few days later asking her to text his brother.

*Sorry. I've been busy doing chores and working. I'll text him soon.*

They messaged back and forth a few times. He seemed nice and polite, and two weeks later he asked for a photo. They exchanged selfies and his scar didn't look bad. After a few weeks, Grace was fine doing her solo thing, having no need to meet, but he wanted to.

*I have the day off to write,* she replied. *Would you be free later? We could meet at the Red Park?*

*Yep, I'm free to meet you. 7:30?* he asked.
*Sounds good,* she texted back.

She silenced her phone and sat on her bed to write. She paused, thinking about her story and anxiety flooded over her when she thought, *What will people think of me when they read it?* Up popped that beat up, *ugly* and scared image of herself from her time in the yurt. Then she was taken into emotional imagery:

Where several men thrust her against a wooden post. She submitted to them in fear as a couple of them quickly tied her hands with raw rope, burning her skin.

She had no idea what was happening or why. She was completely powerless, looking around at the crowd of people watching. They stared in shock, also apparently confused as to what was going on.

A man on a horse came close, pulled out a knife, and cut the full length of her face as she screamed in utter pain.

Another man threw wood at her feet. The worst was happening. Lethargic, her body went limp as they lit the wood at her feet and threw lamp oil on her face, burning her bloody cut.

Fierce screaming and shrieking hit the air as she watched flames around her.

Grace stopped herself right there. She was trembling and sweating like she was spiked on caffeine—and wasn't. She grabbed her phone, hoping to find something to shake the images.

She selected the first video on her YouTube feed and watched it. A favorite astrologer said:

"Today, the moon will position itself in the part of the sky that Neptune was when they had the Salem witch trials."

Grace immediately walked away from the playing video, showered to shake the anxiety then dove into ideas about her story of the mother and sweet boy on the island.

* * *

She went for a grounding walk at Auger Falls and, hours later, pulled into the Red Park. She watched Blake pull up and walk towards her.

When she saw the scar, she thought, *It's not too noticeable, he shouldn't worry about it so much.*

"Hi," she said sweetly and hugged him.

"Hi, Grace. I have a confession to make... we know each other."

"Really?" Grace said, taking a longer look at him without staring. She thought she might recognize him.

"Yeah, I lived down in your dad's basement duplex with Sam. We were good friends," he admitted.

It all came flooding back as she recognized him.

"Oh, yeah. You always picked on me!" she said honestly.

"I'm sorry," he said. "Man, I was hoping that wouldn't be the case."

"When did you realize it was me?" She asked, looking up at him.

"I thought of you when I heard the name Grace, and I put it together when my brother said he worked on some plumbing in your dad's rental. I didn't want to tell you because I was afraid you wouldn't meet me today."

"Well, honestly... I wouldn't have," she said frankly. She didn't like being in his presence. "I think you should have told me it was you when you realized who I was."

"I know what kind of guy I was, Grace," Blake said. "I've had a lot happen to me and I've changed for the better. I

~195~

would love a chance to show you that and treat you the way you deserve. Either way, I respect you and your decision." She could hear the honesty in his voice. "And I should have mentioned that we know each other."

Grace glanced down, wondering what to do next. "I'm going to give myself time to contemplate before I go any further. Ok, Blake?" Clear as day, her internal voice said, *move forward*. "I like you over text and your scar doesn't scare me, I just want to keep moving forward. I've gone through heartbreak and I need to trust my gut. I have to be upfront. My gut says I'm good on my own for now."

"I understand," he said as he looked down from her gaze.

She gave him a hug, then he walked her to her car and opened the door for her. He was standing very close. Not in a harmful way but a little too close. She looked down at her keys and backed up from him then saw a flash image of the man on the horse as he leaned over to slash her face. Grace blinked the image away, feeling a strong internal stop sign.

"Blake, I'll be in touch. Okay?" she said as she sat down on the driver's seat with an uncomfortable feeling.

"Okay, Grace. Thanks for meeting with me," he said as he closed her door.

She gave a goodbye wave and drove away with her radio up loud.

While she headed home, she soaked in what had happened, not knowing what to think. *Another flash of soul memory. One after the other. Men, they all have to do with men,* she thought to herself

# 15

## Going Back

June & July 2017

Grace decided to go to her childhood church the following Sunday. She hadn't been since eighth grade with her grandmother, who'd passed. She didn't see herself as religious; she was more spiritual. But she wondered if going to church would cleanse her or bring healing somehow?

Maybe there was some strategy to help her cope with whatever was going on, or ground her spirit? She went with an open heart and an open mind. Maybe something there would put her at peace… couldn't hurt.

Grace pulled up to the church building, 30 minutes out of town. She was stunned, glancing at the building from her childhood as she walked inside. She saw a reflection of herself in the glass door, glancing directly at the obvious tattoos on both her ankles. They showed off what came across as *tainted*.

She sighed and said to herself, "Here we go!"

The main hall had seats facing the pulpit. She scanned the crowd and saw her grandmother's friend, who they called "grandma Noni" while growing up. Grace walked towards her and Noni recognized her right away.

"Grace! Sit, sit." She patted the seat next to her.

"Are you ready for the great solar eclipse everyone's been talking about?" Noni asked, sounding up to date.

Grace sat. "Yes, I've been looking forward to it for a while." She thought back a year ago when she first heard of it.

Noni had many questions for Grace. The last time she'd seen her she was with Cray. She wondered about their relationship and Grace summarized what she could for Noni.

"Well, Grace. You need love in that heart," she said matter-of-factly. "And what about Kai? He needs to see you love again."

Grace laughed. Noni lightened the mood for her, which she appreciated.

"If you could wish for anyone to marry, who would it be?"

Grace sighed and thought about her first crush. Noni knew him, so she said confidently, "Tyler Fox, hands down, if he weren't married."

"Ha, you and every other woman."

Grace laughed and sighed at the truth of it. Tyler was 10 years older than her. She met him when she was seven. He was in a play Grace performed in and was so kind to her. Every time she ran to him, he met her with a warm smile, enthusiasm, and attention.

He never got annoyed with her. At that age, that was all she remembered about boys. They were always annoyed by her or didn't care one bit about her interests. He was different and she was sure he radiated that to everyone.

He loved God and he didn't come off religious, judgmental, or preachy. He was simply *Christlike*. She wanted to be like that herself.

Plus, he was good-looking. He had long blond hair and bright blue eyes. He was slightly hippie and had a smile that could catch anyone's attention. His kindness and attention he paid to everyone enhanced his charm.

The last she knew he was in Argentina, volunteering with his wife for a year. They couldn't have kids, so they traveled the world working in schools and orphanages and getting clean drinking water into rural third world villages.

Grace saw Tyler a few years ago at a play. He came over to talk during intermission and her heart pounded in her chest, saying, *Let me at him!* It was ready to leap from her chest into his.

Grace had bashfully kept the interaction short as she couldn't follow their conversation. She was unable to maintain focus on anything but the rapid thumping of her heart, even though she had no chance with him.

Coming back to the present moment, Grace enjoyed sitting next to Noni. The song was about to start, as they followed the prayer with singing.

She pulled out the songbook and flipped to the correct page number. She saw the name of the song, "Love One Another"—out of 340 pages, it happened to be her grandmother's favorite.

Grace thought, *Of course…* And they started into the hymn. Grace teared up, unable to hold them in. Noni sensed it, reached for her hand, and squeezed.

Grace was *living* in her grandmother's house, in *her* bedroom, sleeping where *she'd* slept. Yet she felt her grandmother more intensely through the music than she ever did at home. She was grateful for the hymn and release of cherished emotion.

When Grace left the church she blamed God for breaking her childhood family apart. They believed so strongly in God and the value of family, but they ended up splitting when she was nine, out of her control.

It wasn't devastating, but it hurt. Grace had expectations for her youth and it didn't go that way. She thought God had everything to do with the destruction of her family and wasn't supporting her family or nudging her parents to focus on harmony and love.

She asked God for all-encompassing forgiveness that day. Something she didn't know she needed but was glad she did. It was nice to soothe her scars and she looked forward to church the following Sunday.

The following work week was long and she was glad to not have garden responsibilities this year. Last year's growing season was an endeavor!

She was grateful for the time spent being productive in it as it helped her work through her emotions, but a break from hard labor was good too.

On Sunday morning she was pleased to go back to church. She walked straight to Noni while sensing someone watching her. Noni put her hand on Grace's lap and said, "I'm singing in the choir today, honey."

"Oh." Grace said.

"You stay right here. I'll be back after the song," Noni said while patting Grace's lap.

After the choir finished she scooched over for Noni to sit. She immediately leaned into Grace, "You see who's here? Sitting in the back with his family?" She whispered, "Tyler Fox…" shifting her glance towards the back of the room.

Grace's nerves flared up and she went numb. She wasn't about to turn and look, no way. She crouched closer to Noni and said, "What? I didn't know he came here. I thought he was in Argentina?" She was half ecstatic, half panicked.

"His mom comes every Sunday," Noni replied. "They just got back from their volunteer trip. I'm going to go say hi," she said before adding, "You must've summoned him, Grace!" As if it mattered.

Grace thought, *odd he showed up the same day I'm here.*

She saw Tyler and his beautiful wife as she walked to the next session. Everyone crowded around to welcome them, curious about their adventures. Grace walked out quickly, through the opposite side of the chapel, headed straight to her classroom. She was the first person there.

Waiting for the teacher and classmates to join, a man

walked past and said, "Grace, class has moved to room 204 today."

"Oh, ok." Her brow furrowed. *How would I have known that?*

She walked down the empty hallway, turned the corner, and *bam!* Tyler Fox was striding directly towards her, on the same side of the hall. Her nerves startled with anxiety, hoping he wouldn't recognize her or even smile nicely, but nope. He just wasn't that kind of man.

"Grace!" he said loud and clear. His eyes peered straight into hers. She didn't have a choice.

"Tyler! Welcome back."

Again, her heart began to beat rapidly. It wanted to jump into him just as it did last time.

He admitted that he followed her on social media and asked about yurt living. He and his wife were very earthy. He thought that way of living was so interesting and wanted to know more. He asked questions while her boisterous heartbeat made it difficult to have the conversation.

She answered one question and politely said, "I'd better get to class. Enjoy your family while you're here." She made it to her lesson before they'd started.

After class, she thought how nice it was to see Tyler. There was no denying her attraction to him, but mostly she wanted to be like him. Confident in herself, living that life of service to the world while having enough love inside to spread it to those in need. The humanitarian soul. She wanted it to grow inside of her.

* * *

That week she spent all her spare time in the canyon, stopping at the juice shop on her way down. There was always a new place to explore: dirt trails, boulder fields, or the river's edge.

She celebrated the river's radiant energy. Nature was a grounding comfort, embracing her as she was. It enhanced her imagination, enabling her spiritual freedom as a dreamer.

Her favorite was sunbathing, welcoming the lovely rays as they filled her with pure light. A different God enveloped her with love through sunbeams. Grace often thought if she lost everything, she'd be content basking under the sun on a warm rock.

# 16

# Leo New Moons

July & August, 2017

Grace continued going to church on Sundays. It was bringing trust back into her life. Trust, recovery, and a healing of her past.

This Sunday, she wanted to experiment after following her astrology. She was in the habit of taking notes as to what was happening in the sky, when, and what energies it held.

She recalled the new moon in July would be in the zodiac sign of Leo, the lion. It rules the heart and is the sun's sign. She was excited to see what would present itself the day of the new moon.

Sunday, July 23rd, she went to church and was cozy there with Noni. She noticed Tyler and his wife were still in town and she went straight to class after singing to avoid interaction with Tyler. While sitting in class, she was sensitive. There was a profound depth inside her chest, openness expanded outward from there, and her heart was open. She couldn't dismiss the powerful expansion.

Her teacher said, "I've invited a couple to help us with

the lesson today." As she said that, Tyler Fox and his wife came in and sat right next to Grace, adding to her sensitivity.

Tyler and his delightful wife, Jade, sat on the other side of Grace. She got nervous. It started again, her heart pounding in her chest. They both said friendly hellos to Grace. And it got even louder.

They got into the lesson and the teacher started crying. She was feeling the open-hearted love too. The room was saturated in it.

She looked to Grace, "Grace, I'm going to ask you a personal question. Feel free to answer it if you want. Why did you come back to church? What are you in search of?"

Her eyes teared up as she looked up to keep her cheeks dry and glanced towards a couple who were also tearing up. Her heart was even more sensitive and sensed the love of God, Jade, Tyler and everyone else in the room. It was flowing from her and within her and everyone else.

That had to be her answer. The answer she sought in every situation.

She took a breath and softly said, "Love," as everyone sniffed and wiped their tears.

Grace sat still in her chair with her hands in her lap, her heart pounding throughout her body as she received sacred, unconditional love.

It was self-love encompassed in God's love for her.

In that moment, young Grace was given the opportunity to bestow innocent, childhood love she'd kept towards Tyler. It was welcomed and freely experienced, innocently and unattached.

She knew the moment was as fleeting as a train leaving the station. They were unable to stay, but something told her Tyler could feel it, his heart received it and his wife could sense it too. The love was free. There was no taking anything, just allowing it to pour where her heart had wanted it to go. Everyone was sniffling as she wiped her tears.

An older man in the class nodded and said, "You hit it right on the nose there. Love!"

In the next class, Jade sat next to Grace. The teacher asked a question to open with, and Jade answered. When she was talking, Grace watched her hands move. Jade's wedding ring stole all of her attention. When she laid her hands down, Grace's gaze hovered over her honey amber stone in a tarnished ring.

She *knew* that ring. The phantom ring River gave her in the meadow. She studied and stared at the ring. She knew it inside and out. It was an illusion, but that *was* the ring!

Grace yearned for answers to what these blurred lines of reality meant.

When the class was over, Grace walked straight to her car, feeling fast and tall with a flame of inner agitation. She was free for the rest of the day and decided to go for a drive. Driving enabled her thoughts to flow with the movement of her fiery red car through the rushing wind. It kept her from not getting caught in an idea too long. It was a cleansing process, like watching the river take her thoughts away.

As she started the car, loud music immediately played, "Love Is Like Ghosts." The words to the song fit too well within the moment; spirit was speaking to her, through the music. She embraced the sensation of having a loved one envelop her.

"Yes," Grace said out loud. "Love *is* like ghosts!" Agreeing with spirit.

She thought, *What is this world that has cracked open to me? There's a lot of soul growth going on... whatever it is, Keep trusting this process.* She was a detective, following the clues in a direction of her own evolution. And that's the kind of work that's real to her, a broader fulfillment of *purpose.*

Grace drove around the outskirts of Twin Falls, out in the valley, fields, and hills, simply *being* with herself while she basked in her music, the movement of the valley, fields, and hills, and getting lost in the landscape.

Grace continued loving herself, nurturing her heart, and letting go. She was always trying to find a productive way of looking at situations like this.

A few weeks later she saw on her weekly astrology video that August's new moon was also in Leo. It's rare to have two new moons in a row in the same sign. It was all gearing up for the North American solar eclipse in Leo, the day after the second Leo New Moon.

The astrologer said, "Expect this new moon is

to have the same energy, just a step deeper, than the last one in Leo."

Grace thought, *Okay, well let's test this theory out. I wanna see if Tyler Fox and his wife come into my class again in a few weeks on the second new moon.*

Grace followed astrology every day and knew the eclipse was coming—so did everyone else, but she knew about it from a different angle, and she was looking forward to it moving across her area of the world. The last time a total eclipse came through was 99 years ago.

The next new moon in Leo would be right before that popular eclipse, and she knew it would eclipse major things out of her life.

She got ready for church that Sunday, went to the main chapel for service, then walked gradually to her class. She saw Mr. Fox ahead of her, walking alone and heading right into her classroom. She continued walking and looked into the room. He made eye contact with her, and she smiled and kept wandering. She didn't want to have a lot of time to themselves before class started, so she walked to the bathroom. She looked in the mirror and said quietly to herself, "Whoa, the Leo new moon… They've been gone for two weeks in a row and he's in my class again. He's not in my class… what's he doin'?" She took a deep breath to prepare herself to go back. She went in and sat down six seats away from him.

"You're in this class?" She asked.

He replied, "Well, your teacher is such a great teacher."

"Aw, yes. She is." Grace said, "How long are you guys around? I thought you were visiting for a little while."

"Oh, we made an offer on a house in Wyoming. We're waiting for it to go through. Jade is there right now getting all the paperwork settled," he said.

"Ah!" she said.

He asked her questions about living in the yurt and wanted to know about the area along the river where they'd put it. She answered all his questions. She told him he should live that way if he craved it.

The teacher raised his eyebrows to find Tyler in the class again.

Grace felt a dark side of love. Nevertheless, she sensed a release for the desire to have him. There was something sensitive about letting go, but Grace knew he was revived and brought back into her life to let him go, making room for something else.

She walked out of the church, and again Tyler was right there in front of her. She got into her car and Tyler turned back and waved his friendly wave. She waved back as she played, "Always Right" by Alabama Shakes.

She rolled down the windows to a summer breeze and rebelliously turned the music up as she drove out of the parking lot, adjusting her rear-view mirror. She took one last glance at her childhood church and Tyler, grateful to have been guided to church to heal and wrap up her past.

She thought back to the time she fell for Tyler in her youth so many years ago. He was so kind and warm.

Grace cranked the volume to maximum, swiveled all the mirrors to her as she drove, a friend in herself. She noticed how her long hair looked with the tight black t-shirt dress and her tan skin, then her reflection looked back and said, "I'm me, I'm free, I love me the way I am… me, I love *me* with all my wounds." She had her own back and loved herself no matter what.

She drove for miles with the song on repeat. She sang and danced in place with such vitality. She was letting it all go and knew this was goodbye to a phase of life.

Grace was getting comfortable with a new way of experiencing life, one where her inner voice was learning how to speak up to herself and her ears were getting better at listening to her inner voice.

She sensed a push of power, feeling Internally strong, dealing with all this stuff coming her way. Her bravery was building towards something. She wondered if the energy from the eclipse was to thank for the burst of empowerment? The eclipse, yes. She was ready for the long-awaited eclipse, tomorrow.

# 17

# The Great American

# Solar Eclipse

August 21, 2017

Grace was so excited to take her long lunch break to watch the highly anticipated North American Eclipse. It would be totally visible there in Twin Falls. There hadn't been a solar eclipse in Twin for nearly 100 years and there wouldn't be another for 100 years more.

Grace kept an eye on the clock, and when it hit 12:00 PM she grabbed her stuff and ran out the door, jumped in her car, and drove to grab her freshly pressed "green juice." Then headed towards the homestead with her eclipse glasses and a smile.

As she drove up to the red light, there was a young man

begging on the corner. She stopped, thinking, *I've seen this guy around.* She rolled down the window, and held five dollars for him to see.

He bounced over and said, "You can see me?" He jumped around. "You can see me! Can I take a quick ride with you down the street?"

"Um," Grace nodded slowly. "down to the next corner?"

"Perfect!" He opened the door and jumped in. She was big eyed, and the cars behind her were honking for her to take advantage of the green light. She quickly drove north, instead of east to the homestead, thinking, *I could drop him behind Costco...?*

He didn't care for the money, so she dropped it in her lap.

"I've been in this town for four months now and nobody ever engaged with me." He folded the visor down and combed his dark brown hair in the mirror. He looked her age or a little younger.

"Well, I've seen you several times on this corner. I've wanted to give you cash but didn't have any 'til now."

"You've seen me before today?" He turned to stare intensely. "Before today? You've seen me?" He looked around. "We're close to the canyon. Have you ever been to Auger Falls?" he asked as she passed the next corner.

"Yes, I walk down there all the time. Where do you want me to drop you off?"

"Auger Falls."

"Really?" She was a bit shocked since it was a lot further than she'd promised.

"Why are you questioning me?" He asked with erect posture.

"I'm not questioning you. I told you the next corner." Grace glanced quickly at his bright green eyes and long, thick lashes—any girl would love to have them. He was cleanly dressed in a plain black T-shirt, Carhartt pants, and new boots.

"I want to take a quick walk along the river," he demanded.

"You really know how to push for more, don't you?" She shot him a sly look. "Well, I'm going to watch the solar eclipse on my lunch break. It's a time-sensitive, rare event that I can't miss! I've been looking forward to it all year."

"Wow, a whole year. My Goodness, try a lifetime."

She examined him, wondering if that was true.

"Come with me. Inside the canyon is a great place to watch the eclipse!"

"Why can't we watch it up here? I have two pairs of Eclipse glasses."

"It's spectacular down there," he said. "Is it me you're worried about? I see you have pepper spray on your keychain."

Grace peered at it in the ignition as they neared the canyon. "You have full permission to use the spray on me, if you so choose," he said with such confidence as he broadly gestured with his hands.

Grace wondered if the guy was on drugs, but something told her to trust him. Still no internal stop sign. Besides, she appreciated that he was so different and eccentric.

The way they interacted with each other reminded her of how she was with her brothers or cousins, warming her to the plan.

"Well, I would love to see the eclipse down there, but I have to get back to work right after," she said.

"Don't worry 'bout me! I can take care of myself after the eclipse. I'll just stay down there afterwards." He slapped the center console, clearly glad she was open to the idea. "It's nice to have someone acknowledge me."

"Well, it's crazy that nobody else has noticed you."

"Crazy, maybe. Or I've been waiting for you."

"Oh? What if I was waiting for you?" Grace said, just to mess with him.

She got to the bottom of the canyon's grade, driving past Centennial Park then along the golf course. After driving five minutes down the dirt road, she came to the new parking lot where there were plenty of cars parked, indicating that there were people around, and she felt it would be safe.

She put the five dollars away and grabbed her keys with pepper spray before they walked down the dirt road towards the river. He led her on a mountain bike trail along the water where Grace glanced around at the familiar landscape then back at the vagabond.

"What brought you to the Twin Falls area?" she asked.

"You have music on that iPod?" he asked.

"Yes."

"You should listen to it," he suggested.

"Why?"

"I noticed you brought it. You must enjoy listening to it? Don't you love to do that?" he asked.

"I grabbed it out of habit. But what about you?"

"Don't worry about me. You still have that spray?"

Grace patted it inside her pocket.

"Good! You feel safe?"

"...Yes," she said, knowing there were others around as she saw bikers and others walking.

"Good."

She watched him walk ahead of her as she put her headphones on. He appeared to be her height or maybe a bit shorter and definitely a quicker walker—he was full of energy, set on his destination with drive and purpose. She could tell he was used to walking.

"Turn that music up!" he said, interrupting her thoughts. He'd turned around, showing the sweat beadlets scattered across his youthful, freckled face.

She adjusted the volume, then he was no longer there. She put the iPod back in her pocket and the upbeat music switched to a sinister symphony; it was dark and full of frightening tones. She pulled her iPod back out to change it but the screen was stuck. She looked around as the music got louder. She started to panic.

Then she heard his voice in her thoughts. "Keep going!" She was startled and jumped in fear, realizing that standing there wouldn't help. So she obeyed his voice.

She focused on the warmth of her heart instead of the loud, eerie music full of moaning, and she heard his voice again: "Feel the sun's light."

She imagined the light filling her entire body, radiating from within. Regardless of the heat and bright sun, the music was giving her chills and the air cooled around her.

Figures materialized along the trail, scary dark soul ghosts, as the song's moans grew louder.

Dark soul figures materialized along the trail, lurking nearby. As the song's moanings grew louder, these ghostly men followed her closely, coming straight at her. She walked straight through them as she focused on the light pounding inside her heart, quickening her pace—away from them.

Her leg pain shot into her foot, pushing her to move quicker towards the waters edge. She grew cold as she passed ominous trees and shadow after shadow. Finally close, mist appeared ahead.

She made her way down the rugged five-foot wall to the water. The music calmed with a woman's gentle voice, lifting the heavy darkness as she approached her favorite spot in the canyon. She was relieved to be there and rid herself of her socks and shoes for a chilling foot soak that numbed her pain.

She stood in the river, looking around, breathing slowly to relax. She jumped as she spotted the beggar standing on the cliff above her, looking at her. She took one headphone out.

"Where'd you—?"

"What did you learn from darkness and fear?"

"What did I learn?" she looked away "That there is a deep love inside of me that cares for the light and trusts the love it provides, even though darkness is scary. I had no doubt I'd make it through the fear."

He then pointed above the towering canyon wall.

"Keep those headphones on."

"Why?" she asked.

He shot her a perturbed glance and Grace followed his orders. The woman continued singing her lovely song while the beggar swept his hand across the stunning view, changing the bright sky into deep shades of purple and blue. She gazed in awe as the stars and planets in their full beauty drew nearer. Her jaw dropped, overwhelmed by the loving comfort of the universe. Her eyes glued to the heavenly vast scene, scanning every detail.

The beggar above, to her left said, "This is the sky, arranged the moment you were born."

A twinge of satisfaction tingled throughout her, smiling proudly at the thought she was part of this skyscape— enveloped by the pure, grand beauty of the universe being shown to her. She could not move her eyes from the view. The music added to the experience while standing at the edge of the world as if she could reach out into the heavens above the rim.

It seemed too big, too powerful to be a part of her. Yet,

she could happily take ownership of it.

"Your soul chose this sky to be born under," he said.

*Chose?* Grace thought.

"You. A recipe of your soul, your mission, your desires, your personality, the dreams you've always dreamed. The level of beauty you wanted to have, the sorrows, the heartbreaks, the life you wanted to write and the lovers you've wanted to experience. It shows the way you love God, the gravity of your path. You. Your heavenly stamp. We all chose a stamp. We're all different," he said.

She was looking into her childhood, the feeling of her first memory. Her heart was beating, was in love, not with anyone specifically, simply standing in true love for the first time. She was within her inner child, a space of innocence, wonder, and hope. She senses her dreams, the creation of herself, and the love God had for her—all at once.

She just stared, soaking in the sight and the magnitude of every planet, their weight, the different vibrations from each, even the sounds they hummed as they moved. Standing in her river at her spot, sensing the feeling of the universe, the phenomenon of her life in motion.

"There's someone who wants to talk with you." he said from the cliff.

Standing still, unable to look away, Grace didn't register what he'd said. Then her hands were grabbed, and her body was pulled to the side. She leaped quickly out of the water. She was being dragged around by a man her height with white hair, who was laughing. She kept spinning with him until he let go and grabbed her shoulders, positioning her to face him. Giggles.

"Einstein?!" she stared at him, confused.

"My dear girl!" he said.

"Now I know I'm hallucinating!" Grace said, feeling sedated.

"I am so proud of you!" he said as he shook her shoulders. "Love, true love. Light is love and love is light… it's born out of darkness. That's all you need to know, my dear soul," he said in the tone of a lullaby. He chuckled close to her face. Her mind glitched at witnessing his presence. He grabbed her solar glasses, put them on Grace, and turned himself around, taking her with him.

The sun was already halfway eclipsed by the moon. "Isn't it wonderful?" he asked, "The father of light meeting the mother of night precisely in the sky. To kiss a grand kiss!" His mustache curled from a smile… she had completely forgotten about the eclipse. She felt the cooling temperature of the sun being blocked and the shadow across the landscape. She could feel it all the way in her heart.

She watched for a while in awe. She heard the beggar say, "Ahem. There's someone else who wants to join," taking his eyes up the river.

She looked at him as she took her glasses off, saw his gaze upstream, and took one look at Einstein and back at him to say, "Who, Jesus?!" Jokingly. As she finished the entire turn, her view was filled with a bright but not blinding light. She saw him walking in a natural cloak on the river towards her with a huge, handsome smile. She dropped to her knees on the rocks, half in the river. She started to cry, and he walked up to her. He put his hands around her upper arms to lift her up. She tried to stay planted to the ground, not feeling good enough to face him.

*My soul is not ready,* she thought. *Not ready.* She repeated it as she squinted her eyes, her face nearly in the water. He tried again to pull her up, gently but firmly. As she was lifted, she knew she couldn't keep the resistance up. She saw flashes of the women crying at the cross. At his bloody feet, later wrapping his body with a robe after cleaning him. Sobbing, she looked up at him and saw images of her at his feet while he was on the cross. That love, that sorrow returned to her heart as if she had been there, and she wept as she looked into his eyes, afraid too.

He had loving, bright, pure eyes, those eyes nobody could ever portray… he pulled her in for a hug, and she felt enveloped by light. She gave in, surrendering to him. It was expanding out beyond her, through her, into the world.

She had an understanding that this person was the essence of God in an image she could comprehend.

Her body dissipated, feeling only light and love. No judgment of her path but an acknowledgment of what her soul had learned.

Her iPod was playing beautiful music, and she didn't

want to leave. She was done with this life without this bright light and without the sky showing itself, without answers. She wanted to stay there forever. Like a little kid enchanted by childhood, not wanting to grow up. He pulled her away a bit, but she pulled back and was her little five-year-old self, being held in his strong arms.

In her lap was the exact photo of him kneeling on a rock in prayer. Next to it was her sparkly snow globe with a carousel horse that was playing the tune of "Somewhere Over the rainbow." Her short blonde hair dangled against her cheeks. She held those two items, recalling the specific memory she had with them at that age. She made a promise to him and herself. She looked at him, knowing what her young seed of a soul intentionally wished, during that memory long ago.

He smiled, knowing she acknowledged the memory. He nodded in the direction of the northwest sky. Still showing its heavenly bodies completely. She could see Saturn lit up. It slowly moved into the sign of Capricorn, then it quickly moved out and around the sky, through all the other zodiac signs, ending back in Aquarius, followed by Uranus moving into the constellation of Taurus. She looked back at him as her little self and nodded, knowing what he was hinting at, even though she didn't know exactly what it meant.

She remembered her soul's promise as a little girl. She leaned in for another long embrace that filled every part of her physical body with light and deep love. She felt water on her left leg, the one that was hurting her on her walk to the river.

The one that she'd wrapped in bandages while living in the yurt. She reached down to feel the water even though she was up in his arms. She looked down to see why the water level was rising quickly. She saw that she was looking at her hand in the water as she was lying on the ground, on her back. She sat up while she pulled her hand out of the water.

She looked around and nobody was there. One iPod headphone was still in her ear and she looked to see only her two eclipse glasses sitting next to her. She put one of them on and looked at the eclipse. The shadow was just coming off the sun. it moved off then she lay back down on the rocks to support her. With her left leg still in the river she rested, crying happily, fulfilling tears with "Wandering Star" By Lisa Gerrard playing in her ears. Grace felt so at peace, so comfortably strong. Healed from the heart.

She got up, put her shoes back on after allowing them to dry off, picked up the solar eclipse glasses, and patted her keys to make sure they were still with her. She walked with her music to her car. Her ankle felt better, but it was not cured of all pain, no.

She drove to work to finish the day. She saw the patients at work in a different way. They were even more precious. *There should be no stop sign blocking a human from any kind of healing their body, not money, not status,* she thought. *Nothing. We should help one another heal, share our gift of love and healing.* Pulling finances from the sick or suffering made her nauseous.

*People should be our investment, they would heal better, stronger, and quicker if it was done out of a pure heart.* She wanted to see that in her lifetime. She wanted to see people care for one another, just to care. We are so much greater than we allow ourselves to be.

She remembered the beggar. How long was that beggar standing there begging on the street? What sort of beautiful moments had she missed trying to follow a straight line through life?

#1 Shadow Hunter by Lisa Gerrard.
#2 'Wandering Star' By Lisa Gerrard playing in her ears.

# 18

# The Planet of Power and the Planet of Karma

## Move Forward

Saturn direct August 25, 2017
Pluto direct, September 28, 2017

After the eclipse, Grace realized the grand power and potential of shifting heavenly energies. She didn't understand all of it, but it gave her the desire to dive deeper into their system. The Friday following the eclipse, Saturn was moving direct into the sign of Sagittarius.

"See what Saturn brings you," said an astrologer on YouTube. "When Saturn, the lord of karma, goes retrograde [moving backwards in the sky], it's a double dose of karma. When Saturn goes forward, it heals your pain and sets up an optimistic future. It also brings karmic lessons to see if you've learned from your past.

Karmic balance is found as debts are repaid."

She'd been contemplating getting a used fifth-wheel trailer. Thinking it'd be fun to park it at the lower end of the property during the summer. That way she could have her own space and rent the entire homestead, bringing in more income. Plus, she wanted to grow a garden next year right outside of her bohemian home, imagining opening the door and walking straight into the garden.

She had her eye on one on Craigslist, a 30-foot, 2003 trailer with a wood burning stove inside of it, and two pop outs.

Two days after the eclipse, she went downtown to look at the RV. It was nice, and a great deal. She thought it over and decided to make a cash offer. She didn't have a truck, so the guy selling it offered to deliver it for her.

Grace was more stable knowing it was available just in case she needed to move from the homestead. It was always a possibility that her dad, aunt, and uncle might want to sell the place, and she wanted to be ready. She had tried to buy a house but couldn't get a loan for more than $65,000. There were only three homes in town around that price, and they all sold before she could make an offer.

Everyone in town who knew about the homestead property said, "DON'T SELL IT!" Twin was growing, and that area was a prime location. In town with plenty of acreage. If it were Grace's, she would never sell it. She'd grow organic crops and build her a little house on the northern part of the property, rent out the big house after remodeling it, and live there until she passed, just like her grandma and grandpa did.

The idea of the gypsy RV made her feel adventurous and connected to her Czechoslovakian, Bohemian roots. The man was ready to deliver it, but at that moment, she wasn't getting along with her dad.

She sensed she was on shaky ground with it being on the property even though she could move it whenever. So, she had the man deliver it to her cousin Sam's property in Glenns Ferry, an hour from Twin Falls. She figured that was the best decision.

She was going to focus on her writing and if she wanted to move her boho wagon to the homestead later, she could. It would be good to have options!

The tensions between her and her dad were pretty high. Things were going up in the air with the homestead; her family was thinking about selling, and Grace knew it wasn't hers. She figured it would be good to move herself out of the equation so that the three owners could make a clearer decision. She'd tried to buy her uncle out, but it seemed they couldn't get a deal made or a contract, plus six acres of land was a lot to take care of for a single woman! So, it was a plan to head to the boho mobile by spring, after winter.

Friday, the 25th came along and Saturn was moving direct. She was waiting to see what it would bring her. She went to Auger Falls to write, since she had the day off. She found a spot to sit at the top of a big mound of volcanic rock, wanting to feel the wind gently whispering by with inspiration.

She was lost in motivation as she wrote about the beggar on the day of the eclipse, remembering how interesting that was. After hours of writing, she lay back to bask in the sun.

She walked back to her car in the evening and drove home. When she pulled up to the house she heard the sound of a social media message. She thought, *Hmmm, who could that be?* She hardly ever got messages on Messenger. She checked, and it was Seth Higgins. A friend of her older brother's growing up. She met him the summer after her Sophomore year in high school. He stayed with them for 3 weeks that summer. He was a Marine and he was *deployed* to Iraq.

He was so cute! She remembered his bright blue eyes and big smile that made her girlfriends melt!

He had a serious girlfriend when she was in high school, and Grace thought there would *never* be a chance he'd like her, even though he'd tease her and flirt with her. She thought he was just picking on his best buddy's little sister.

His message said, *I had a very surreal dream about you last night. Let me know if I'm stepping over a line here.*

Grace replied with *Hi Seth! Long time, no see. You're only steppin over the line if you're a married man!*

*I'm single,* he immediately replied.

*Oh! Well, If you told me about your dream to get my attention, it worked. What was it about?* Grace asked.

*You would have to meet me for coffee one day to catch up. Then I might tell you 'bout the dream,* he said.

*Gottcha. Well, I'll meet you for tea someday. You're back in town?* she asked.

*Yeah, I'm living in town and have two little girls. 6 and 5,* he said. *They're my life.*

*Aw, how nice. Well, it's nice to hear from you. I'll give you my number and we can go get coffee or tea one day?*

*Sounds good, Grace,* he said.

Grace couldn't believe this opportunity had come along. It would be interesting to catch up with him again.

A few days later Seth invited her to get tea from a local coffee shop. He came to pick her up. She was in the backyard moving sprinklers and she'd just gotten off work, so she was dressed nicely in her teal-green form-fitting dress with her hair down. She'd told him she'd be out back.

She turned around and he was there on the back deck. He looked strong and tan, and he had on a white t-shirt and his aviator sunglasses with a newsboy flat cap hat. He walked across the deck and out onto the grass.

Grace told herself to be confident. She was. She stood tall, firm, and sure of herself. He walked up to her, and as he did he seemed to get shorter. She didn't remember him being short. Grace was barefoot, so she was her normal height.

"Boo!" she said as he walked over.

"Boo!" he replied.

They both gave each other a hug. "Whoa, this is a beautiful place, Grace!" he said, looking around.

"Thanks," She said. "It's my grandparents' place. My grandfather was out here every day working on projects, taking care of the yard and house. I'm not that handy all on my own but I try."

"It's beautiful! What's that hill over there?" he asked while focusing his gaze on it.

"That?" She pointed north towards the canyon edge. "That's Evil Kanevil's jump."

"What? It's right there?" he asked, stunned.

"Yep. Been there my whole life."

"Cool, well, can I take you to get tea?"

"Yeah, let's go," she said as she grabbed her flip flops.

He drove them to the coffee shop. They were chatting along the way, and when they got there it was closed, so they decided to go back to her place and make tea to sip on the back porch.

"So, have I earned the right to hear your dream yet?"

Grace asked while enjoying the view and comfort of the back deck.

He said, "Yes!" and he jumped right in. "So, I have this recurring dream where I'm always at the canyon edge, looking down. I sometimes turn into an eagle, my spirit animal, and fly down the canyon. It seems like the same place every time. Over on the west side of the bridge. This dream started the same way as usual, me looking down into the canyon. But something different happened. I saw people down in the river. The river was full of them, and they all needed help. I flew down and started helping the people out. I could tell that there was another person helping me pull these people out, but I couldn't see them. I could only see another set of arms, but no body or face. We kept pulling the people out and when we were done, I saw it was you. You were the only other person there helping these people. I looked at you and you were all smiles, glowing and happy even though we were dragging suffering people out of a bad situation. You gave me a hug, and the feeling was so warm, happy, and loving. I woke up with that warmth, and I had to find you and tell you!"

"Whoa, that's a great dream," she said. "It's right up my alley. I spend all my free time down at the river and I like the idea of 'spirit animals.'"

"Yeah? What's your spirit animal, Grace?"

"Well, I'd like to earn the deer as my spirit animal," she said honestly.

"Deer. I could see that. Quiet, motherly, natural, and a

sight to see."

Grace flushed

They chatted into the late evening, and then he said, "Well, it's time I say good night. I have to get my girls."

"Alright," Grace said as she stood from her seat to give him a hug. "Stay in touch."

"I plan to," he said and left.

She could tell Seth was a bit saddened and weighed down by life. He'd been through some things, but he was trying to be better, to make better choices and be with his daughters more.

The next weekend he had invited Grace to the Boise Zoo with his two daughters. It was a two hour drive west. It was a fun day and a good way for Grace to interact with the girls. She carried the oldest, who was getting sleepy, to the car afterwards. She called her "Momma." Grace thought that was cute, but Seth said, "That's not your momma. That's Grace!"

She said, "Momma" again.

Grace asked her, "What was your favorite animal at the zoo?"

"The kangaroo."

"Aw, yeah. That's a good one." The little girl clung to her even more. "Roo, Roo." Grace said. "You're a Baby Roo, Roo."

"Momma," the girl said again.

"Roo, Roo."

They both enjoyed bonding. *How nice,* Grace thought, *I*

*could do this… be in their life.*

The girls slept on the way home and Seth and Grace chatted. He drove her car while she sat and slouched sideways with her legs reaching over his lap.

The older girl awoke cranky just before they took the exit to Twin. She had to go potty, so they stopped. Her sister stayed asleep. Seth took her into the gas station, they came back, and they pulled out. She was already yawning, ready to get back to sleep. She yawned again, eyes closed, snuggling her head into the side of her seat and said, "Grace?"

"Yeah?" Grace said, turning to look back at her.

"You're pretty." And she fell asleep.

Grace looked at Seth, smiled at her, and all she could say was, "AWWW!"

They made it to his place and put the girls in bed. Grace said goodnight to Seth and he grabbed her, pulled her into him, and planted a firm kiss with his full lips. He was so purposeful. He pulled back with a look of fulfilled satisfaction and said, "I've been waiting 17 years to do that." Grace smiled, and he kissed her again.

She thought, *I had no idea he liked me back then.*

After that kiss, they became joined at the hip. They barbecued together, made healthy meals, and played with the girls when they were with him. The girls would go to Grace if they were sad or upset. They'd want to show Grace their "look what I can dos." It was all going pretty well. Grace was grateful for this experience.

She was so distracted by them that it was weeks before she realized she hadn't been writing. She needed to get back on track with that! She even put off moving to her trailer. Her dad said, "Stay at the homestead through the winter at least." Grace was okay with that.

Seth invited Grace over one night for a movie. "I got what I could from Redbox," he said while putting in the movie. It was Sam Elliot's new movie *Hero*. Sam was her favorite actor, as she had discussed with River. The movie was about a 70-year-old man who fell in love with a woman in her mid 30s. Grace thought how similar her story was to the movie's. At least most of it.

The male character even asked her why she was there with him. She asked him if he wanted her to leave, but when he thought about it he said, "No." She was appreciative for Sam Elliot and the lead actress for playing those characters, to make it a little more acceptable. How nice.

Grace got a text message from Cray during the movie, out of the blue. He said he was getting married on the 30th. Grace wished him the best. *Another ending*, she thought. She was feeling good about her own path; she knew to keep going at a slow pace with Seth. There was no rush.

Grace asked Seth if he'd like to go to Hagerman for a nice dinner then soak in the hot springs on Wednesday night.

He liked that idea.

Grace was watching what was going on in the heavens that week. There was a new moon in Capricorn, her sign, Pluto would go direct Thursday in Capricorn. Uranus will square Pluto in Capricorn that day. Grace had no idea what any of that meant, but she made her little plans anyway. She would just watch. Be the observer, like always.

On Wednesday evening, they drove Grace's car to Hagerman to have a light dinner at the restaurant before going to the hot springs nearby.

Grace noticed on the drive that her leg and foot hadn't been hurting so much lately. That was incredibly appreciated.

They sat down to eat at the restaurant, and Seth ordered a glass of wine. It was the first time he'd had a drink around her. She knew that she'd be so dehydrated if she drank before soaking in the hot springs, so she decided to decline.

He started acting a little funny, flirting with the older waitress, and he ordered another drink.

"You know, that first day we got together, in your grandparent's backyard? When I walked up to you, you were towering over me. So tall, I didn't remember you being so tall," he said as though he were talking to himself out loud.

"Funny, because I was trying to feel confident and tall. I noticed it too. I felt tall when you came up to me. But we're the same height, if you're not a little taller," she said.

"Interesting… Grace, why are you so nice to me? What have I ever done for you?" he asked.

She was caught off guard by the question. "I guess I'm pretty patient. I don't know. You want me to get pissed at you?" she asked.

"No," he said. "Grace, I can't give you babies. I had the surgery, and I know you want a little girl."

"Hmmm. Ok, well, I'm sure your little girls will fill my needs of having a girl," she said truthfully.

"What if I told you I didn't have the surgery?" he asked.

"Well, have you, or haven't you?"

"Waitress?" he called out and held up his card. The waitress walked up, annoyed at how he called for her, then she took his card and walked off. There was a moment of silence at their table.

The waitress quickly brought the card back and Seth asked, "You ready Grace?"

"Yep," she said, a bit agitated.

They got in the car and headed to the hot springs down the road. Grace decided to drop the subject to enjoy the evening. They soaked and chatted about the girls, her book, her wishes for the homestead, and his dreams. Then they got out and drove back to her house. It was fully dark out.

He stopped in her driveway. It was late and he was acting odd, stressed out. Grace climbed over to his seat, straddled him, hugged him, then kissed a real good kiss. Hoping to help him relax and come back to the moment.

She pulled back, looking at his face for relief. He had his glasses on and a white t-shirt and jeans. He looked all comfy.

He grabbed her promptly and started clenching her shoulders while looking past her. He pulled her into him and back towards the steering wheel again saying, "Who are you, is someone there?" And he looked outside, a bit panicked.

"Are you alright?" Grace asked, noticing the playful vibe quickly changing to worry. "You want me to get off your lap?" She thought he must've been really dehydrated after his two drinks and over an hour soak in the hot springs.

He said, "No, this is a dream of mine," referring to her sitting with him in the driver's seat. He pulled her in closer, hugging and cuddling into her.

"You need some water! Come inside and I'll get you some," she said.

They both got out of the car and went into the kitchen. She gave him water with a pinch of sea salt and lemon to help hydrate him. He sat down and started bringing up the conversation about having a vasectomy again.

"Seth, it doesn't matter if you have or haven't. Just tell me the truth," she said. They hadn't been intimate; Grace didn't plan on that for a good while.

"I can't tell you," he admitted. "If I tell you I have had the surgery then you won't want to be with me. If I tell you I haven't then you'll want one soon," he said, looking into the future with a bit of weight on his shoulders.

"Well, I don't think we need to worry about that. That's not why I'm dating you, and it's not a reason to end our relationship either," she said, trying to reassure him.

"I can't tell you yet."

"Alright, Seth. That's fine, just don't try to mess with me

about it, alright?" She sighed as she reached over to rub his back. "I think you need to go home and get some good rest. I'll add some more water and salt to your glass before you go."

"Thanks!" he said as he hugged her.

She got up, filled the mason jar, and handed it to him then hugged him, and said, "Goodnight" as he walked out the garage door.

"Night, Grace," he said appreciatively.

She cleaned up the kitchen and headed to bed. She locked the door to her room every time since she had two roommates who lived in the two spare rooms. She lay down to go to bed, tired and relaxed from the warm soak.

A half hour later, she heard a knock on her bedroom door. She got up with her duvet blanket wrapped around her. Opened the door and Seth was standing there with his guitar. He asked, "Can we talk, Grace?"

She looked at him and said, "Sure." She welcomed him into her room, not turning the light on.

Seth sat on the bed, hunched over his guitar. Grace sat on the edge next to him.

He said, "Grace, you're so happy all the time. It concerns me that I haven't seen any other emotions yet."

Grace noticed she was breathing deep and feeling strong. She said, "Seth, I haven't had any reason yet to be any different. You want me to argue with you?"

"No." He leaned in for a kiss. A passionate kiss. Grace didn't mind that, but she was confused.

In order to calm herself down to rest, she turned Pandora on before he returned. His favorite song came on Pandora— "Tuesday's Gone." He said, "I love this song. It's such a sad song!" Then he giggled, put down the guitar, and grabbed her playfully. A big bear hug took them both off the bed backwards. Her head hit the floor first with all their body weight. It hurt her neck. She thought that was too rough. Then he rolled over until he was on top of her, hunched over in the dark. The duvet was still wrapped around her, and her hair was stuck under her back so she couldn't look directly at him.

He pushed himself up. "It would be so easy to beat you into submission and kill you..." Grace couldn't believe what she was hearing. At the same time quick flashes came of herself in a little dark room with a man in a dominating stance, only a window letting in enough light to show the marine's suit hanging on the wall.

Grace lay under Seth calmly, knowing she was protected even though she had all the right to be worried. She knew not to panic. She could feel a cloud of protection surrounding her even though she was ready to react if needed.

He said, "It would be so easy to strangle you." Another flash of her pinned under the strong man forcing himself on her. Image of blinds evenly spaced, vertically in the window as if they were bars imprisoning her. Grace felt these stories coincidentally overlapping.

He moved over and leaned against the bed. "I'm sorry," he said while putting his head in his hands. "I shouldn't have done that to you, Grace."

Grace could see the little boy in him. Confused by his own behavior. She turned the light on and knelt in front of him with the blanket wrapped around her. He looked at her and said, "Sorry." Then he grabbed either side of the blanket, pulling them tight around her neck. "It would be so easy to strangle your slender neck."

Grace reached out to stop him.

"Seth, you need to leave," she said firmly.

He got up and said, "I'll call you tomorrow." Calmly.

She slammed the door and bolted the door. She could hear her roommate in his room next to hers, thank goodness.

Grace lay down. She picked up her phone, looked at the last person she texted other than Seth, and texted everything that just happened.

Her friend called right away. "Grace, are you okay? You need to call the police!"

Grace began to cry over the phone. She didn't think she was that shaken up, but she was! She was crying intensely. Shocked at what had happened.

She heard a knock on her door. "I think he's back."

As she took the phone down, her friend shouted, "Call the police!" Grace walked over to open the door.

Seth was standing there. "You're crying! Who were you talking to?"

"Nobody," she said.

"Grace, who were you talking to?" he demanded.

"My friend. I just told them what happened and started crying."

He walked in as he hugged her and cradled her head in his hands. Grace felt so uncomfortable with him.

He said, "Finally showing emotions! Now you know who you really are." As he rubbed her back Grace thought, *I'm only crying because of what you've done.* She pulled away, reached for his guitar, and handed it to him. "You need to leave right now, Seth. I will call the police if I need to."

"I'll talk to you tomorrow, Grace." He took his guitar and left.

Grace went to work the next morning. They only worked until 11 AM that day and she made sure to get her neck worked on by her boss. It hurt from being taken off the bed with Seth. She told her boss what had happened, mostly to make sure she wasn't suppressing it.

"*Run!*" he said, "Men like that don't get better, Grace. Maybe if he were younger, you could work through that behavior, but I would run!"

Grace shook her head in agreement.

"Plus, you wouldn't want Kai to have to experience anything like that."

"Yes, I'm very grateful that he wasn't there to see any of that."

When she got home, Seth was in her room, asleep on her bed. He must have watched her put her hidden key away before and unlocked her door. She went out in the backyard to think for a bit. She knew what she needed to say. She needed to voice some things to him.

He texted her. *Hey, Grace. I thought you got off work early today? I'm lying on your bed.*

She replied, *I know. I'm in the backyard, in the raspberry patch.*

She picked a few berries and ate them, trying to summon her courage to confront him and tell him face to face how she felt.

She felt Pluto moving forward in the sky and knew she could use it to empower her. After all it was in her sign of Capricorn.

Seth came out and walked across the lawn over to her, looking like he knew he would get in trouble. "Grace, Are you mad at me?" he asked her.

"Seth, let me ask you a question. What would you do if you knew that a big guy did what you did to me last night to one of your little girls?" She crossed her arms. "Would you allow that to happen or let her be with him?"

"Grace, I don't remember anything from last night!" he said.

She looked at him with a sideways glance. "What?"

"I remember parts but not everything that happened, no."

Grace proceeded to tell him everything that happened

last night with a quick-paced voice.

He said, "Grace," as he walked too close to her. A foot away. She stood firm as he continued, "I take medication for my PTSD, and when it mixes with alcohol it causes me to lose my memory and act a little off. I'm sure being dehydrated didn't help. It's happened to me before. I did the same thing with my last ex-girlfriend of two years. I tried to strangle her at her house while her new boyfriend was there. I drank after taking my meds and I didn't remember!" he admitted as though it made him innocent. "Her boyfriend intervened."

Grace looked at him. "*What?*"

"Yeah, I'm actually going to court in a couple hours. I was accused of 'Attempted Strangulation.' I find out my sentence in an hour. I could be going to federal prison in a few hours, Grace!" He said all this with enthusiasm, as if the information would save him and make it all better.

The thoughts going through Grace's head were all over the place. Looking at this man whose fate was unknown, she had compassion for him, but at the same time an even stronger feeling that these were all consequences of *his* actions. This has nothing to do with *her*, other than her learning to stand up for herself and stay firm.

"Grace, will you wait for me?" he asked.

"Wait for you?"

"If I go to prison?"

Grace's awareness went out and above her body, even though she was clearly looking through her eyes. She was now the observer of this situation. The flashes of her having lived through a similar experience to the one last night were not to be ignored. Her soul had experienced this force of power over her before, and she had Pluto, the planet of power and transformation, with her this time.

"Seth, you threatened to *kill* me last night! I got an adjustment on my neck at work today from you thrusting us off the bed. Whether or not you remember, I do! You crossed a major line and I'm afraid of you! Afraid of you! Why would I sacrifice my life and potential relationships for *you* when these are *your* consequences?! I gave you a clean, clear shot at having a healthy relationship with me and you proved yourself untrustworthy!"

"So, it's over?"

"Yes, it's over, Seth!" she said. "And… you should have been upfront in the beginning and told me about the situation with your ex."

"Really? Grace, I'm not going to accept that. It's not a reason enough to break up," he said.

She couldn't believe he said that. "Seth, it is! It's more than enough. Why would I knowingly put myself in a position with you where this could possibly happen again? Especially after knowing that you tried to strangle your last lover. Last night's preview was plenty of warning!"

She looked at him and his pretty face. It wasn't so handsome anymore. She could put up with a lot, but she'd learned to love herself enough. She mattered more to herself than to allow situations like that to continue. There was no going back from this.

"Well, I have to go get ready for court. Wish me luck," Seth said.

"Good luck, Seth!" Grace said as he walked to the front of the house.

Grace watched him the entire way—full of inner power. He was nearly gone when he shouted, "I love you Grace! I will always remember you standing beautifully, out in the raspberry patch."

She looked around the garden, alone and strong. She felt Pluto shifting the energies above and Uranus bringing his "unexpected" events. She also thought back to the day Saturn went direct, the day Seth first messaged her.

The lord of karma hadn't brought her the soulmate of her dreams as she had hoped for. No, the ringed planet demanded Seth to pony up his karmic debts and had given Grace a repeat lesson from her past.

She had certainly learned her lesson this time! Both occasions were similar in the way that a man aimed to have aggressive physical power over her. She did not take action in her last situation, but this time, she would.

She waited until Seth drove away then called the police to fill out a report. Grace had no doubts in that moment that her voice had value. She was proud of her present response, bringing healing over the wounds of her past, stimulating growth within.

* * *

In astrology, Pluto represents the shadow side of human behavior. He dives deep into psychology and requires all of us to own our power. He won't let you do the superficial relating, stay on the surface, and ignore the elephant in the room or the problems in your relationships. If you wanna just stay quiet, swallow your feelings, to keep the peace... Pluto won't let you!

If we swallow our feelings and not stand up for ourselves then we're not living to our fullest potential. And we are not allowing ourselves and the other to grow either. Relationships are for mutual benefits. Mutual growth. Our soul's evolution.

# 19

## Jupiter's Ingress Into Scorpio

October 9, 10, 2017

Grace stayed a few nights in her bohemian home after saying goodbye to Seth. She'd bumped into Matt Haze, her old boss who invited her to join him on the last day of Ketchum's market. He had to deliver hay to someone and she jumped at the chance.

The day before Jupiter moved into Scorpio, she journaled to document her emotions.

> *There's a blanket of shadowy emotions swirling inside my chest. I'm completely aware that I am alone, but I want to be held and escape in the comfort of a loved one's embrace. This leaves me on the vulnerable side.*

She wished the heaviness would pass as she continued writing.

> *These sensations are strong and the opposite of what I've been experiencing lately; I've been stable in my independence and*

*newfound strength after my recent experience with Seth. ~ Maybe my empowerment was a front, to get me through the situation?*

She'd stayed the night at the homestead and followed her morning routine while listening to the astral weather. She was curious to know what shifts were happening in the sky—It had become an enjoyable habit for her.

The astrologer who created the app was becoming a good friend. He had no idea she existed, but she saw him as a genuine pal who looked out for her.

"Jupiter in Scorpio brings blessings! See what she brings as she shifts signs today,"

The astrologer said while she finished brushing her teeth, placing her toothbrush near Kai's kiddy toothbrush. She straightened them in a caring way then glanced at her star chart, taped to the wall to familiarize herself with it.

The first house on her astrology wheel was Taurus. Jupiter in Scorpio would be moving through the opposite house of relationships and other people. This is where you can find your marriage and business partners, contracts, and your open enemies.

"This shift can bring up past romances to revive or bury deep—never to uncover again. On a collective level, it can bring out dark sexual issues and the most interesting relationships. Wherever Jupiter goes, it will expand. Even if it brings a tough situation, Jupiter expands our experience to somehow benefit you or the collective."

Grace was thrilled, readying herself for market and positively affected by her good-vibe tunes, playing aloud. She slipped on her skinny jeans, a long sleeve top and kept her hair down, half-scrunched in a clip for a messy look. Then checked two incoming texts from her dad. The first was the usual To-Do list for the rentals and homestead and a surprising note of gratitude for all she's done. She zipped up her puffy vest confidently, ready for cool weather if that'd be the case.

The second said: *I bought you guys tickets to visit us in Florida. We got passes for Disneyland to celebrate Kai's birthday. You'll fly out at the end of the month. I also put $250 in your account for travel expenses.*

She made a fist pump, saying "This Scorpio season is starting nicely! Jupiter *does* bring blessings," she said, putting on her tall boots feeling pleased, adding to her confidence.

She checked the mailbox on the way to meet Matt and pulled out a little package. It was her antler ring she'd ordered a few weeks ago and had asked the shop owner if it was deer or elk antler. They said there was no telling if it were elk or deer since they'd mixed them.

*Perfect, Two birds with one stone,* she thought, pleased to receive it on that specific date. She put it on her ring finger, fancying how raw and natural it appeared on her slender finger. She committed to her inner doe and elk soul mate, out there somewhere.

She parked at Barnes and Noble to wait for Matt—just like old times. While she waited, she wrote in her green notebook.

> *Jupiter is in Scorpio today. Kia and I are going to see dad! Antler ring! Let's see what else she brings.*

Then she wrote about how sunny it was and how the birds were flying all around. They seemed to do well with the Scorpio energy too, looking so free as they easily glided through the air with magic.

Haze showed up with his truck full of straw and she hopped in like the good ol' days. They spent their drive catching up and she thought of the possibility of reuniting with River if he happened to be there. She was ready for whatever would come, looking forward to reuniting with her market family.

Matt asked about Seth since she'd just introduced them a few weeks prior at the Twin Falls farmers market. She went into full detail about what happened and said it was a shame that it went in the direction it had but splitting up was for the best.

"You need to get a restraining order on him!" He said.

Grace knew he would say that but she knew Seth was being taken care of and wasn't worried.

When they got to Ketchum, where she was eager and nervous, she was solid and confident, sturdy and ready to face anything. Haze stopped to let her out in the alleyway while he went and parked the truck.

She headed to their old booth space where another farmer from Buhl had taken it over. Grace was close to the family and looked forward to seeing them and their kids.

Carrying her reusable bag, she glanced around a truck and a trailer, seeing River with his tidy sweater over a collared shirt and cap with his white hair poking out the sides.

He hadn't seen her walk into the market, so she went straight to their old spot that was nearly set up, kitty-corner from him.

The family who was selling produce in their old space was delighted to see her. All three kids came running up to her.

"Grace!" They shouted, hugging her fondly.

She was sure River heard them crying out her name while she gave them hugs. Then she helped unload a few boxes of veggies on the tables, getting a kick out of being in the booth again. Her soul would always love the market. It was simply beautiful with its abundance of food and great, down-to-earth people. The weather was perfect—the hot summer sunshine was now turning into that fall kind of glow.

"Hi, Grace!" Sawyer said, walking up to the booth—the lizard spirit guy who had her pull her deer card nearly a year ago.

"Hey!" she said as they walked to his family's booth where he introduced her to his new puppy.

"Remember you texted me the day before the full moon eclipse at the beginning of August?"

"Yeah."

"You said something will climax, come to fruition or end."

"Uh-huh," she said, remembering that.

"Foxy got run over the next day. On the eclipse."

"Oh, I'm so sorry Sawyer!" she said as she rubbed the puppy's ears with new awareness.

"It's alright. She was my best bud! I just couldn't believe you said that the day before and it happened."

"I hope I didn't manifest that terrible accident," she said, sorrowfully patting the pup.

"Oh, no! I found it interesting and couldn't help thinking about your text."

"Well this puppy is wonderful and I hope she helps to heal your heart, Sawyer."

"She already has," he said proudly, rolling the puppy around on the grass.

They giggled about the playful dog's energy and talked

about growing vegetables. He reminded her of the popcorn she'd grown the year before and had shared some with him. He had grown both varieties this year and was selling it in their booth. There were two kinds: a little yellow corn and long kernel purple corn. She favored the purple variety, it made a delicious snack.

"I took seeds from both and planted them last year. They cross-pollinated and created mini purple corn. I called it, "Sawyer's purple thumb.""

She was thrilled he had done something with it and appreciated his enthusiasm for gardening.

When they finished their conversation, she walked straight south towards River. His back was facing her, standing at the front corner of the booth, straightening up some pottery.

"Boo, you!" she said.

"Hey, you!" he said, turning around.

She gave him a big hug and squeezed tight, noticing his familiar lemony fresh laundry soap scent.

"Ouch!" He yelped and pulled back.

Grace promptly backed away as he pointed to his clavicle.

"I broke my collarbone… feel here." He grabbed her hand and rubbed it over the break.

"Ouch, I'm sorry," she said, thinking he was too close and towering over her.

"No worries. How's the homestead?"

She was intimidated by his closeness and wanted to pull

away to hear herself think. She took a few steps back into the main walkway and he followed. She didn't know what to tell him, and he picked up on her struggle.

"It's alright. You don't need to tell me."

Then she walked them to the other side of the street, making sure he was standing on lower ground and her on the higher ground even though he was taller. She didn't want him making her feel small.

Together, they were magnetic. The attraction pulled at them both as he was now standing back from her.

"I like your bracelet," he reached over, taking her hand to get a better look. "Where'd you get it?"

"My stepdad's shop, 15 years ago."

"Nice that you held onto it for so long."

She gently took her hand from him and adjusted the bracelet, glancing at it. It did look pretty, and she felt pretty with it, but more than that, she was strong in herself.

"So, what happened to your collarbone?" she asked, changing the subject.

"Was mountain biking with some friends and crashed, landing on my shoulder."

She was still fiddling with her bracelet as he continued looking at it and then at her ring.

"And this?" He pointed to it. "Tell me 'bout that!"

"It's an elk..." —She felt him collapse a bit— "I mean, a deer antler ring. I've committed to my inner doe." She looked up at him with the pine-covered mountain and blue sky in the backdrop.

He just nodded and said, "Inner doe, huh?"

"Yep."

She told him about her boho wagon and that she was planning on living in it.

"I'm in my grandparents' room for now. I had a boyfriend who kinda distracted me from my book for a month. I had to call the police on him… so, I ended that and got my ring."

He sunk his head as though he were thinking she shouldn't give up on her pursuit of finding someone. She didn't care what he thought anymore.

She mentioned how her dad and she were butting heads and her home on wheels might help lift their tension.

"But he just texted me this morning, appreciating me and all I've done." Grace grabbed her heart and said, "It makes my heart happy!"

"Huh, he wasn't appreciating you?"

"Nope." Then she added, "He's flying Kai and me out to Florida in a couple of weeks."

"Nice! How is Kai?"

"He's great, thanks for asking."

"I'm going to go see my boys for a couple of weeks, next week."

"You're not spending all winter there again?"

"No, not all winter. I'm gonna be up there on that mountain, where I belong." He motioned his glance to the ski hill behind him and she smiled happily for him.

"It's also my last market, Grace."

"Really? So, today is your grand finale?" she asked, a bit shocked.

"Yep. I'm going to travel and spend time with my boys while I'm up and at it."

"Well, that's good for you, River," she said, nodding. "I'm sure you'll enjoy your summer freedom!"

He leaned back, studying her, and said, "You look good. Skinny as ever."

Grace sensed a little piece of him enjoying the attention she was giving him in front of all their market friends. Then Willie, the nearly toothless market customer in his 50's whom she'd known since her first market, saw her. He walked straight towards her, eyeing her while River moved to the side to welcome him.

"Willie, you're lookin' good," River said. "You dress up 'cause—"

"Cause I knew *she* was comin'!" Willie pointed at Grace.

River carried on… "You dressed up knowin' *Grace* would be here."

Willie walked closer to her and nudged his shoulder into hers, giving her a wink.

"Remind me your name."

"—Grace." River piped in.

"Grace, be my—Grace." He bowed.

"Come on now." River said as if he'd all of a sudden

claimed her.

He seemed to have an issue with another man flirting with her and they got into a bit of a scuffle with each other while Grace was slightly pulled towards River. She was focused on the way his hands moved, talking with influence.

She slipped into a daze as the breeze gently blew her fine hair across her face, swaying with the current as their voices faded. Her awareness turned inward, hearing a sound from within—

A hammer was driving a nail deep into the wood of her heart, in sync with the now loud banging. She saw an image of herself, hair down long in a beautiful, light peach dress and cowgirl boots— hammering nails one by one into a wooden board, experiencing every nail. She finished nailing the board onto a tall, wooden wall on River's round horse training arena. She was sealing up the doorway to the inside, where he taught her how to ride Luna. The mountain hills were reverent in the background with the bright blue sky above. It was such a warm sunny day. She picked up another tall board while gripping a few nails in between her lips. Her hammer in hand and a calm expression, pounding each nail into the last board sealing the arena closed. She ran her hand along the boards, making sure they were on tight. Her hair glamorously curled as if she were headed to a formal wedding.

She was sturdy and accomplished, holding the hammer firmly, shaded by the tall arena wall, then leaned forward to peek through a hole in the new boards. She saw herself inside, dancing a beautiful dance with her flowy dress, displaying a delighted smile across her face. This made her smile then River came into view through the hole, following her in the dance, reaching for her hand. Then gently pulled her in for a kiss.

She pulled back from the whimsical image through the peephole, accomplished knowing they'd be there dancing in her heart. She'd leave it boarded up like Fort Knox, forever.

She backed away from the wall and walked with full esteem through the corral. Flashes of her turning into a strong, elegant, red-haired bull—a Taurus bull with a sturdy, majestic gait, moving on. She *was* the steady bull with the world under her feet, walking to the beat of a catchy new song she enjoyed, through the gate and out into the sagebrush hills.

Moving on. Alone.

River jolted her out of her vision, when he said, "I should go, but let's talk in a bit."—frustrated about Willie.

She shook away the faded images of her inner film, making no promise to converse again, and was left to chat with Willie. She had a chuckle chatting with him then proceeded to float the market with a sturdy heart, pleased. Willie passed her again and said, "You're gorgeous."

She smirked, continuing through the crowd knowing her attractiveness was beaming from within, and joined Matt, who was diagonal from River's booth. She stood to talk as he was in a group of older men who were catching up with him. They started talking with her, then one gentleman shook her hand and kissed it.

Shocked, she said, "Nobody's ever kissed my hand before." then looked at Matt, wondering what to do.

"That's something unusual for you?" the man asked.

"Yeah, it is." she laughed and politely pulled back her hand.

"Well, you're beautiful," he said kindly.

She couldn't help but look over at River. He could hear it all and acted like he wasn't watching. She wondered, *What is this?* A jackpot of older men showing her positive attention? She saw it as somehow a "good karma-kick-back" in her favor for being loving and open with River. Or at least she'd like to think so.

She knew they had little time, so she paced the market one last time before Haze caught her attention.

"Ready?"

She shook her head, though she didn't want to leave, she was ready. Matt walked them behind River's booth.

"Goodbye," she said as they walked by.

"Leaving, already?" he asked, holding an expression that

showed he wasn't ready. He had wanted to chat again, but they were headed out. "Can I give you a hug?"

They hugged quietly and he pulled back to say, "' Til next time."

"Yep!" she said as she walked towards Haze, seeming she'd left him hanging and she did.

She knew it was their last time seeing each other, using Jupiter's move into Scorpio to her advantage, burying him away. Or better yet, board him up, in his arena.

As she sauntered out, he said "Goodbye" twice. She looked back once with that sturdy bull gait and waved empowered as that song came flooding loudly into her mind. The beat added to her strength as she walked away from that heartache, transforming into more security in herself.

\* \* \*

On their drive home Grace found a new freedom. It seemed that Jupiter's ingress had given her many gifts, but the greatest of them all… was that freedom. She could see River had his reasons for not being with her, and her heart had allowed him to go. She was ready to move on—ready to fly wherever the energies would carry her.

She noticed all the birds along the ride as she had that morning. They were so free too, flying as if this Scorpio energy gave them something they didn't have before. It gave them an extra burst of flight and wind at their backs.

*Note: this is the time frame when the "Me too" movement...
Jupiter in Scorpio vibe.
*"Trying So Hard Not to Know" by Nathaniel Rateliff & The
Night Sweats

# 20

# Barnes and Noble

Friday, November 10, 2017

Grace spent the day writing at her beloved Barnes and Noble cafe, in her favored spot—a two-seater table next to the windows, enjoying the bright sun.

A strong sense of gratitude welled within her and she wrote a brief "thank you" note to the universe. Afterward, an impressive magazine cover caught her attention with a close-up of Saturn.

*How stunning!* She thought as she flipped through its pages at her table, in awe of its beauty. She was grateful for the chance to see the majestic planet in great detail, feeling connected to him even more than before. She cried, enveloped by his brilliance as nearby cafe customers gave her a look of concern.

She picked up her pen, hoping a bit of writing would ground her but she couldn't turn off the floodgates. With hindered vision, she put the pen down, trying to focus on the caring sunshine. That only intensified her emotions with its unyielding affection. She struggled to allow it all in, finding herself trying to push it away, unable to manage the incredible force.

Tears ran down her cheeks as she wrote through them, using her napkin to wipe her face just to have them continue, so she walked to the bathroom. Once she was alone and in the privacy of a stall she leaned against the wall for support to let the tears flow.

The sensation didn't fade after leaving the sun's rays—it was just as intense, concentrating into her heart.

*This love couldn't possibly be for me*, she thought, wanting to give it to someone more in need of it—which amplified the sensation. She slid to a slouch, working on embracing the flow, sitting with a sensitive heart until her emotions stabilized.

*Why now? Why today?* She thought. Either way, she appreciated whatever it was and was glad she was able to get back to her table in the cafe, resuming her writing. She found it interesting how she'd fought the sensations as she sensed eyes on her and her attention was drawn to a man walking on the sidewalk.

It was the beggar strolling his stress-free stride—in no hurry, wearing the same Carhartts, a black shirt, and boots. His thick, dark hair was down to his shoulders, looking clean as he came through the doors and straight to the magazine racks.

His bright green eyes were shocking as they met hers. She smiled shyly, waving and he walked towards her as she offered him a seat.

He was calm and collected, shaded by the pillar in between the windows.

She made room on the table, leaning her notebook against the window on the floor while he glanced at her empty teacup.

"I'd fill your cup," he said, "But they don't take smiles as currency" and smiled at her.

"I'm good." She said, "I just finished my tea. Would you like some coffee?"

"I brought my own, thank you." He said, holding up his Thermos and turned silent, in no hurry or concerned with small talk.

"When you walk all day, where do you go?" She asked, breaking the silence.

"I don't walk, I travel." He said, matter-of-factly, peeking at his digital watch and around the cafe.

"Oh," she said, wondering what to say, "When's your birthday?"

"Today."

"Really?" Grace asked skeptically.

"Yes, today is the 100th birthday of the Marine Corps," he said, sounding like a commercial.

"So, your birthday is on the Marine Corps birthday?"

"Not really, but that information is irrelevant."

"I was just going to see what your—."

"Again, irrelevant," he bluntly interrupted.

Grace allowed there to be silence, while he checked his watch again.

"My job is to serve and protect this one nation under God," he said as though he'd repeated it thousands of times.

"What are you protecting it from?"

A glance of agitation crossed his face then stared at her with potent eyes.

"Can you protect me?" She asked, playing along.

"There are many on my list to protect." He said, pulling out a weathered pocketbook, allowing her to glance at the neatly written information then looked around.

"That's a lot of people."

"Yes, it is."

"Were you protecting me the day of the eclipse?" She asked, making eye contact. "The Great American Eclipse."

He jumped to his own question.

"What was the promise you made to 'the man in the *robe*?" He asked, holding up quote fingers, "And what's with the snow globe and picture frame?"

Grace was surprised he'd picked up on her illusion the day of the Leo Eclipse and thought, *Odd… it's a Leo moon today.*

"Look who's all of the sudden full of questions," She said sarcastically, as he gave her a deep stare. "Well," Grace cleared her throat, "when I was about five or six, I was praying in my room holding my photo of Christ and a snow globe that played *Somewhere Over the Rainbow*. I was asking to be someone who could touch the hand of God, to be pure and love the way we were meant to. I wanted to continuously be within God's love.

My soul yearned to BE the sensation that comes across every soul when they experienced love. I could live a life in the physical world, but what I *wanted* was to become that tender energy. I promised I would be that as best I could and help others know they're adored to the fullest."

She kept his interest while he said nothing, so she continued.

"But... growing up has shown me it's not that simple. I know I haven't been able to love everyone—even myself like I'd wished." She paused, his eyes still watching her. "How can I help others feel that when *I* have difficulties?" she asked. "I experienced that penetrating emotion here, this morning, not knowing why." She looked away as if she had been speaking to herself.

"Thank you for sharing, Mother," he said, eyes still locked on hers.

She peered at him and decided to skip over the "Mother" comment.

"Beautiful heart, Grace," he said, it was a genuine compliment and not the response she'd expected.

"Why do I keep having these odd relationships where I'm giving love and I seem to end up needing to learn a lesson or needing to move on?"

"What did you experience before I got here?" he asked.

"An immense inflow of love pouring into my heart

through the rays of the sun," she said in one breath with her eyes closed, using her hands to express the emotion.

"What more do you need?" he asked. "A tangible man never came up and made you feel that way, did he?"

"No," she admitted.

"What you want is companionship from the opposite sex," he said. "The emotions you experienced earlier were from a higher source, and that's available any time. All beings are free with their priorities. You are no different."

He stared at her then shrugged his shoulders.

"Your love... is a form of currency. You can't buy tea with it, yet..." He looked around the cafe and back to her. "See your love or the time you invest in someone as a pearl. You wouldn't throw a pearl to swine, they would eat it because they don't know its value. A swine is a swine; he simply eats what he's given."

"So, men are all pigs?" she asked playfully, squinting one eye.

He rolled his eyes as she snickered then gave him her full attention as she sat back in her seat.

"What if God were alone, Grace? And he *was* pure abundance, able to do anything. You would think he'd create a place where he could give an infinite amount of soul selves the opportunity to experience limitations, restrictions, and a sense of lack. You know, change it up?

He *was* the creator of the light and came from it. He is also of darkness. And his desire to experience the universe from *your* perspective grew out of an intention from the combination of both."

*I'd never thought of it that way*, she realized.

"God had all the time to create and design a place to experience—you," he said to her, "and just because you're here, the dark will naturally transform into more light. You're expanding God and giving the light and darkness what they want as well. One day you'll return to that pure light, and you'll know you've been loved the same as you are now—as when you first began and as you will ever be."

"God is lonely..." she said, "so he created us through light and dark in order to interact with different parts of himself and feel less lonesome?"

He shrugged his shoulders as if to say, why not? "It's the true gift of the veil."

She was captivated and said, "Well... that makes the concept of oneness easier to grasp."

"Once again, I'd fill your cup, but they don't take smiles as a form of currency... yet," he said again, hinting at something.

She wondered what he was getting at with that statement? His responses evoked additional questions within her, and she moved towards the edge of her seat.

"Recently... I've been having flashes of past lives. Mostly in the last few months or so. These images are incredibly *real* as if I've lived them and now I'm remembering them. Certain events trigger the memories—I'm usually a woman with a lower rank in some way than a man. The images are so tangible, I understand the woman's emotions as though they're mine."

"Ah, the divine feminine wants to have a conversation," he said, peeking at his watch then back at her. "I'm going to give you an analogy. Say there are three specks of dark particles stuck together—6, 6, 6." He held up a finger with each six, giving her a look of "you picking up what I'm putting down?"

She couldn't help but glance at the once bright sky with a cloud moving over it, blocking the sunlight—oddly coincidental.

"These particles are so small they can travel through your nose and lungs without you ever knowing it. —Carbon—" he said, as the lights in the entire store went out.

She looked around thinking, *This had never happened.*

He nodded in recognition of the lights and cloud cover, continuing, "Carbon binds to anything and everything. Let's say you breathe in a speck of dust with the three dark specs bound to it. They go into your lungs and body. Let's say your body is a system with a lot of minute specs of dust floating around, some with these carbon specs, some without. They are looping around in the system." He held up his pointer finger, drawing a closed-system cycle in the air. "And when one dust spec binds to the carbon it becomes aware of the system."

She was listening carefully.

"Now, the spec is aware of the system, while being stuck in that system, aware."

"You said the divine feminine wants to have a chat. Are you referring to darkness as the feminine?"

"That's how I've experienced darkness," he responded, "it's our throttle towards growth."

"So… darkness gives us higher awareness?" she asked.

He looked at her, acknowledging her interpretation, not wanting to intrude on her train of thought.

With this realization, she grabbed her writing notebook and tossed it on the table.

"Is it even worth it?" she asked in a stern voice, holding her hand out to present her work.

"Is *what* worth it?" his eyes widened, sitting back.

"*This*… my story? If there's only awareness to be found… then why even? WHY…?" she asked in frustration.

He looked at her with alarm and said, "WHY?… Why is infinite." He stretched his arm out as far as it would go. "Why, why, why, why,"—showing the question went on forever. "Why not…" His hand dropped firmly on its side next to her notebook. "Ends your questioning right here." pointing to her notebook then pulled his hand back to his lap.

She picked up the notebook half in frustration and brought it to her face. As it bent to her chin, the sun broke out of the clouds and a shimmer from its rays hit the metal spine, reflecting it into her eye.

"Did you see that?" he asked, nearly jumping from his seat, then pushed a button on the side of his watch, looking at the time, and said, "The fourth hour on the forty-fourth minute, forty-fourth second on my forty-fourth click! How's that for synchronicities, Grace!" He showed her the watch and slapped his knee.

444 was one of Grace's special numbers. She told herself when she saw it—spirit was saying, "I love you!" Or "I'm here for you, I support you." He didn't know that, but she appreciated the playful interactions and the sun coming out to shine again.

"I love seeing the time 4:44."

"Time is all we have, Grace," he said, reaching for a napkin while she glanced at Saturn on display, remembering how he's the planet of time. Then she waited patiently, watching him tear a small rectangle from her napkin.

"This is a soul's life." He turned the rectangle into a ring. "This is one life, whole and complete. We all have a choice: to live a whole life fully and be done, or..."

He pulled the ends apart, twisting it into the infinity symbol, and continued, "We can choose an infinite amount of lives, one after the other." He unwrapped it from a figure 8 and laid it flat on the table then made two more rectangles, laying them next to each other. "You can live as many as you want until you choose one and that is your end." He made another ring. "Your wish, Grace..." He pointed to her notebook. "Is your wish. It's not God's *task* for you, although God does love when you stand up and say, 'Me! I was meant to do this!'" He calmed his voice, "Your past lives can flashback when, let's say, veils are thin. Why not give that five-year-old Grace her wish?

Share the love you've found and the way you've found it." He motioned his open hand over the notebook and said, "It's a way to give what you've received."

And the lights come back on in the store. He looked up at the lit ceiling, smiled, and stood to say, "I feel blessed to have shared my birthday with you!"

Grace rose to hug him, not knowing when or if she'd see him again.

"Thank you! Can I give you a ride somewhere?"

"I'm good at taking care of myself. Thank you, though." He walked away without turning around and loudly said, "April 3rd… the day of my birth."

She smiled, a bit amazed by the conversation, and sat thinking about what was said. Curiously, she pulled up Google on her phone to see they were celebrating the Marine Corps' birthday. Then she searched for the atomic number for carbon, which was 6...

Grace smiled as if she'd been on a thrill ride then continued her writing in the bright rays of her devoted sun with new perspectives.

# 21

# Neptune Direct

November 22, 2017

Neptune direct in its home sign of Pisces gives us the ability to see into our lovely fantasy world from which we escaped reality. The planet protects us from our harsh existence and gives us faith, spirituality, and dreams.

\* \* \*

Grace prepared herself for work, aware that Neptune would be moving ahead. She'd been looking forward to it since the day it went backward, when the tiny yellow plane landed in the field.

The sun was shining into the office with a warm glow as she glided through each room, readying herself for patients —open to the possibilities of what this transit could bring.

She was careful not to have expectations since that caused anxiety but she had hoped for more clarity and a higher sense of love. She hadn't been there ten minutes when the gal at the front desk summoned her.

"I just got a call from the daycare. They said Kai is sick, I'm guessing you won't be back 'til he's better?'"

"Yep..." With no hesitation she grabbed her things and drove to the daycare, looking forward to snuggling him all day.

When she tiptoed towards the "Tot" class, he was standing near the garbage where he could throw up. She tried hiding near the side of the doorway to surprise him but was spotted immediately.

"Mom!" shouted her tiny 5-year-old son. He was running towards her at full speed with a giant grin.

She lowered herself to his level and embraced her cute, shaggy blonde boy who nearly knocked her over with his powerful hug. She wrapped her arms around him warmly—just as she had 30 minutes prior.

"Bubby!" she said through her smile. A flood of love filled her as she teared up. "Looks like we get to spend all day together."

"Mom, you cwrying?" He pulled away and looked her straight on.

"Yeah..." She wiped her cheeks, "Happy tears, Buddy, happy tears."

"I missed you, Momma!" he said in his peppy, high-pitched voice.

"I missed you too, Bud!"

"You dot hewre so fast, momma! I phrew up on da

dwround and you dot hewre so fast, like a wrace cawr," he said with his adorable slurred words, pretending to steer an imaginary car.

"I did?" she asked while picking him up, not wanting to let go. Then she carried him over to grab his coat and sign him out.

When she flipped through the history of sign-in sheets, Cray's signature showed up every other week.

*Cray...* she thought, and memories of their lives together flooded in: their beautiful wedding in the Stanley hills, the long bike rides together, the birth of their son, and the loving chemistry they once shared.

Then, she remembered the collapse of their ten-year marriage and the anger that boiled up while living in the yurt. She wondered, *Why... Why did it fall apart?*

She pulled Kai even closer. He fit just right as she walked to the car and she buckled him in, taking her time then gave him a tender kiss on the top of his head, so glad for his presence. She drove away with her special gift, delighted to spend the day with her guy.

They were heading to the store for Pedialyte when she asked, "What is your favorite memory with Momma?" adjusting the rear-view mirror to see his face.

"All of dhem, Mommy!" Grace laughed as he continued, "Um, um, the day the wred balloons were at da top of da ceiling inside da cawr. My favowrite colowr. WRED. An, an, da wiiiiind... blowing dhem all ovewr in da cawr! An, an, one flew out the wiiindoooow... Haha!!" he said loudly, with his funny kid laugh.

Her grin broadened as she watched the road then looked back to him.

"An we went to da wred pawrk, and I gotta eat wred gummy fish candy!"

She remembered that day clearly. The balloons were bouncing all around inside the car. Kai was laughing so hard when he told her a balloon flew out the window. She glanced at the side mirror and watched the balloon get swept behind them. Its bright red self gently bounced into the sunny yellow sunset, blazing its beautiful hues.

She chuckled at his full-on kid giggle as the balloons bobbled all over, causing the hairs on their head to rise. She recalled the warm wind coming through the windows, what a cheerful memory full of vivid laughter. There was a permanent smile across her face while she reminisced.

She parked at the grocery store and asked Kai if he wanted to go in or did his tummy feel too sensitive? He thought he'd be fine so she took him in, grabbing a plastic bag just in case he needed to use it.

They walked straight to the Pedialyte and raw coconut water. *This will keep him from getting dehydrated,* she thought, then grabbed some bananas and plain yogurt for ease on his stomach while he spotted a mini theater-style popcorn maker that was bright red.

"I want Santa to bwring me a poptorn makor."

Grace often made buttery popcorn for a snack with coconut oil, and Brewer's yeast, Kai's favorite treat.

*Christmas…* she thought. It was coming up, and this would be a special one. One where he was old enough to understand what was going on, and it would be their first Christmas with just the two of them. It was also their first year putting up a tree and lights, so she planned on going all out, making it a holiday to remember.

When they got home, she laid him down in the corner of the room on a child's mattress, next to her bed. She tucked a bunch of fluffy pillows and a duvet blanket around him. He fell right to sleep as she snuggled into him, looking at all his sweet features while lightly running her fingers through his hair and along his exposed skin.

She was caught by the same questions from earlier. *Why had I pushed Cray to the back of my thoughts?* Then the answer: *It was painful...*

Curious, she pulled out her writings from the yurt and read a few lines, making sure it was the right one, then sat back next to Kai to read. The first entry was July 2015 and it had toddler scribbles throughout the pages, making her beam.

> *I've had ideas for a book flooding into my mind for a month now. I just gotta write them down!*

It had a title at the top of the page in bold uppercase writing. She quickly read the entry. It was a story narrated by a twelve-year-old boy who lived on Ritter Island, an actual island Grace enjoyed discovering and lounging on. It was several miles downstream from the yurt.

## RITTER ISLAND

*The boy lived with his mom, who was sick, and his father was not around. But someone always supplied a survival-stash-of-cash, inside a tin cup in the cupboard above the stove.*

*Our house was a tiny, gray shack that had no insulation. You'd walk into our wooden house through the northwest corner, entering the kitchen just big enough for a small, two-seater table in the center. The kitchen had two open doorways on either side of the corner, opposite the entrance.*

*These doorways led into an L-shaped side room—My room.*

*On the east there was a single twin bed, permanently billowing with white bedding, where my mother slept. Mom was beautiful to me. Her hair was dark brown, long, and wavy. She was tall and thin with bright, beautiful eyes and a tremendous smile.*

*Her part of the room had just enough space for a neat nightstand next to her bed, and right against that was a cabinet that took up all the space on the north end wall.*

*The doorway to the south side of the kitchen opened to a couch where I slept. In between her bed and my couch was a tiny wood-burning stove. The other side of my couch was the door to our narrow bathroom.*

*The house was dainty with the bare necessities, but love was in full bounty.*

*Mom slept most of the day and through the night. When she was awake, she made sure to provide enough energy and love to me and was full of beauty and grace.*

*Her sole focus was me. I felt like I was the sun and she was a close planet, revolving around me, and while she was awake, I was whole and complete.*

*Her hair was full and would flow with her white nightgown as she moved around the house. She was angelic in her presence and would embrace me fully, enveloping me in hugs.*

*I so loved being in her arms; nothing was better. Life seemed sunny when she was up. Even if she woke in the middle of the night, I'd wake to be with her. And I'd take as many opportunities to snuggle her as I could while she slept. I enjoyed her warmth as she dreamed her life away.*

Grace glanced over to Kai, who was probably dreaming away too. She wondered if she had written about her tendency to escape? *Was* she escaping the pain? Grace let out a heavy sigh, returning to the story.

*I wondered what kinds of places she was exploring while asleep and whom she was loving, constantly curious if I appeared in those magical dreams. I looked forward to her being awake with me, but I knew rest was exactly what she needed for her strength, to be that light while awake.*

*When she rose, she always asked if I had breakfast, even if it was the middle of the day or evening, and asked if I wanted "eggs, waffles, bacon, or a muffin?" Every day was the same list of foods.*

*I'd tell her what I wanted, and she'd add some ripe, delicious fruit too. I kept the fridge stocked with these items so she would always feel the abundance and never worry about food.*

*While she cooked or did dishes, she stood in the tree yoga pose, with her left foot up to the top of her right thigh. She was comfortable that way and would take this time to ask me questions about school, friends, and the neighbors, always picking up from where we left off. We never mentioned anything about her health. I usually asked about her adventures in her dreamscape.*

*She'd jump in happily with great detail. I loved her creative mind and enthusiasm when she spoke of her inner world. It seemed real, so pure, so… just right for her. I was lucky to be the solitary person she interacted with during her waking life.*

*Some days she would surprise me with red balloons, knowing I loved red.*

Grace glanced at Kai thinking, *I started this story to escape the state of my marriage. Could I see it coming, a life with just Kai and me… and me, lost in my imagination?* Grace held a paused look of contemplation then went back to the story.

*One summer day, she woke me from a nap with her face*

*right in front of mine and said, "Come here!" She ran to her bed giggling then slid under the lumpy white sheet. I curiously followed, making it to the edge of the bed, and she chuckled uncontrollably. I smiled, pulled the edge of the sheet up and climbed under, chuckling too.*

*We were surrounded by red balloons. The overflow bounced out from under the sheets as we made more room. Our hair was standing straight up from the static we created, rubbing against the balloons.*

Grace stopped, looking at Kai once more. He was so peaceful tucked into his nest of blankets and pillows. She noticed how beautifully perfect he was, how immensely appreciative she was for him. She leaned over and snuggled into him, tickling his arm, and back again.

Feeling cozy, she drifted to sleep for a brief moment, then woke to her open notebook and continued reading.

*After we giggled and played with the balloons, she pulled a book into our fort, showing me the front cover. It was a book about space. She knew I loved space and was intrigued with astronauts. How she got the book, I didn't know, but she read page after page with eagerness, her face lit with animation. Something I'd admired. Then we switched back and forth from page to page, reading until we finished the book, accompanied by a few staticky balloons.*

Grace took another breather, remembering their trip to Florida to visit her father, Kai's Pop-Pop. They went to celebrate his 5th birthday, visiting Disney World and NASA. He appreciated NASA more than she'd expected; he had to look at every rocket ship and took his time scanning the old astronaut suits.

She glanced back at her writings and read again.

> *For the next week or two, I'd come home and there would be a red balloon floating from the headboard of her bed. Today, there was a note attached to the balloon. In big, bubbly cursive, it read, I love you to Pluto and beyond.*
>
> *I whispered, "I love you beyond Pluto and back!" Her note made me smile, she made me smile… I looked down at her notorious yellow notebook and checked to see if she was in a deep sleep. As usual, I opened the notebook to see if there were any new writings and read them. She had a wonderful dream state with great adventures and lovers. Afterwards, I'd test the pen to see if it worked, and if not, I'd replace it.*
>
> *She had over a dozen spiral notebooks full of writings tucked in a drawer. She never wrote in front of me, always making time for me while awake. I appreciated that.*

That's all Grace had written about that story in the first notebook. The rest was plans on traveling to see her mom and stepdad in California with Kai. A plan to get away from the drama of the yurt neighborhood, stresses about finances, and the car breaking down on her and Cray.

She was taken aback, slightly light-headed, not wanting to re-experience all the hardships.

Shortly after was the pow wow Cray, in her garden about her going on a spiritual journey. He was uninterested in participating and she saw them growing in different directions. This is where the breakdown with Gretchen intensified. Her hip and leg pain was at its peak, causing her to limp, and she recalled being on edge, even in her sleep.

The wasps were entering the yurt throughout their final days, stinging Cray and Kai at different times but on her last day, the yurt was filled with ladybugs… something she took as a positive sign, looking forward to her month getaway in California.

She closed the notebook, thinking back to all of it with a heavy heart, then remembered the ladybugs that followed her in the rental van to California, despite the November weather. She had googled the meaning of the ladybug: *Happiness is on it's way.*

Since then, every cheery red bug would put Grace at ease.

She reached over to caress Kai's forehead and thought, *Here it is… The source of pain from which I escaped. I ran to River to get out of my crumbling marriage. It worked but the wreckage was unbearable.*

She swallowed a dry, hard swallow, thinking she loved her little guy so much and was filled with guilt for the destruction her intense emotions brought into his life.

Clarity was what she had hoped for today and clarity was what she was getting, in a way she hadn't expected. She lay down, snuggling closer to Kai, beyond grateful for the gift of him in her life.

She thought back to the farmers market while pregnant with him... he was the engagement ring she'd so proudly shown off at the farmer's market all those years ago. Looking at him now, she wanted to show him off all over again.

Her focus was on him, which comforted her heart. She had deep gratitude for the lucidity of her past and emotions, revealed at this time. A feeling of peace, faith, and trust in the process was finally appearing, front and center. She had an expanded sense of "self-empathy," and forgiveness took over her.

# 22

# Saturn Comes Home

Saturn into Capricorn. Dec. 20, 21, 2017

The ringed planet, Saturn, had moved into its home sign of Capricorn the day before. This is where he does his best work, so she anticipated a substantial shift but hadn't detected anything out of the ordinary. However, she did see the green-eyed beggar while out shopping for Kai's presents.

He was on the same corner as last time, holding up a sign that read, *Enjoy this time of year!* She watched his breath billow into the winter air, wondering if he really was enjoying it? He flipped the sign and pointed to it—*Your slate is wiped clean, Grace.*

She approached closer, giving him a "thank you" in sign language. He responded with a thumbs up and a "bye-bye" wave.

*Well… that was specific!* she thought, waving back while driving through the light.

The next day, she started off, ecstatic to have Kai with her for her birthday and Christmas. She turned up the heat in her room and started wrapping presents, leaving a few unwrapped for an instant surprise. Then she played an astrology video relating to the grand transit of Saturn into Capricorn.

> "For the next three years, structures will fall and be rebuilt. Taking a historical look back—the Berlin wall was built when Saturn was here and came down 28 years later when he arrived back in Capricorn."

*Will the homestead be sold during this transit?* she wondered, but she didn't want to premeditate such permanent loss.

> "This could be a time when new traditions are started and governments will likely experience prominent changes as Saturn and Capricorn both represent the government. The devil may come out or we could see a darker side of politics or our leaders. I'd also say the 'rightful king' will surface and rule."

*We are having a U.S. election in 2020, just before Saturn leaves his home sign... But the rightful king? We don't have a king*, she thought, then she looked up when Saturn was last in Capricorn: 1988-1991. *I was 4, 5, and 6, the time I made my promise to God, my wish of becoming the sensation of love.*

"This is all too heavy and important for wrapping presents," Grace said aloud as she turned on a cheerful holiday channel.

The next day, her grandparents on her mother's side took her shopping for a tree and lights, such perfect birthday and Christmas presents. She was grateful to them for being so thoughtful. They helped her set it up and left a gift for Kai, a sturdy train. She put it under the tree, thinking it could be the beginning of a holiday tradition from now on, creating even more excitement for when she picked him up.

Before she went to get him, she kept the tree lights on so when they got home, it would be all lit up—ready to decorate.

At the daycare, he glanced straight at her and ran in for a hug, clinging to her all the way to the car.

"Momma, I missed you!" he said from the back seat.

"Aw, I missed you too buddy!"

"When I'm not with you, I feel you next to me,"

"That's so sweet, Kai." Grace blushed, making eye contact with him in the rear view mirror.

"When I eat food, you'wr thewre, when I sleep, you'wr thewre, when I watch a show, you'wr thewre, when I go to daycawre, you'wr thewre..."

"That's because I'm always thinking of you, loving you."

"Yep," he chuckled.

His comment warmed her heart, and just as suspected,

while she drove down the lane Kai spotted the tree in the window—where her grandparents had placed theirs every year.

He jumped out of the car, ran directly to the lower living room, and checked it while Grace captured his reactions on video. This was their first Christmas tree since Cray requested they not have one.

He walked up to the tree slowly and said, "Beautiful, so beautiful," lightly petting the branches and making Grace choke up.

His attention went from the tree to the train. Without any help, he figured out how to turn it on. It had realistic train sounds that gave her delighted goosebumps. He played with it until they fell asleep.

They woke the following day to three inches of snow covering the landscape. She cherished the years when the season's first snow fell on her birthday. It was a gift from heaven, making her world white, peaceful, and beautiful for her day.

They went out for a special brunch then tried out the new climbing gym, staying as long as Kai was actively having fun. She was happy to spend the day climbing indoors then home for snow fort fun. They finished the day inside with homemade pizza and Kai got to unwrap *How the Grinch Stole Christmas,* which he thought was fun, then they listened and followed along with the audio CD of Jeff Bridges reading *The Night Before Christmas.* Kai played it over and over while flipping through the beautiful pages.

After indulging in the new holiday books, they took their blankets and pillows under the lit-up tree, moved the train and laid next to each other. They gazed through the branches and lights.

"I love sleeping undewr the twree, Momma... I LOVE you momma!" He hugged her firmly.

"I love you too, Kai, more than you'll ever know. I'm so happy to spend my birthday and Christmas with you!"

"Me too, Momma. Momma? You'wr beautiful."

"Awe, you're so sweet!" She snuggled into him. "That's the BEST birthday present ever, Kai." And they fell asleep in each other's arms.

They woke on Christmas Eve to more fluffy snow. Grace could see her breath, so she turned on the heat so Christmas morning would be comfortable and took Kai back to her room where the heat was on low.

They made cookies for Santa and decorated the tree with all her childhood Christmas ornaments. Kai played with them just as she had with her brothers during the holiday season. Keeping with her family's tradition, she let him open an ornament and he went wild realizing it was Spider-man, who joined them at the dinner table.

Her roommate set up a Christmas tree in the upper-level living room. She thought it was lovely having two sparkling trees in the house.

"Should we write a note to St. Nick?" she asked, getting out a nice piece of paper and pen to write it.

"Yeah! Can you tell him I want a poptorn makor and please mawrry my mom, because she has a bwroken heawrt."

Grace was surprised that he'd picked up on her emotions without them being discussed.

"You think I have a broken heart?"

"Wriver bwroke it."

"Oh…" was all she thought to say, beginning the note.

Afterwards, she took him to a church gathering to sing Christmas songs together. He looked so cute, in his white linen button up shirt, sleek jeans, and a thick red scarf she had knitted ten years prior. The kids got up and sang, "We Wish You A Merry Christmas." It softened her heart, watching him walk up without fear, singing with a smile and trying not to giggle.

He sat back down and they listened to the pastor then sang a few songs. He became fidgety, so she held him despite the pain it caused throughout her back. She sang in his ear, which calmed and relaxed him. He snuggled into her and she relished the connection and spirit of the season.

She thought, *It's a good thing we made cookies and wrote to Santa before we left,* since he passed out on the way home. She carried and laid him down in her room then went back to the kitchen where she replaced Santa's cookies with a black frosted ninja cookie her coworker made for Kai. She took his sweet note and wrote a very swirly reply in red ink at the bottom of his letter:

*Dear Kai, Merry Christmas to you and your mom. I didn't know what tree was yours, so I hope you find the present I left for you. Have a great Christmas and thanks for the cookies. Here's a cookie for you!*

*P.S. Your warm hugs and sweet kisses will heal your mom's heart.*

*Love, S.C.*

Grace put the wrapped popcorn maker under her roommate's tree then put a dozen presents under their tree. She hung his stocking from a side table drawer knob and made sure the train was set and ready to "choo, choo," first thing upon waking.

Once everything was set up for morning fun, she sat in front of the lit-up tree with all the presents. She glanced at all the hanging ornaments she'd accumulated over her youthful years and yawned, ready to join Kai in dreamland.

When he woke, it seemed like she'd just closed her eyes. It was still dark outside and she knew there was no going back to bed. He was all excited and ready to see what Santa brought.

"MOMMA, LET'S GO SEE IF SANTA CAME!" He ran to the kitchen and turned on the light to see if our cookies had been eaten.

"He ate my tookies, and he left me a ninja tookie!" He was yelling with excitement.

"Oh, look, he left you a note too." Grace read it out

loud.

"He doesn't know what twree's ouwrs?" he asked, running to her roommate's tree, still chewing his ninja cookie. He looked at the tag on the present.

"To Kai." he read.

"From Santa," Grace read.

"From Santa! I hope it's a poptorn makor." He ripped part of the wrapping paper off. "It IS a poptorn makor! Santa bwrought me what I wanted." Again, he was shouting with pumped energy, not even finishing unwrapping it before he was off to their tree.

"WHAT?!" he shouted, following him into the semi-warm room. "Thewre's MOWRE?" He ran to and held up an unwrapped present. "This is what I was talking about, Momma!"

"You have to start with your stocking." she said, getting the train going.

He ran over and pulled everything out of his stocking by name.

"A banana, an owrange, a toothbwrush, and nuts." These were items she got in her stocking as a kid. Then he ran over to the tree and had so much fun opening present after present.

When he was done, Grace made breakfast with the friendly sun shining into the kitchen windows. She took the food back to the messy room where they ate before playing with his new toys.

They made Legos, did puzzles and read books, colored with scented markers, then listened to Christmas music. Grace kept sensing a metal on metal feeling and thought, *Slate... My slate is wiped clean*. It was like two pieces of metal were rubbing together. She wondered why and then remembered the beggar's sign saying, "Your slate is wiped clean."

She walked into the kitchen to make an early dinner and thought, *Hhhhmmm... that is how I feel*. Is it Saturn transiting over my natal sun?

After dinner they made great flavored popcorn then slept under the tree again at the request of Kai. She celebrated those moments and slept there every night until he went to Cray's for a week with dad.

# 23

## A Tale of Grace

December 2017

Grace took their Christmas tree down after taking Kai to Cray's, and she spent the rest of her long New Year's break writing, staying up late every night, making significant progress. When she realized she'd been so immersed in her story that she skipped dinner, she went to the cold kitchen and made a hot bratwurst sandwich with sauteed spinach.

She took it back to her warm room and scarfed it down then lay on her bed in exhaustion, unaware of the time. The waning gibbous moon peered through the window and she stared at it until her heavy lids closed.

Her mind drifted to River without an ache of heartbreak. She didn't want to think of him, really, but the dream proceeded anyway.

He got out of his truck and adjusted his shirt as he crossed over the wooden bridge onto the island.

When he did that, her view switched to his perspective, walking in his shoes. He was tall and strong, with broad shoulders. She was swept away by him. He passed the big house and the heat of the summer was heavy. The sprinklers were significant as she felt the cool spray on her skin.

He made his way through the shady yard to a gray shack, the little house where her story's character and his mom lived. He opened the screen door to a simple kitchen and walked in, looking at the woman sleeping under a thin white sheet in her white nightgown. Grace had a full understanding of his love for her.

A glass of water on the nightstand stole his attention and he tiptoed to her side, curiously brushing his fingers against the yellow notebook. There was a red balloon attached to her headboard, floating near his head. He tapped it and it swayed.

His glance shifted to her, and he wished her the best then took her glass into the kitchen and filled it with fresh water. He quietly took it back to her side, pulled a flower from his shirt pocket, and laid it on the sunny notebook.

As he left, he opened the cupboard above the stove and put a roll of bills inside an old tin can then closed the cupboard quietly. He accidentally allowed the screen door to slap shut after he walked out.

He stopped, waiting to hear if he'd woken her, then continued on.

A big grin appeared on the mother's face as she stirred. Her smile turned into a giggle and she snickered herself awake, opening her eyes, continuing the chuckle. Out came a yawn as she sat up and took a sip of water, noticing the slightly swaying balloon. She tapped it with a graceful finger, shrugged her shoulders, then reached for her yellow dream journal.

She smelled the dainty flower and put it to the side, thinking it was from her son. She pulled the notebook into bed with her and wrote page after page, whispering every word. Inside, she finished with *The End,* and a big smile ran across her face. She closed the notebook and wrote, *A Tale of Grace* on the front with a permanent marker.

Just then, her son walked in and she jumped up to hug him.

"My boy. My boy," she said, embracing him.

He hugged her with the same adoring response.

"Let's go kayaking. Take a little float?"

"You sure, mom?"

"Yes, I'm feeling up to it."

They kayaked around the island, coming into a clearing with half a dozen swans floating on the cool water.

"Oh, my goodness. They're so beautiful." She

put her arm out. "Wait, wait, wait, let's watch."

"You remind me of a swan..." Her son said. Then he whispered, "Graceful."

"That's sweet of you." She choked up, experiencing the beauty of nature with her son. "I'd love to be a swan."

Grace woke with warm emotions at peace with River and a part of herself. All she wanted was happiness for River Billings—as she wanted for herself. That realization let out a healing release.

# 24

## Soul Soup

January 10, 2018

Grace was deep in her dream state as a princess with a lavish green dress on a fine horse, atop a grassy hill. Her feet nudged the horse, who galloped into the woods where sunlight flickered through the foliage. Leaping over fallen logs, between bushes and trees, she let out a liberating laugh as they rode strong with her focus ahead.

A rider with a deep purple dress crossed her path then slowed for a better look before circling back. Grace realized it was her twin with skin slightly more bronzed than hers, bright blue eyes, and brunette hair as long as hers—panting as if she'd been the one running.

Grace stared curiously at the Princess who seemed to have something to share.

"Come on," she said.

Grace promptly followed through the obstacle-filled forest, falling behind. The woman came back to giggle in her face. She chuckled back then took off chasing after her, laughing carefree.

The landscape opened to flat terrain, where they reached top speed. Her royal look-alike slowed to offer water and she thankfully drank from the waterskin as it was snatched from her playfully. Grace nudged her back, snickering till the girl shoved her off the horse, laughing.

The Princess hopped down to tease and wrestle lightheartedly until their steam ran out, then together they gazed at the blue sky.

She treasured the reflection of self-love. It was magical—taking all the seriousness out of the equation to play and love a version of herself.

"You know your search for purpose after Africa?" the twin asked, breaking the cheerful vibe.

Her face turned serious, remembering the emotions, and she nodded.

"Follow me," the Princess said, and they rode towards and through a large castle's stone walls, slowing to a stop inside. They entered a soup kitchen where townspeople in tattered clothing were eating together. In awe, she got in a line where a voluptuous woman was serving soup. She had the warmest presence. Her generous soul was glowing as she cared for these people.

She offered a bowl to Grace, and Grace responded with a thankful nod before taking a sip, swallowing pure comfort and satisfying warmth.

She glanced at her soup with a few veggies and slivers of meat. Spiritually nourished, she glanced back at the crowded room and the woman serving. She knew her purpose was to grow food for this soul soup. The intention of sharing nourishment propelled her forward, switching scenes to one where her blue-eyed twin led her through wide hallways within a majestic palace. They passed rooms and corridors full of luxurious art and came upon a door at the end of the wing where her twin quietly led them in.

The room was full of delicate, appropriately placed golden furniture that stood out from the fancy wallpaper. Dainty bedding matched up with billowing curtains. The open French doors allowed in ambient light, adding to the golden glow.

An elderly woman stared into the autumn landscape from her wheelchair on the back patio, dressed in a light white nightgown. A long silvery-white braid wrapped around her neck, resting on her chest. Grace was taken aback when she saw her older self.

"What happened to her?" Graces asked while the woman's gaze never strayed, remaining focused on the landscape—disengaged.

"This lovely woman spent her youth preparing for a righteous king to devote herself to and rule next to."

Grace's thoughts went directly to her King's dream, and she knelt near the woman.

"Once married, she did what she'd aspired to do: lived for and stood by her king, serving her people generously, striving to bear a son. Although she never conceived, her love found a way into the hearts and lives of her people. They were grateful for her and continue to mourn her."

Grace placed a hand on the arm of the Queen, whose gaze was unwavering. The touch flashed her back to the King from her dream and memories of her life as the Queen: the way she loved the King, her confidence and support for him. Every moment spent with her town's people fluttered within and how her heart was replenished through their exchanges. Then pain overwhelmed her spirit as she experienced the moment she shut off after witnessing the King's intimate interaction with another.

She re-experienced the shattering of her soul, knowing no matter how powerful she had been, there was no controlling what happened, nor an ability to change her past souls' fate in her choice to terminate her daily life.

"You see it all?" her twin asked.

"Yes."

"60 years of silence."

"She could have done so much." *What a shattered waste*, Grace thought.

"Is your life a waste?" her twin asked, caressing the woman's braid, unraveling it softly.

"No."

"She is very real within you today, deeply connected to your imagination, and she has passed on the strength of her mental solitude to you, to put it in use now." She paused to give Grace a chance to soak it in. "Your desire to serve those with little emanates from her."

"And the King?" Grace asked, trying to connect him with her friend Sky.

"The King has passed from this life with the Queen. His soul is with you, unable to leave your side— watching you with your son. He desires to be with you both but cannot. His soul chose to stand by you in this life, as you did for him. It will bring his soul back into balance. Your life is doing the same."

Grace peered at the queen's legs, wrapped in a blanket, and she sympathized, thinking, *All these years of quiet stillness—alone.*

The Princess combed her fingers through the elder woman's hair and began re-braiding.

"The King loved you, Grace. He missed your

support and was deeply regretful," she said, hearing her last thought. "You are free from obligations to him now. Praise the gifts that she never experienced; you were destined a son," she said as if to take credit for it. "You have freedoms that she did not. Your love for nature… the way it rejuvenates you, is residue of this life."

Grace studied the landscape, allowing the information to soak in when a heavy pulling woke her.

Her eyes were glued to the ceiling of her grandparent's quiet bedroom. She was grateful for what was revealed to her—making her way to the bathroom with warmth in her soul.

The left half of her body was released from pain. She stopped to praise the moment. Her glance took her to the golden swirly edges of the white cupboards, connecting her to the Queen's fancy room. She was blessed for all she had, looking out to the land, knowing there was no mistake: she was there to grow food for her community.

# 25

# Apricot Landing

Grace took the day off knowing the temperature would be in the 60s, which was completely unusual for a winter's day in Idaho—with the warmth and clear, sunny skies, it was optimal for an outdoor venture. The perfect opportunity to execute her desire. So she loaded up her paddle board, longing to connect with nature and the spirit of the eclipse. During last summer, the Great American Eclipse took center stage in the sign of Leo. Tonight, the moon would disappear behind earth's shadow in the same sign.

What would the mother of the night bring? She couldn't guess but planned to perform her spirit animal dance, wrapped in elk hide, as she set out to do years ago.

Before returning to the canyon where the idea originated, she'd carefully drawn henna designs on her forearms and calves in delicate detail. Her hair was down long with a mini bun on top where a skinny braid dangled. Feathers were sewn throughout her hair, and she wrapped the hide around her chest as a dress. Then sewed feathers to spare pieces for a belt and ankle cuffs.

*I feel more myself than ever,* she thought, adjusting her attire.

After driving through Buhl and parking at the hot springs, she grabbed her nature pack with a thin wool blanket, fire starter kit, and iPod with speakers.

Paddling downstream, she appreciated the calm float in the afternoon sun as her own solo tribe, headed to connect with a more expansive one: earth, spirit, and the heavens. The soothing current created a relaxing moment as the river took her where she needed to go.

Her paddle slightly disturbed its flow, creating a lovely sound as the sun glistened from it.

"Hello again," she sang to her beloved canyon. "I miss your cliff. The river, the birds… your waterfalls." The falls were iced over and melting methodically from the warm sun. Her gaze followed the dampened winter scene of sleeping trees and sagebrush, all in earthy browns.

The center island passed by, and she wondered what creatures inhabited it, then squinted towards the clear sky, enjoying the soft rocking of the board, open and free. Nature had been a healing home, a *comfort* zone for sure.

She peered overboard to her reflection, placing her hand in the icy current to connect. Gradually, her landing bench came into view—tucked on the ridge of the canyon. She first visited this spot years ago, always wanting to come back.

Gleefully, she guided her board to the riverbank and heaved it over the edge, leaving it on even ground. She made it through toppled dead grass and bare sagebrush, passing her favorite landmark—the apricot tree. It had to have been planted ages ago since Idaho wasn't its native home; she was thrilled it continued to survive, beautifully out of place and such a sight in full bloom.

Last time, she'd named the spot Apricot Landing and smiled walking past "the sleeping gift to the desert."

She came upon a dry patch—perfect for a fire pit and to lay her pack. Someone had left a bundle of firewood, sufficient for keeping flames burning all night.

She gathered rocks, branches and twigs for the fire. Then followed the clear spring, which provided fresh watercress. A vibrant green against the winter background and a crisp, peppery snack. A spot beckoned her to lounge in the sun and eye the landscape before dusk, where she slipped into a comfy catnap in her blanket.

The evening's air woke her, reminding her to get a fire going. Once it was roaring, she played a tribal-sounding album at top volume while she sat, tending the radiant fire. Lost in the flames, rocking to the beat, hair blanketing her back.

The music urged her to dance, and she moved within, open to summon the spirit of the elk. She beckoned the celestial bodies to accompany her in their far-out twinkling seats. Welcoming them to participate in the performance they'd inspired within her.

Their vibrational existence wove throughout the same energetic fabric she was, delighted to experience a moment in the physical through her.

One with her body, she moved quickly as songs changed one by one, surrendering to the trance dance with a proud smile and creative flow.

She drummed her feet on earth's drum, causing a bellow of dust. Her hair twirled out, fluttering feathers in the air, and she was grateful for the gift that kept her alive—pounding strongly in her chest. Thankful to every beat. Sweat gathered along her body while pure satisfaction traversed her face and ambient light intensified her sensual side.

The rhythm was wildly a part of her, delighted to share this with the earth and cosmos. She spun, merging with the tempo, when a brush of dirt caressed her skin. A heavier portion sprinkled her legs without interrupting her flow. She opened her eyes to a faint dust cloud and swept her hands through as the dirt brushed up again.

*Let's play with this dust,* she thought, directing her hands towards the earth. The powdered dust picked up, magnetized to her hands.

Grace went with it, thrusting her hands once more towards the ground in sync with the beat. A hefty mound of earth erupted instantly, enhancing her dance—she grinned ear to ear, fully satisfied.

A force of energy emerged throughout her body,

forming a magnet in the palms of her hands. The music strengthened, growing louder as she flung her hands towards a lifeless nature scene—instantly transforming toppled dead grass into a tuft of fresh growth. She threw her head back in pure delight, power exuding from her.

Bringing her head level and hands together, she faced the fire, forcing the flames into the dark sky with the music. They grew instantly in that direction as crackling sparks exploded above.

Feet planted firmly, she asked for more and the energy built strongly as she thrust her palms down and another mound rose to meet her. She spun her arms out, knocking it down with vigor, completely elated.

Then slowed to meet the apricot tree beyond the flames, smiling at the sight of it—the tree instantly blossomed!

Grace laughed, spinning deeper, eyes closed, knowing this may not be real but refusing to doubt the magic, relishing the moment. Unable to hold it in, she let out a raw and alive giggle, whirling through the boastful child-like laughter as her *true* self.

The playground spun and spun as she drummed the earth, opening her eyes to the dancing flames, immersed in vivacious energy. The music was intense and fast. She swirled nearing the fire when the music stopped and her untouched iPod switched to a sauntering tune, prompting her to halt.

Her gaze hooked a set of wide antlers then she leaned to the side of the flames. A muscular figure stood tall, with soft animal eyes and the mane of a buffalo.

Firmly grounded, maintaining her sight on the creature, she walked towards him, gaining height and courage with every step. Once she was around the flames, more of him was visible. He carried a robust man's body with pecan brown skin and the face of an elk with long lashes and hooved feet. His breathing mirrored hers as if he'd danced alongside her.

Still, his eyes told a gentler story of inner peace and knowing. Wise eyes. She stood in front of him, unable to look away from his slightly flaming mane. His breath appeared in the frigid night, and she was in awe and inspired to touch him.

His skin shocked her fingers, prompting her to pull back.

Drawn to him, she steadied herself, trying again. This time bracing for the zing, she ran her fingers slowly up his arm, glancing at his beaten body.

He let out a groan and sunk his shoulders. Her fingers moved up while scenes of people suffering played in her mind.

As she focused on the movement of her fingers, the images continued. They were lost and depressed, striving to handle moments of struggle. There was every type of person: wealthy, poor, young… multiracial. Old, famous, homeless, sick… no one was left out. She'd understood everything about them, even experienced pride when they'd managed their suffering.

Her gaze moved empathetically towards the elk, who appeared to be the sole vessel for this distress. His emotions were hers—she was an amplified receiver of these immense sorrows. She watched his chest rise and fall heavily, and she took a few steady breaths, mimicking him. Her heartbeat slowed as she gazed back to her fingertips, seeing her younger self crying alone, re-experiencing everything her young self had. Scene after scene of every difficult moment throughout her life.

The creature bowed, seeming to sense her approaching his heart. The flashing images slowed to a single one. She focused on his heart, watching the difficult moment replay.

She swallowed hard watching it drag on then pressed the palm of her hand to his heart, grounding herself.

He lifted his head as the images weakened her, and she met his tender stare knowing he had been there. On her darkest night, he was there, loving her.

It was over.

She blinked rapidly, internally numb. Although disturbed, she'd made it to the other side of that experience and was alright. He slumped while her tears dripped down her cheeks, falling as he softly caught them.

He was deeply intertwined with her. Their connection was difficult to comprehend, but she was grateful for the proof in her vision that her soul was heard and never abandoned. It was known that she was loved, even by darkness.

His warm hand reached up to support her. The other took hers from his heart and pulled her close. He provided a sturdy presence, leading their clasped hands above, twirling her sweetly with the music. He stopped to firm his grip, dipping her back. Her toe pointed into the dark sky and emotions purged effortlessly.

She was swept up, catching a glimpse of earth's copper shadow draping the full moon.

*How on point,* she thought, guided to his side. He brought her near, heat radiating from him—guarding her against the cold. She glanced at the smoldering flame throughout his mane and a crackle of light boomed within her.

The loving light pierced through her shadows at lightning speed, into her chest, inspired with words.

"You are loved," she said warmly, her voice carrying a vital force, familiar to them both. It gave great comfort as he released, resting his heavy burdens. A slight moan expelled from him and she shuddered from the power of it.

"You are loved now, as you were the moment the first spark of you began." The force went into a whisper. "I could never love you any different."

He slouched deeper, liberated. Her tears rose from his fierce emotions which they now shared, both appreciating the fabric of God's interwovenness.

The elk grew warmer, holding her tighter. The heat penetrated through, quickening her heart. His head bowed in healing, her spirit rapidly expanded out, hitting a boundary beyond and back.

The totality of the outside world suddenly attached to her in one plane of energy.

The beating of her heart was loud and fast as the energies morphed her body into his. She was him, realizing the "devil" of a creature was merely a mask, a muddied version of God. He was there, always in everything, within the darkest and the purest souls, mainly the part we blame. He'd come to her on the mountain with Cray, while living in the yurt, and in her most difficult times. He could never not hear her.

The light filled her sight while the pulling energy continued then the brightness dimmed. What appeared was a heavenly universe with beautiful shades of colorful hues over a canvas of black. She was one. One with God, with the vibration of earth, existence, past, present, future, and eternity.

More alive than ever. The physical was no longer. She *was* the eyes and presence of the universe. Suspended in all of existence and nothing at once. With this realization, the enveloping light returned, showing her individual particles of light suspended gently together. Each one played its own remarkable melody while a black speck equal in size attached itself to a glistening particle, causing it to diminish.

It nearly burned out then rapidly grew in light, consuming the speck, then expanded so brilliantly, expecting it to fully envelop her as her awareness was directed to the earth.

She stood with bare feet surrounded by hoof tracks. She blinked, taking in a stabilizing breath before glancing at the luminescent glow which was now the sun—ascending above the ridge.

Her gaze fell upon the smoldering embers and burn

marks spanning beyond the rocks. Then to the erupted mounds of earth and tuft of fresh grass. She stood in awe when a small branch broke. Her head swiveled in the direction of a beautiful doe, nibbling from the ground.

Unable to hold in her emotions, she cried—blessed with bountiful gifts from spirit. She released, knowing he was with her. Inching towards the deer she reached to caress its neck. The wind carried a white blossom between them as the elegant creature allowed the embrace.

*The tribal album: *Zaba*, Glass Animals
*The song playing before switching itself: Walla Walla
*The slow song the iPod changed to: Lord Huron, "The night we met"

# 26

## As Above So Below

Aquarius solar eclipse, February 14, 15, 2018

Grace was digging the solo vibe on Valentine's Day; it was a refreshing way to spend it after years of relationship ups and downs. She knew being single wasn't forever and encouraged herself to relish her current freedom and independence. Throughout the day she got a kick out of watching the ladies receive bouquets from their honeys, and her workday passed with a breeze.

She returned home excited for a date with herself, where she made a delicious lamb dinner and sauteed veggies. Then went to *The Greatest Showman* at the theater. The music instantly grabbed her chest, sparking adventure and fun within her. It was fully entertaining and drew grateful tears for the message of love and acceptance for who we are.

She thought, *What a perfect movie for the Aquarius moon and eclipse tomorrow.*

Aquarius is the humanitarian of the zodiac. It's responsible for the "bizarre" in life and it also represents the people, including their differences and uniqueness. The film was *clearly* celebrating the beauty of each character's individual strangeness, accepting them as a success. Even the circus was Aquarian in its roots.

She left the theater thrilled and immediately got the soundtrack, listening to it as she crashed—head to pillow, with an enthusiastic heart.

The next morning she went to work with a gung-ho attitude while "This Is Me" played repetitively in her head. Inspired by the movie, she set out to accomplish her desires, starting with a request of two days off a week to focus on her writing and prepare the garden. Surprisingly, her boss accepted her plan that day. She would only work two days in the office, making headway with her personal goals the rest of the week.

Ecstatic for the chance to refine her story, she aimed to post the first four chapters to a blog for friends and family by May 15. This was when Uranus would move into Taurus. She had three months to get ready.

When she left work, it was nearly dark, and she knew she'd be lonely at home in Kai's absence, so she grabbed a bite to eat and drove near the South Hills to play her new album on repeat.

The skies were clear, so she pulled over to gaze and connect with the heavens. She thought back to being alone on Valentine's Day and how it hadn't dampened her mood. She felt she was being nudged towards strengthening her relationship with the universe and self. While sitting with the heavens, she peered at the twinkling bodies, appreciative of how her life had unfolded, both good and bad. Then she realized the eclipse was happening across the planet at that moment.

She wanted to get back to the thrill of driving with the music since it moved and inspired her. So she headed past Nat Soo Pah—a natural mineral pool she'd enjoyed as a child. She'd intended to park near the mine where she often sat to write and gaze at the sage-filled landscape and open skies. But when she came upon the turn, she spontaneously continued to the right. She was glad she had since the sun had melted the snow everywhere, except this section. It was lightly covered in untouched, pristine powder.

The virgin snow took her back to the first visit at River's after their walk, when he'd driven her back to her car. The way the shimmery crystals interacted with the headlights was just as magical here, if not more.

The song switched to "Come Alive," and she experienced every word and tonal vibration, welcoming it to bellow through her.

There was an epic moment building, driving on her version of the Yellow Brick Road from *The Wizard of Oz*. This was more of a runway into her dreams since the road curved up and over the hill, appearing as if the earth dropped off. It was more fitting to her story than a yellow brick road, thinking back to her glitter globe as a child, which ironically played the tune of "Somewhere Over The Rainbow."

It looked as though God opened an enormous version

of it and shook it all over her runway. Grace giggled at the personalized gift, accepting it graciously as she took flight into her dreams. She said, "Thank you... universe! Thank you."

* * *

The next day she was up early, ready to write. Busy typing away, she received her star chart reading via email. Excited to see results, she immediately listened to the recording from an astrologer on YouTube. He shared his interpretation of her birth chart:

> "Your Sun, Moon, Jupiter, and Neptune are in the 9th house, this is a stellium or a lineup of planets in Capricorn. Saturn rules Capricorn and takes 28-29 years to make a full cycle back to where it was when you were born. Saturn-born people, especially ones that have Saturn in the 7th house, which you do, tend to get married when they are older and if they get married young, marriage can get rocky when Saturn returns to the place of your birth. The seventh house represents, 'the other,' or what we call the 'relationship house' and 'marriage' house."

Grace was taking notes, looking at her chart in more detail while he continued.

"Saturn also rules the father, father figures, and grandfathers. You might be attracted to older men in relationships or choose a Saturn ruled partner, such as another Capricorn or Aquarius type. Saturn in the 7th can strongly signify past karmic relationships. With your south node here as well, that makes it an even stronger likelihood. You could have been married to someone with power, or a significant title in past lives. These indicate you are karmically meant to be in the relationships you're in."

Grace was already overwhelmed by the information, but that didn't cancel out her excitement.

"When Jupiter transits a person's 7th house, which it's here for you now, this is when you can attract your partner or get married. When it goes retrograde, someone romantic from your past could come back, to revive the past connection, giving it new life, or, especially being in the sign of Scorpio, it can bury it forever."

Grace thought back to the first day Jupiter went into Scorpio when she put on her elk ring and boarded up River in his metaphorical horse arena.

"When Jupiter transits your south node, which

is here too, it tends to take something away that's no longer needed. It's the largest planet and can see the bigger picture. It wants to expand whatever it touches, whether it's hard to let go or not. It will benefit you in the long run to let go of whatever is leaving during that time, because it'll go anyway."

*Note to self—Look up when Jupiter will transit my south node.*

"You're a Taurus rising, this is your first house, representing your image, persona, and how people see you. Taurus is an earth sign ruled by Venus. You needed this earthy Taurus appearance and demeanor to get done what you came to do this lifetime. Your north node is here as well. You would do well to focus on *you*; your skills, your art, your projects, your creative outlets, your appearance, and... loving yourself.

"When planets transit this house, it could change your appearance or the way others see you. For example, when Jupiter comes through here you can physically expand either by gaining weight, having a big personality, lots of attention, or often women expand by becoming pregnant.

"The asteroid Ceres is here on your ascendant, and when anything conjuncts your ascendant, you embody that energy. Ceres is in Taurus here, fully at home in this sign. You *are* Ceres; you are the personification of her—the goddess of agriculture and fertility. She rules over the harvests and is also the reason we have winter. I don't know anything about you, but I would say, if you grew a garden, I'd bet so much money that your garden would be a great garden, even if you didn't know how to garden!"

Grace gleamed.

"Chiron is also in your first house, not on the cusp or in Taurus but in the sign that follows which is Gemini. Chiron is the wounded healer, so you yourself could be someone that was hurt by love since it's in the sign of Gemini, representing the lovers. In past lives your soul may have been badly crushed by a lover, or you could have wronged someone in love and this life is for you to heal that wound. It can also indicate shyness as a child, maybe stuttering, or it may have been difficult for you to speak your mind around others. This is your soul's wound. It came to heal itself this lifetime. Since it's in the first house, you might be someone who could help others in healing the same kind of pain, since Chiron is the wounded healer.'"

This resonated with Grace fully. She was terribly shy as a child, blocking her from living to the fullest. Then her mind flashed back to her past life, the silenced Queen. The astrologer continued,

"Some words of advice... get ready! Uranus is about to enter Taurus, your first house. You're gonna come out in some way. Uranus rules the heavens, and it's the ruler of Aquarius, the sign of the water bearer—the humanitarian—it rules the sky, lightning, electricity; it rules people and the future, the internet and networking. They say to expect the unexpected when it comes to this planet because it's a rebellious planet.

"Uranus is different and unique compared to the others as it lays on its side rather than upright, and it rotates around the sun in 84 years—I see you were born in '84—interesting numerology there. Uranus has been in the sign of Aries since 2011, working its way through your 12th house of the hidden and what's now behind you. It'll move into Taurus and back into Aries for a few weeks then enter into Taurus for the next seven years, so get used to it disrupting you and your plans, but also look forward to being seen differently, or shocking in some way.

"The love interests you choose might shock people. You'll be electric, guided and loved by the universe. You'll be future thinking or connected to 'the future,' led by the heavens. Not only that, you have Saturn, who just came back into Capricorn, which will change your foundations from the last 30 years and start rebuilding for the next 30 year cycle."

Grace was overwhelmed with all the inspiring and technical information. She paused the reading to study her chart with new eyes to dig deeper into it. Something the astrologer said made her think of a new way to look at her chart.

He said, "Saturn-ruled people may experience separation or a disruption in the foundation of their marriage, if married before their Saturn return." She looked up the dates when Saturn was last in Scorpio. October 2012 – December 2014 and retrograded again last in September 2015.

Hmmm, Grace thought to herself, My father's dad passed the first time Saturn returned in my chart. That's when I thought of my own death bed, unable to see Cray there, that's when I first questioned my marriage.

"That's when it all started falling apart at the yurt. We left after Halloween in 2015," Grace murmured. "Well, I can't make conclusions based on a couple coincidences... but it is interesting." At any rate, she was having fun, investigating this new way of looking at her chart.

She thought about her son, who was a Scorpio, having been born during this transit. He would forever have his natal Saturn in Scorpio too. His sun and Saturn fell into her seventh house of relationships. She had no way of telling the exact degrees Saturn was during all these life changing shifts, but going forward, she could keep an eye on the current alignments and watch for them. She also wondered if Kai was one of her karmically bound relationships?

Curious, she thought, *Well, what's the next significant transition coming up in my chart?*

Jupiter was just a few degrees from transiting her natal Saturn, which meant it would transit a few days from today. Grace knew Jupiter was in Scorpio but was unaware that the degree mattered until now.

She confirmed that Jupiter would retrograde March 9, at 23 degrees of Scorpio, where her natal Saturn was parked. So, it wouldn't only pass over her Saturn once, but it would stop there, go back over it for a couple days, then move forward in July, making its last move over it in October. *I'll definitely be watching to see what happens.*

"So, it'll move forward on my Saturn, go backward and move forward again," she said aloud while drawing it out on paper, trying to soak it in... *I don't want to wonder what will happen when Jupiter transits my south node at 27... I'll wait till then to worry about that.*

*Knowing what transpired when Saturn came through here the 1st time, now I want to look back and see what happened when Jupiter came through here last.*

Digging further, she looked up the last time Jupiter was there, October 2005 through November 2006—the time frame she had gotten engaged then married to Cray, remembering her mother's grandfather passed away the week of their wedding.

*Hhhmmm, well I know I'm not going to get married when Jupiter hits 23 degrees in a few days… I don't know what could happen, but it'll be fun to see what takes place when it's exact. I'll be documenting it, for sure.*

It seemed she'd opened a treasure box full of information kept from her until now. She was having fun "playing around" with these jewels.

She looked up Jupiter's last transit through Taurus. It was 2012, transiting through her first house when she *did* get pregnant and physically expanded.

These coincidences gave Grace a new toy feeling, motivating her to keep researching dates and events, even though she had every intention to spend the day writing before picking up Kai.

She couldn't stop digging for more clues to the cycles since it seemed these heavenly alignments coincided perfectly with her major life moments. She felt like an investigator having light bulb insights going off, getting a kick out of immersing herself in this new language.

\* \* \*

That Aquarius eclipse brought so many astrological answers for her. After a week passed, she took Kai to Barnes and Noble to hang out in the kids' section, something they both loved to do. She found a beautifully illustrated children's book on Greek Mythology and flipped through.

"Hey Kai, this book looks fun! You wanna read it with

me?"

"I wanna look at Paw Patwol," he said, pulling all the Paw Patrol books off the shelf and starting to look through them.

"Okay," she laughed and flipped through while he browsed the other kids' books, turning page by page, not realizing how much Greek Mythology overlapped with Astrology.

After reading about a few gods and goddesses she happened upon Ceres, the asteroid that was directly on her ascendant. She remembered the astrologer saying: "Ceres, the goddess of agriculture is on your ascendant. You *are* the personification of her. I bet if you ever grew a garden…"

She read: *Ceres controlled earth and its fertility, wheat was her main harvest, and her hair mimicked long golden strands of wheat. Her smile made flowers blossom.*

Wide-eyed, Grace grew goosebumps, remembering the apricot tree blossoming when she smiled on the night of the lunar eclipse. *What an interesting coincidence,* she thought, purely thrilled.

She loved how the universe was placing breadcrumbs in front of her like a game, recognizing her relationship with the cosmos was growing stronger. It wanted a bond with her just as she wanted one with it. There was a childlike wonder in the moment, a rarity in the "grown-up world." She relished the magical essence of loving creativity.

"Can you wead to me?" Kai broke her trance by plopping half a dozen books on her lap. She happily read him half the books then let him pick out a few to take home.

While walking out, she noticed the store hours showed they didn't open until 9 AM. She had plans to meet a friend here in the cafe the next morning. He needed to meet early since he was leaving town, so she texted him right away.

*Let's meet at Java, 8 AM*, he messaged back.

She groaned internally, not exactly fond of this coffee shop. It was the most popular place in town, and everyone from high school who came back to town got their coffee there. Her brothers had to go there while in town and Grace wasn't as much of a fan.

She decided to meet at Java anyway, despite the probability of her past flooding back. Maybe she was being too picky about it anyway?

# 27

## Jupiter in Scorpio Brings Blessings

February 23, 2018

"The moon is in Gemini today," said the astrologer from her daily video. "This one can draw in your twin lover, since Gemini represents the twins."

Grace was getting into the shower and thought, *Yeah, yeah, they always say stuff like that...*

"It can also bring together business partnerships..."

The astrologer continued as she turned the water on, drowning out the video. *Good to know,* she thought, *I'm meeting with a Gemini to talk business and possibly partnering but I doubt there's an intimate connection since he's only 19.*

After dropping Kai at daycare for his week with Cray, she pulled up to the coffee shop right on time for her 8:00

meet-up. She expected it to be busy and sure enough, she had to stand right inside the door at the end of the line. She spotted her friend then looked at the menu ahead, ready to order a steeped yerba. Her eyes fell to the front of the line and she took a second glance at the guy ordering.

*Is that...* She watched until she got a better look... *Piper? It is! And he's got a man bun, nice.*—He kept it short and spiky in high school.

She saw him years ago at the Ketchum farmers market and wanted to catch up but he was in a hurry and out of reach. She'd tried to befriend him on social media but it was obvious he hadn't been on there in years.

The barista handed him his coffee, and she knew it was now or never. It was out of character for her to reach out to her high school classmates but while he walked towards her, her courage took over and she leaned to the left as he got close.

"Piper!" she said, aware that everyone in line would hear what they'd have to say.

"Grace!" She was met with a surprised smile.

"How are you? It's been 15-16 years."

"I'm good," he replied happily. "And you?"

"Good. Are you living here or are you just visiting?" She assumed the latter.

"I live here," his wide smile continued. "I moved down from Ketchum a while ago to build houses with my dad."

"I wondered if you'd been up there. I saw you walk by the farmer's market and thought, 'Is that Piper?'"

He looked at her as though it was possible, but he didn't recall the moment. "What about you, where do you live?"

"Off of Falls Ave." She pointed in that direction.

"Oh, here in town?"

"Yep."

"What do you do these days?" he asked.

"Organic farming and gardening." She kept it brief since the line was moving.

He gave her an unexpected high five. She wasn't used to such a positive response. It made her stand a little taller. Usually, she was met with more questions, like "A farm? How do you sell your produce? Is that a tough gig?" Or "Do you have pigs?"

"You have any little ones, Grace?" He held his hand out to measure a kid's height.

"A five-year-old boy. His name's Kai."

"Nice!" He made a pleasing face.

"He's a hoot and full of energy. You?"

"Nope." He admitted, "Never had kids or a partner."

"Why not?"—remembering how much she'd liked him, knowing he was a catch.

"I'm lazy and don't go out much."

"I don't go out either, not much of a drinker, and that's what most people our age wanna do. Are you on Facebook?" she asked, knowing he'd say no.

"I have a profile but I don't use Facebook," he said, sounding disappointed. "I'll give you my number, though"—

turning enthusiastic again—"we can catch up."

"That would be great," she said, patting her pockets. "I left my phone in the car though."

He turned to the side counter and wrote his number on a napkin, "Here you go."

"Thanks!" she beamed optimistically. "It was good seeing you, Piper!"

"You too Grace. Have a great day."

He gave her another white grin and she thought, *That's the first time I've seen his smile without braces.*

"You too!" thinking, *I'm so glad I reached out, even if nothing comes of it.*

She was next in line and chuckled to herself as the guy taking her order had been in her first yoga class. They said hi and made small talk, then he handed her a steamy yerba mate.

When she sat to greet her friend, she saw two teachers from grade school and junior high.

"Geez, it's like walking into my past when I come here." Grace cheerfully shook her head as a lady from her art class walked in. She had to give Grace a hug and a quick chat.

"Whoa, it *is* like walking into your past," her friend said after eavesdropping and the lady walked away.

"I saw my first kiss too." She sat back down.

"Your first kiss? Really, cool."

Then the two of them caught up, sharing plans for their gardens and foodie aspirations. They both planned to grow organic veggies and promote locally, but Grace's intentions were strongly centered on educating about gardening and, most of all, donating the harvest.

She got a kick out of her experience two years ago when she invited the refugee center to harvest what was left in her garden. She wanted to expand in that direction. She'd also planned on inviting her neighbors to participate.

Gemini liked her ideas and was already gaining momentum selling his produce and eggs to local restaurants. She'd done that with Matt Haze and wasn't interested in doing that as of now. She was set up where she could be of service and welcomed community participation.

He offered to help in any way and they planned to keep in touch, wishing each other luck.

Before leaving the coffee shop, she let go of all expectations and texted Piper, not wanting to lose his napkin. That way his number was on her phone.

*This is Grace. Chat me up if you'd like to hang out sometime.*

\* \* \*

Grace reflected on her meeting as she pulled up to Barnes and Noble and thought, *It'd be nice to have the trailer parked right next to the garden so I can walk out of my tiny abode into my garden. I can garden, write, play with Kai—repeat.*

She was thrilled to write the rest of the day next to the big window in the cafe. After hours of productive writing, she took a break in the children's section and read more from the Greek Mythology book. She flipped through the pages and thought, *interesting how the gods and goddesses are intertwined with astrology.* She didn't know the connection but enjoyed the read.

She found a similar book on spirit animals and she flipped through, curious if they had the deer.

> Divine Spirit called the gentle, loving creature up to Holy Mountain, but a terrifying beast blocked the deer's way, scaring everyone who tried to visit. Deer was unafraid, having so much love even for the beast that he disappeared, opening a path to Divine Spirit for all others.
>
> Gentleness cultivates love and compassion for both the light and the darkness in order to find harmony.

Grace thought of her experience with the elk man at Apricot Landing. Further curious, she turned to the swan, symbolizing *"Grace"... How interesting!* She thought, continuing to read.

> Ugly duckling flew into Dreamtime alone, concerned by its dark whirlpool. "What is this?" she asked.
>
> A voice replied, "the portal to imagination, illusions, and the future. If you enter, you must receive

whatever the future offers as it is presented, without changing Divine Spirit's plan."

Swan looked down at her ugly duckling self and said, "I'd be happy to *surrender,* I won't resist Divine Spirit's plan and I'll trust what's offered." She was absorbed, appearing later, graceful and white.

"What did you learn, Swan?"

"I surrendered to Divine Spirit and saw the future on Holy Mountain. My faith and acceptance have changed me, learning to accept the state of Grace."

The word *trust* really stood out to her as she then found the elk which was much shorter.

The Elk represents stamina; if the elk spirit has entered your life, prepare for the long haul and plan to work on a project for a lengthy time.

The description made her think of the process of writing her book. *It's definitely been a long process,* she thought, then flipped through some other books, staying in the store until closing.

Once home, she saw Piper had replied to her text.

*Hey, I'm busy for a while. Would you like to meet on Sunday, have some coffee? Or I could take you and your son out to breakfast?*

*Breakfast sounds great. Kai is with his dad for the week, so it'll just be me.* She was surprised that he had responded at all.

*Okay... Do you like Buffalo Cafe?*

*Yes! It's my favorite breakfast joint. I usually go on Sundays with a friend.*

*Great! I'll pick you up around 9?*

Grace thought, *Hhhhhmmm… He wants to pick me up…?*

*Perfect, I'll text you the address Saturday night.*

*Lookin' forward to catching up.*

*Me too!*


\* The animal card book: Medicine Cards by Jamie Sams and David Carson

# 28

# Buffalo Chip

February 24 - 27, 2018

*February 24, 2018*

*I've had a lot of downtime to reflect and sift through my thoughts today. I didn't write much. Instead, I enjoyed escaping in contemplation. It gave me clarity and peace as I came to strong conclusions.*

*I reflected on what's transpired in my life these past years and saw what could be on my horizon. It's an important time as the present energies are similar to the time my grandfather passed in the fall of 2014. There was a stellium peak of planets in Scorpio and I had my first Saturn return.*

*Now, Jupiter will make its way over the same ground starting tomorrow. She'll transit over my natal Saturn at 23 degrees Scorpio through March 9th and retrograde at the end of the degree. My south node will be graced over this fall at 27 degrees.*

*All this activity is happening in my 7th house of relationships where the "other" is represented, opposite from the 1st house of "self." This is why I say it's a pivotal moment, based on a repeating pattern that came before, generating life-changing events.*

*I love how life is showing me the light and giving me direction. Let's see what else the universe has planned.*

*Astrologers say wherever Saturn is in our chart, we are asked to calm our ego. I know I would benefit from taking a more humble approach as I interact with my dad, especially as Saturn represents the father. Interestingly, when I had my Saturn return, it took my father's father.*

Grace carried on journaling about missing her grandparents and how it was as though she were living in their tomb. She wondered if she'd overcome that or would it always be that way? Her goal was to buy the homestead in the future and have her gracious garden thrive, intending to make her roots proud by caring for the land till she passed.

She ended on a positive note, switching gears, and watched an astrology video.

"This is a unique planetary alignment here on the 15th"—referring to last week's eclipse—"The Aquarius Eclipse will suddenly trigger those born with Aquarius energy." Her Mars and Venus were in this sign. "These people will let go of their ego to embrace something for the *world*. But how? The rulers of Aquarius are Saturn and Uranus. Find these planets in your chart. Through these two planets, you will cleanse your ego. Also, find your north and south nodes, they will show you where to go."

Grace paused to study her birth chart, giving her best attempt to comprehend the information.

"The ego and the individual needs will go away and the focus will be on the people. Saturn in Capricorn is representing structure and sacrifice for others. It's also saying—you must do things *yourself*."

She resonated with that statement, thinking, *I see this in my life as I care for the homestead and carry on as a single parent. I garden alone and write alone...*

"Mars in Aquarius is saying, take action but take action for other people." This was the sign her Mars was in. "Jupiter in Scorpio is saying, teach and counsel people for the betterment of others. These humanitarian energies will bring in money but not for a personal salary. They will do something where the entire public will benefit."

Grace was overwhelmed, excited and under pressure, as

these aspirations were her driving force. She thought, *If only my grandparents were here.* The more she thought of them, the more she missed 'em. With that heavy thought, she laid her head on her notebook full of writings, and her eyes closed.

* * *

Her face stuck to the pages of her journal when an incoming voice jolted her awake.

"Piper!" She grabbed her phone and responded, *Sorry, I forgot to send my address last night* and gave it to him.

She put her phone down and wrote a quick documented entry of how the morning started, with Jupiter at 23. She checked online to see where it was, and it was right on the dot.

*February 25, 2018*

.

*Jupiter transiting my natal Saturn starts this morning in my 7th house. The planet of expansion will move forward 13 days then turn retrograde over that same degree until March 20th. Then turn direct again in the summer, hitting 23 degrees a third time October 5-10, for a total of 29 days on my natal Saturn. Nearly a month, lucky me...? Something profound will occur, I'm guessing. Saturn coming home in my chart took grandpa, and on his deathbed, I deeply questioned my relationship with Cray for the first time. All that's over, so how will Jupiter moving over the same place manifest?*

*The astrological energies are ringing true so far, my first intimate partner is meeting me today. We are going to breakfast.*

*~We shall see. Will the universe bring it up to rekindle and reconnect us, or will it bury our connection for good?*

*I'm so glad the moon is in Cancer too, the vibe is so homey and cozy.*


Piper drove up the lane and she met him in the driveway. *Funny, his Toyota Camry reminds me of his Honda Accord from high school.* Once in the car, they were back as teenagers except Piper was now rocking a man bun.

They drove to The Buffalo Cafe, chatting the whole way, then waited in line out in the cold wind. It was worth the wait.

He asked about working on the organic farm and about her garden. He told her he grew a garden in his mom's backyard the year before and shared photos of a very organized and clean patch.

"Nice work, I bet your mom loved it!"

"She did. I'm thinking about growing another one this year," he said, putting his phone away.

"Great idea." There was a pause in communication, and then she asked, "Do you remember I left high school?"

"Yeah, I remember wondering where Grace went?"

"The social scene was too overpowering. It wasn't productive for me at the time and my mom worked at the

College of Southern Idaho. So I started taking classes there. I graduated with honors in two degrees, so it's not like I didn't want to do the work. High school just wasn't for me."

"Gottcha," he said. "Not many people consider alternative options at that age," he admitted.

The line moved into the waiting room where two maps of the world were posted on the wall. People had pinned the places they'd traveled to and from. Grace showed him the two pins she had placed on it. One in Zanzibar and one in Arusha, Tanzania.

"Why'd you go there?"

"I volunteered in an orphanage."

His jaw dropped slightly. "You'll have to tell me more about that sometime." And they were directed to sit at a booth with two menus.

"Do you have a favorite dish you like to get?" he asked, picking up the menu.

In unison, they said, "Buffalo Chip."

"Buffalo Chip."

"Yep, with no egg," she added and they both smiled.

"I have a confession to make," he said.

"Oh," she said.

"I thought about the Ketchum farmers market and I remember seeing you, thinking... Is that Grace but I didn't know for sure. You guys set up your booth right next to my buddy's condo."

"Oh, really? I'm glad you remembered. I guess we

weren't supposed to catch up until now. What was your friend's name?"

"Dave."

"Oh Yeah, Matt used to leave him a bag full of steaks and veggies on our last day of market every year. It was his way of saying *thank you* for putting up with the market all season."

"Yeah, he's a good guy." he said, "speaking of not meeting up until now… can I ask why aren't you with anyone?"

"I was married to Cray for 10 years, together for 12, but we split when Kai was 3. I'm still learning lessons from that relationship. What about you?"

"Ah, I was dating a wonderful, sweet girl, and I broke her heart which broke mine. That was 10 years ago and I've been working on myself ever since. That was my biggest life lesson."

It seemed that was all he wanted to share on the topic for now, which was fine. She didn't need to pry or make it uncomfortable, they were having a good time. It was so fun sitting there across from him. She'd never imagined this would happen and was beyond grateful for the chance to reconnect.

When they finished eating he drove her home, since he had a prior engagement with his brother. He was coming up too fast on her street.

"It's right here." She pointed quickly as they passed the turn.

He continued driving and playfully said, "I'm not taking you home yet."

"Okay," she said, enjoying his playfulness.

He turned left next to the LDS temple and asked, "See that empty lot?"

"Uh, huh."

"My dad and I are building a house there this spring,"

"Nice," *So close to the homestead,* she thought.

"Ok, now I'll take you home." And he drove in the wrong direction again. "I'm not taking you home."—grinning at his joke—"You're mine now!"

Grace laughed, enjoying the butterfly-inducing flirting. They overlapped with their high school selves as he drove around the block, making it to the homestead to drop her off.

"What are you doing around 6?" he asked.

"Not much. Text me when you're done, and we'll see where we're at." He nodded and she went inside, busying herself with house chores and writing.

He came over later and they talked for hours next to each other on the couch. She remembered a moment in their first year of high school where they met.

"I have to tell you about an experience that I had while standing next to you in PE." she said.

"Go for it."

"I have to be honest, on our first day when we were put in line alphabetically by last name, you were put next to me and I thought—this guy's going to eventually flirt with me. I didn't like to be flirted with so I always avoided you. You were nice and tried to talk to me and one day, you were talking to the person on your left while I was looking straight ahead. Even though I could see you in my peripheral vision, I felt a definite tap on my shoulder from your direction. I thought that was odd and I looked at you without being obvious and was instantly attracted to you from then on."

He nodded warmly.

"What do you think that was?" she asked.

"Our future children," he said sarcastically.

Grace laughed. "You were my first kiss," she said. She'd been waiting all night for the right moment.

"I had forgotten about that," he said, smiling. "Not the kiss but me being your first kiss."

"We got together on our birthday, I turned 16, and you 15."

"I do remember that. You kept saying you were scared, but that was your shyness."

"You told me, 'Don't be scared,' then kissed me." she blushed, "I remember all the fear completely melting into lovely sensations. You made it easy."

"I remember all that too," he smiled.

"Well, you did a good job. I've been told I'm a good kisser," she said playfully.

He laughed and Grace pointed out three deer in the yard. He looked out the window to see then turned back to kiss her. Grace was again taken back in their past to those hormones and sensual sensations... She was comfortable and safe in that kiss, back in a time where our youthful innocence was in its purest state.

* * *

Monday morning she woke up on cloud nine, driving down the lane with her l delightful music, ready to get to work. Her mom called from Oregon and Grace thought, *Mom doesn't call often. I better answer.*

"Hey mom," Grace said over the speaker.

"Sorry to bother you this early. Are you headed to work?"

"Yeah, but I'm stopped at the end of the lane. What's up?"

"I just got a message saying Grandpa went into the hospital yesterday morning. He has an infection in his foot, and it moved into the bones, his organs are shutting down and he's in a coma. I wanted to let you know."

"What?"

"They say he might not make it through the day," her mom said in a tender voice.

"Okay," Grace said, not knowing how to process the news.

"I'll let you get going to work, sweetie."

"Alright, love you, mom."

"Love you too."

They ended their call and she drove to work dumbfounded, thinking, *I just saw him last week and told him to try an Epsom salt soak. Now he's dying?*

When she got to work, she tried to hold onto her emotions. But as always, her dear coworker asked how she was. She repeated what her mom just told her, unable to grip her emotions, and cried realizing what was happening. All the gals at work hugged her at once. There were only 10 patients on the schedule that day, and everyone told her to spend the day at the hospital. They were supportive and loving towards her, and she was grateful for that.

While driving to the hospital she couldn't help but think, *Jupiter's at 23. The planet of expansion is taking my mother's father. Saturn took my father's father when he came through and the last time Jupiter was here, she took my mother's grandfather. It's the same theme.*

When she found his room her grandma embraced her and asked, "Would you like to take a moment with grandpa? They say he can hear you, so say what you need to, honey."

"Thanks, grandma."

She sat next to his hospital bed and held his hand—hooked into IVs. All she said was, "I love you. Thank you for being my grandfather."

He struggled and out came coughing. She decided to speak to his spirit from within, inspired to play a song. She held his hand and scrolled through her music, finding a slower warm song and pushed play. She felt the tears come, still stunned she was sitting there saying goodbye to grandpa, knowing without a doubt he loved her and she loved him. She was filled with love, and their spirits embraced.

She whispered "Goodbye" as tears streamed down her cheeks. Her uncle entered the room and Grace wiped her tears. She kissed her grandfather on the forehead and allowed them some time alone.

There was a seating area near a large window where she soaked in the sunshine. She pulled her journal out and wrote,

*Jupiter's taking my grandpa Jim*–crying as she wrote. The sun warmed her, overwhelmed with spirit. It wasn't an awful, unfair feeling of grief; it was a spiritual letting go, a loving goodbye.

In some ways, she was grateful for another "bread crumb," the universe had sent her. She honored her grandfather's death in that holy moment, connected to the spiritual side of life and him. She saw herself as the dust flake embraced by the three dark particles, making her 'aware.' Aware of a system or a cycle of life, attached to immense emotions of gratitude and grief.

That night, she checked her phone since she hadn't all day. Piper had asked her how her day was. She didn't know what to say and replied telling him what happened.

He couldn't believe it and said he was bad luck.

She offered to meet him for some late evening appetizers, despite being emotionally drained from the day. Piper was a great comfort even though he kept thinking he was to blame. After they said good night, she went home to bed.

\* \* \*

Grace spent all day the next day at the hospital again, sitting and visiting with loved ones. Around 7:30 that night, she asked Piper if she could see him and he invited her to his house. When she got there she sat on his bed, full of exhaustion, and told him how the day went.

Not even ten minutes had gone by before receiving a text: *Gpa had his last breath around 8.* She had him read the message and he seemed to not know what to do or how to support her. She could see it on his face.

He kept saying, "I think I'm bad luck."

Grace hugged him, reassuring him that it wasn't his fault before driving back to the hospital. She stood in her grandfather's room, saturated with dense emotional and spiritual energy. Her family surrounded him, crying in each other's arms, while he lay dignified in death. She sobbed in multiple arms, letting a lifetime's portion of purging out, but simultaneously spirit shone within her. After an hour had passed she asked Piper if she could come back.

*I'd love to have you come over, Grace.*

Her emotions were spent and she was drained spiritually. She didn't want to cry with Piper. She wanted to enjoy him and spend a moment with a warm, loving body. Her grandfather's love was present and she knew he wanted her to have love too.

Grace leaned into Piper for a potent kiss, putting that emotional energy into it. Her body was heightened to the touch as the energy shared between them was powerful. They embraced and she transferred back to her 16-year-old self, kissing her first boy, remembering his braces, and hearing herself whisper, "I'm scared." And he whispered back, "Don't be scared."

The image of young Piper connected with her merged with the now. She remembered the nerves immediately turning into safe, warm, and magically arousing sensations. Grace peered into the dark room. Although it wasn't the same room, it looked the same.

This time, they were able to experience making love in its entirety. It was as though a door had opened back in 2001, teased them, and closed to open again tonight. Grace knew it had something to do with Saturn coming home to Capricorn and Jupiter in the 7th. They were coming home to each other.

She was snuggled against his bare body when Piper said, "While we made love, I nearly cried. I haven't been able to cry in years. I was *so* loved by the universe to have you here, sharing your love with me."

Her heart filled with warmth and comfort as she thought, *this is where the transitions were taking me. I'm sure of it.* She knew her grandfather's spirit was working his magic, aiding her in surrendering to the possibility of loving her "other" again. It helped knowing Piper had put intimate relationships on hold until he was ready. Ten years is a long time to work on the "self," and Grace admired him for that.

* The slow, warm song she played while saying goodbye to her grandfather was "Honey It's Alright" by Gregory Alan.

# 29

## Dreams Inside of Dreams

Jupiter Rx – March 9, Pluto Rx – April 22, 2018

Piper came over that afternoon. They found themselves having lovely conversations and later made dinner. Grace mentioned her passion for writing and told him about the book she was writing. She touched on her desire to grow a service garden that year too.

He was excited about her book and eager to help with the service project. They got started right away by picking out and ordering $350 of organic seeds. Based on the quantity they purchased, the growing space would be similar in size to her first garden. This made Grace enthusiastic, looking forward to having somebody working alongside her.

They talked well into the night and fell asleep on the floor of her bedroom.

Throughout the day the thought of Jupiter loomed in the back of her mind. How it was in its final days of 23 degrees Scorpio before turning backward. She'd been curious to see what revealed itself during this transit. So far, she hadn't noticed anything specific that materialized, other than planning a garden with Piper.

But that night—deep in sleep, Grace dreamt of gardening in the same place she had last year, in front of the house.

She was sitting cross-legged in her usual outdoor work attire: baggy salmon corduroy with a brown plaid jacket and hair in a side braid. The heavenly scenery caught her attention while she was transplanting her seedlings. The wide open space displayed a vast sky and bright sun, shimmering as though the rays were a physical manifestation of the sun's spirit. She basked in its warmth, grateful for the homestead and the family history it held.

Getting back to work, she dug a two-finger-width hole in the ground and planted more leeks the size of a long blade of grass, into the loosened soil. Always enjoyed working with nature. When she reached for another seedling, she noticed the previous transplants had sunk into the soil and tried to pat them securely back in the dirt. They fell through even further as if she'd packed them in quicksand. Bewildered, she wondered if a mole had dug below.

Suddenly, the wind picked up and a storm rolled in. Dust was everywhere in an instant. She stood with squinted eyes, able to peek at the vanishing plants. The holes widened, showing a vast universe beneath. She ran towards the house to escape sinking in and when she made it to the front door, it swung open violently, showing its rapidly crumbling insides.

Grace woke, panicked, looked around, and thankfully saw Piper next to her. What did the dream *mean*? Was it a warning or a sign from the future? Either way, emotions of loss and destruction followed her around all day.

Coincidentally, that evening, her father sent messages of possible changes to the homestead. She began to doubt her plans and the fate of her family's home.

It would be a good plan to get the trailer parked at the lower end of the property and move in, just in case the house situation changed unexpectedly.

* * *

The last week of March, Grace had another conversation with her dad, this time over the phone. Things got pretty heated, there was a lot of yelling back and forth, and she couldn't help but see everything blowing up in her face. After that call, she knew to calm herself and make some decisions. She chose to quit managing the homestead but planned to follow through with her garden project.

* * *

On the first of April, Grace and Kai spent the day moving into the RV. It was tight living quarters, but they treasured their time there together. Grace had five times less stress, not having to worry about homestead logistics. A definite weight had been lifted.

Gratefully, she focused her time and energy solely on Kai, something she'd missed out on, busy checking off to-do lists and working multiple jobs. On days when Kai was with Cray, she honed in on her writing, finding a good balance.

Immense comfort came while decorating her Boho-mobile. She unpacked decorative pillows, pottery, and Kai's preschool-art, surprised how *at home* she was. There was tremendous freedom in her new independence and a release in not having to manage multiple responsibilities. Plus, a bonus from living in the camper was that it made her debt-free. She was finding liberation all around.

Grace took in the panoramic view of the kitchen and living room, from the hallway step into the bedroom, and thought, *Hmmm... it's quite quaint. I could get used to this simple life for sure!*

Kai pulled toys and art supplies out all over, creating messes, and Grace allowed it since they didn't have to consider roommates anymore. Even then, she still had him clean his mess before starting another since there was limited space. It was great not having to worry about him getting into anything he wasn't supposed to, bothering their roommates, or running outside because he was always in sight. This was another freedom for them both.

Kai said, "Momma, I LOVE this place! I'm gonna get a big twuck and pawk this in a beautiful spot in the mountains an, an, when we want to, we tan move it to anothew beautiful place, and then anothew an anothew."

Grace giggled, "Yep, Bubby. You got the idea." She loved that he thought that way.

Time in their no-home was wonderful and mellow. It was a place and time she would remember as fun and adventurous, just her and Kai.

* * *

It was now the end of April, nearing optimal conditions to prepare the garden. Grace had this week marked on her calendar: "service project" and that day's date had *Pluto moved retrograde in Capricorn* again.

Grace, as usual, wrote in her daily notebook, explaining in detail the dream she had last night. It was a continuation of her past life, Queen's dream. This time, Piper was in it as a Knight. The dream was so real, as most of them were.

The Knight, in full armor, walked through the castle uninvited, straight to The Queen's room. He lifted the old royal woman who was blankly staring forward at the landscape.

The Queen was oblivious to The Knight and his

actions while he carried her out of the castle and kingdom. They rode a horse to the top of a lush mountain with springtime trees and foliage. There was a lookout where he placed her to gaze daily into the hills.

The Queen's inner world was the same every day. While she stared out at nature, she was her younger 30-year-old self. The age of her spirit. She watched over the land in the warmth of the glowing sun, streaking its rays across the beautiful valley below.

It was the perfect temperature in her world, always on the warm side, yet snow fell continuously on and around her, despite the clear skies. She noticed every soft embrace of each gentle snowflake. Her feet were bare, standing amongst the sagebrush, in warm snow. Her long, golden locks blew gently in the wind as she watched her beloved planet. Her soul was content, focusing on admiring the grand spirit and essence of earth. She could spend a comfortable eternity here, soaking in nature's beauty.

The Knight often sat next to her and respectfully cared for her. He assumed there was a life playing out inside her and he desired to be a part of her in any way. He often gazed at her while working outside, always wondering what she was experiencing. He wheeled her in every evening and one day noticed she was getting younger. The next day, even younger and the next, younger and younger.

The next day while he sat beside her, The Queen sensed a presence to her left. It was completely unlike her to notice; her curiosity was too strong to deny. She turned slowly to face the present and saw an arrangement of hovering planets, suspended in a system. The late morning sun shined into her face, causing her to squint, urging her to reach for the hovering orbs.

From The Knight's perspective, The Queen slowly peered in his direction with a look of curiosity and looked him over. She reached for his face. He couldn't help but smile back at her.

The Queen noticed her raised hand and before reaching the sphere, brought it back to get a better look. She was growing younger and moving around with ease. There was a change and an awakening from a once frozen space. She brought her hands together, making sure she was seeing correctly and sure enough, her physical body was youthful, returning to the age of her spirit.

Remembering the floating planetary system, she looked back to it, and instead, a long-haired man was sitting next to her in its place. She was surprised by him, and her eyes quickly caught sight of several futuristic windmills spinning rapidly next to a wooden shack behind him.

She looked back at the man who was calmly

watching from her side. She suddenly had a great lust for him, so much that she was sinking back into herself, not used to these strong sensations. She sat and focused on her breathing. It turned into panting and she allowed the desires to be in charge. She hadn't experienced a spectrum of emotions in years, and these... were fabulous.

The Knight admired her youthfulness and heard her heavy breathing, sensing her urges as they vibrated off her. He was experiencing them grow inside himself and leaned towards her steadily. He moved his body slowly in front of her, waiting to make sure it was alright to embrace her, then swept her up and carried her into the hut.

Inside there was a single bed in the corner next to a large window open to nature and pouring in the sun's incredibly luminous light. He headed straight to his bed, but before he got there, he leaned towards her lips, seeing if she would meet him for a kiss. Her lips embraced his with deep passion, and he laid her on his bed, continuing their kiss, illuminated by warm sunshine, undressing each other. They made youthful, passionate love in the light of the day.

Her connection to The Knight was magnetic, naturally pulled together.

As she experienced this, The Queen saw the ghosts of karmic chains fall from her for good. They'd been gripping her wrists after witnessing her lover, The King, with another woman.

When wrapping up her journal entry, Grace mentioned how immersed she had been in warm, stimulating sensations that radiated outward, accompanied with vast gratitude. She was appreciative of all that was involved in reconnecting her with Piper, not forgetting to thank herself for following her heart even when it was painful. And, most importantly, she thanked spirit for her ever deepening connection with it.

# 30

## Saturn's Center Stage

May – June 27, 2018

Grace and Piper returned to the homestead in early May to prepare their garden. The farmer had plowed the land, leaving them a half-acre spot near the irrigation pipe for instant water access. While they tediously raked out smooth garden rows, Grace thought, *It's nice to have help this time around, it'll be a fun project.* She wasn't used to anyone being in her sanctuary and she appreciated it.

While Kai was away, she worked hard to accomplish her goal of posting the first four chapters of her story onto her blog. The aim was to post by May 15, when Uranus will shift into Taurus. She wanted to be prepared since it would be in her first house of "self," May 2021 till 2026 or so, when she planned to have the entire book self-published.

The 15th was around the corner, so she spent the weekend before and the entire day getting the best version of each chapter online with the help from her beloved friend.

They re-edited and finalized her post, having worked their day away in the Barnes and Noble cafe. It was stressful but fun and exciting at the same time. As they walked out just before closing, Grace saw a perfect rainbow in the eastern sky.

"Look! A rainbow," she pointed out. "What a beautiful gift and omen." How poignant; Uranus is the God of the sky and the unexpected. She bounced towards her warm-hearted friend, relieved and enthusiastic, giving her a thankful hug.

Now that her chapters were wrapped up and online, she could focus on the garden project. She decided to make a stopover at the homestead and plan out the next steps for the garden and do a load of laundry. When she drove down the lane, the farmer was working the field in his tractor. She waved, receiving no wave in return, then realized it wasn't the same farmer.

When she walked to their garden space, she saw that the new guy had run the tractor over their garden rows. Her mouth dropped and she leaned forward to pick up a handful of aired soil and pulled out dry bean seeds. He'd just planted beans throughout the entire field.

Grace slumped, sitting her butt in the dirt, looking where their garden had been. A sigh came out, followed by a long, deep breath as she realized her plans vanished. There was no way she'd dig up or plant over the farmer's crop.

*Maybe I'm not supposed to plant here?* she thought, staring at the half-acre while brainstorming on how to deal with this problem. She thought it would be worth asking her farmer friends if they had any space to plant her box full of seeds. She sent a text to everyone who might be open to the idea and received responses within 24 hours.

Her Gemini friend messaged, *Hey Grace, unfortunately, I have no garden space of my own this year. I'm working on getting other gardeners and farmers an outlet for distributing their produce. Try asking your farmer friends in Buhl?*

She'd asked a family who she was sure would have space and let them plant. Mark responded, *Sorry Grace, we would love to have you out here with us, but we are packed tight this year. Try Matt Haze.*

Sadly he had already said there wasn't space and to ask Mark. She even asked Sam if planting next to the trailer was a possibility but he wasn't interested—sigh. She was coming up against stop sign after stop sign. Then Grace met Piper at his mom's and told him all that happened.

"The seeds will be good for next year's garden, won't they?" Piper asked.

"Yes." She slouched at the thought, trying to accept the obvious roadblocks. Although she didn't like the idea of waiting till next year, they were out of time and ideas for starting her beloved service project.

"Why don't we plant some potatoes and onion seeds in my mom's backyard?" Piper suggested.

"Now?"

"Yeah. Just to get our hands dirty. Let's go." There was already a prepared garden space, ready to be planted, and his mom gave the okay, so they began planting.

"What kind of responses are you getting from your story?" He changed the subject. "How's that going?"

"People are liking it." she smiled and blushed. "I've only shared the blog site with close friends and family, and I'm surprised to see what they're saying. My very critical aunt in Australia said it's a page-turner and she would like to read more. I told her it won't be done for a few years. A friend in Ketchum read it and he said it was beautiful and I have 'true grit!' To be honest, I didn't think he'd open the blog site let alone read it."

"See," he said, "Maybe your loving universe is telling you to focus on your book? It's coming easy for you, and you're having a great time getting it written. Maybe it's time to recognize the stop signs and go where the creativity is flowing?" He mimicked Grace's planting technique. "You always have next year for a garden."

"You're right." Piper offered great comfort.

She decided to let go of the project but that didn't change that she wanted this plan as her purpose. She was *supposed* to do this… Right?

"What else are people saying?" Piper asked, seeing that she was let down by the idea of putting it away.

"They all say they like it and ask when it'll be done. My stepmom said, 'It's like you're right there with the character.' She reads a lot and compares me to another writer that I hadn't heard of. It's nice to have *any* feedback, honestly." Grace was excited just by talking about it. She thought, *Maybe he's right. I should focus on writing until I get the green light to garden when the time is right.*

\* \* \*

She spent the rest of her spring and summer writing and bonding with Piper and Kai. Her heart missed connecting with the earth, but she was making good headway with each chapter, enjoying every minute of her process. Writing in nature, connecting to earth that way. Playing with reality was freeing and her creative flow fed something deep within her, fulfilling her.

\* \* \*

While Kai was with Cray for a full week, Piper invited Grace to stay at his place. She spent her time off typing chapter after chapter from his couch.

One night, he got home late and said, "There's a full moon out tonight."

"It's in our sign!" Grace said, looking up from her laptop, all excited. "We're halfway to our birthday season. We get one full moon a year in our sign."

"Really?"

"Yeah, and Saturn's supposed to conjunct with tonight's moon. When we look in the sky, we should be able to see Saturn right next to it. We won't be able to see it for another 28 years until Saturn moves back into the sign of Capricorn."

"Perfect," he said and went downstairs.

Grace continued typing, busy finishing up her chapter when Piper came through the front door again.

"Can I borrow you for a minute?"

"Sure." She saved her work and put the laptop aside.

They walked outside to his telescope, pointed at the full moon. She didn't know he had a telescope and was too consumed in writing to see him sneak it out the back door. Grace smiled big, adoring that he went through all that trouble.

"Take a look," he said, offering her the telescope.

She saw the surface of the bright moon, seeing all its dusty craters and surface details, instantly taking her to a different world. Her sense of wonder was intensified. She pulled away with a giddy smile and said, "Thank you for doing this. That's so fun to see."

"Yeah," Piper said, smiling proudly. He looked into the scope again, moved it to the right, and said, "I think this is Saturn." He held it for her to see.

She looked in, and thought, *I wouldn't know if it was Saturn or not...* until she sharpened the scope.

"It IS Saturn. I can see its rings!" She clapped and pulled back for him to see.

"Really?" Sure enough, he could see them too.

"I've never seen Saturn in a telescope before. I didn't know you could see his rings." A large smile streaked across her face. "The first time I see Saturn is while he's in Capricorn, with my fellow Capricorn on a Capricorn full moon!" she said with joy and wrapped her arms around Piper in ecstatic gratitude.

# 31

# Pluto Direct Shows a Bright Future

Pluto direct, September 30, 2018

Grace was standing on a hallway step, looking into the living room of her new Bohemian home when she received a message from her dad saying, *We are putting the homestead up for sale.*

She conversed with the universe—or rather, she had a one-sided argument with it: "*Why did you lead me to believe growing a garden was my purpose? You could have led me in a different direction before the idea was set in motion!?... I thought I was meant to grow food on my family's land... my plans were at my fingertips!*"

She turned, took four steps, slumped down in the tiny bathroom facing the hallway mirror, and watched her emotions. Giving herself a serious "let it go" look. Her gaze took her to the patterned rug, causing her to flashback to The Queen's castle bedroom. Grace shook her head, refusing to visualize this past life again, as she grew weary of it. Not wanting it to get her hopes up again.

She stood and walked towards the mirror, noticing her

slender neck and shoulders. Images appeared in her mind's eye that were *not* of The Queen in her grand castle, so she welcomed the unfamiliar scene.

A large lotus flower presented itself with stunningly vibrant faces on each petal. These images expanded into a broader view of their world. The people were healthy with elongated bodies and shades of bronze skin tones. Everyone lived outdoors, having minimal, handsomely carved wooden furniture and jewelry. She observed the life-like impressions, admiring the detail of the grain of each wooden piece.

These people lived under the sun, which provided most of their nutrients, having little need for food as though they were fed energetically and what food they grew flourished with ease. The natural state of this phenomenal world was abundance. Love was in ample supply, nature was balanced and lush. Their relationships were healthy and supportive. They didn't need much nor desire much.

They enjoyed and loved one another, spending their time simply enjoying life on our beautifully evolved planet. Their communication was done telepathically; their voices were only for alarm and to create beautiful music. Instead of having one consciousness per body, they had many. Their past lives were completely known to them and a part of their present experience. These humans were majestic.

Grace saw a version of herself thriving on this future earth. Although her appearance was different, she knew the female being shown to her *was* her. Her heart fluttered, moved by this woman and place, knowing it was home. A place she resonated with and had longed for, enveloped by the love and beauty that surrounded them. It was heaven on earth.

The image of the flower petals came back into view, now looking more like illuminated threads of fabric. She knew it was a field, a field of pure intelligence that to us was love. She saw this fabric woven through everything, even rocks, trees, water, and us. Then she saw people interacting with this light web, enhancing it by practicing all forms of love. *This is how we have brought ourselves here as a species, and that's how we will get to the future "us": by strengthening our love together, not separately.*

Grace was overwhelmed by such strong love and peered at her sopping reflection.

Grace saw her current life from a different angle, it was singular and linear. Her future self had multiple consciousnesses all at once and no separation of time, making her a multidimensional being.

This vision gave Grace hope. In the grand scheme of things she saw humanity heading in a fabulous direction, despite her attempt at having her "service garden." It showed that nothing had *really* been lost.

When Pluto had gone backward, she was taken back to The Queen's past life. Having Pluto move forward today showed her a future existence. She longed for this fortunate earth where she had come from and where she would return. She held onto the sight of herself in this world.

Life was showing her that trying to feed the needy to feel "good enough" to be loved by God wasn't the point. Loving men that seemed lonely or needy wasn't the point. Inheriting her beloved grandparents' home and being successful wasn't the point. Seeking fame or riches or being a pure religious person wasn't the point.

The point was this: no matter what, she was loved for simply "being" and having her life experiences, whatever time period she was living in. Even experiencing shame of failure hadn't canceled out the fact that she was loved.

The image of her future self smiled warmly, and Grace smiled back as the vision faded. She said aloud, "I'm going back! Back to a place *drenched* in love." Grace grasped wholly to that idea.

Her voice gained a familiar tone and said, "You are loved now, as you were when the first spark of you began. I could never love you any different." The same voice and words came out while embraced by her elk at Apricot Landing.

Grace looked around the trailer and knew she must offer the homestead to the universe, allowing it to work its bigger picture. She knew she was loved no matter what, as is everyone else.

# 32

# Inheritance

On October fifth, Jupiter hit that 23-degree mark for the third and final pass. Piper had welcomed Grace and Kai to live in his house, so they were busy packing and moving. Kai would be starting kindergarten in Twin, and she looked forward to being closer to his school.

She drove to the homestead to grab a few last items, but before she got to the lane, a *For Sale* sign caused her to stop. She thought back to her astrology reading that forewarned her of the approaching conjunction, *The universe will take something away… Better be ready to let it go even though it's hard!*

This is *not* what she wanted to lose, but it was happening.

She swallowed hard and drove down the lane glancing up at the tall trees thinking, *There's a bigger picture here that's not visible yet.*

She went into the basement, took a good thirty minutes soaking it in, saying goodbye, and a mourning session began.

She allowed it, realizing it was a process, and smiled at the old homestead, "Thank you for the time I've had here and for all the beautiful memories you've blessed me with!" Then she walked to the sliding door. "Are you ready to transform too?" she asked as she touched the rock fireplace then walked out for the last time.

*\* \* \**

Five days later, Jupiter moved over her south node of 27 degrees, Scorpio. The conjunction she had been warned about. She received a text from her father saying, *The realtor made a great offer on the homestead and we took it!*

*Right on point…* she thought. She'd been advised to let go of what was already going. *Well, there you have it… the homestead was the thing to go. I wonder how it's better for me in the long run, having that out of my life?*

Even though she didn't want to lose her family's home, she already started the healing process, appreciative and fortunate for the time she *had* at the homestead.

She was even grateful for the blow-up with Gretchen at the yurt, the tension between her and her father and the ending of her relationships with Cray and River. They seemed to play a role as catalysts for change. Previously, she thought their interactions were simply destructive, and maybe so, but there was a reason for it. She forgave them and herself for what had transpired.

Grace focused on her fresh start and wanted to share her newfound appreciation for the planetary system with Kai. She took him to the Herrett Center to look through their high-powered telescope, wanting to see all the visible planets in the sky; there were several to see.

On this specific day, October 29th, there was a YOD, which is when three planets make a short ended triangle on a chart, astrologers say its "the finger of God pointing us where to go." This was a new idea for her and she was curious to see what the YOD would bring.

The morning started clear. By dusk, it was cloudy, and when they made it to the museum, they'd canceled the viewing due to overcast skies.

Bummer.

Grace knew she would see what she needed to see in the sky that night, and she did. As they drove home, the clouds broke, giving Venus a clear stage, all of her own, along the horizon. The only heavenly body visible was the planet of love.

She thought *That's exactly what I needed to see!* She smiled, showing Venus to Kai, pointing towards love.

* * *

On New Year's Eve, Grace experienced something

profound while writing in Piper's living room. She was overwhelmed with the spiritual presence of her grandparents.

She glanced around the room as it nearly embodied the family room that she and Kai had their Christmas tree in; the lighting in the room took her back to the homestead, to a time when they were still alive. Her couch felt like theirs, she even smelled their home at a time when it was full of life, love, and family. She was comfortable and loved at that moment.

She didn't want to scare the feeling away since she hadn't experienced this even while living alone in their home. It always seemed she was sitting in an empty house where love was once in abundance.

Grace soaked in the moment and said, "Thank you, thank you" under her breath. She knew that this was the place she was meant to be, and everything along the way guided her here. To love and comfort.

Curiously, she walked over to her phone to look at what the planets were doing, and the last planet to move over all this Scorpio energy was Venus. It was at exactly 23 degrees. The moon happened to be in the sign of Scorpio too.

She nodded her head—realizing what was in process. Grateful for the visit from her grandparent's spirit, for their love and help in getting her here, all along the way. She whispered, "Love. There it is, my true inheritance…"

# 33

## The Dew of God

Leo full moon eclipse, January 20, 2019

Grace and Piper take Kai and her mother, who's visiting on a walk to Auger Falls. It's a chilly winter's day, but the sun is shining brightly as they head back to the car. They'd walked as far west as they could, where the calm waters are.

She's content with where her heart has led her: to a place of love, gratitude, comfort and forgiveness of the past. She senses the river calling and is enveloped in that same beckoning she'd experienced in the yurt when her soul embarked on this journey of growth. Naturally, her pace slows while everyone else walks ahead. Piper glances back and she holds up a finger with a "please" expression to say, "Give me a minute?" He nods and smiles as though he knows she's wanting to reflect at the river and she heads downstream.

The presence of spirit grows stronger as she finds herself walking in the same location she'd stood three years ago. After transitioning from the yurt to the homestead, back when she was completely alone and stripped to nothing,

~374~

desperately begging the flowing waters for "*her story.*"

She thinks back on her journey from that point until now, thankful to the universe for listening to her heart and vice versa. Although there's no way to know what the future holds or what the universe can see for her, at this moment she is blessed with an abundance of warm, stable love. She's learned through her experiences to see her heart as a tuning fork, harmonizing herself to the vibration of vast faith and trust. Trust in herself and the oneness of the cosmos, together they make a great team. There's an appreciation of every moment spirit has collaborated with her, including the hard and good times, seeing the value in both.

As she continues towards the river's edge, she thinks back and realizes the purpose of the derailing shifts in her life and the intense relationships that played pivotal roles in causing her to "move" and "go". This is where the universe was trying to get her… to trust where her heart led her—even when it hadn't always gone well.

After hiking down to her favorite area, she sits near the first rapid in the same place she and River shared their raspberry kiss and was later shown her birth sky by the beggar. She removes her shoes and socks, puts her hands and feet in the ice-cold water, watching it flow over her feet.

The rocks glisten and she notices a shimmer in the current. Her gaze moves up, seeing woven loops of metal.

There's a man in polished armor and a fully closed helmet standing in front of her, strong and stoic. They're in the spot she had dropped to her knees two summers ago, during the Leo Solar Eclipse—tonight is the Leo Full Moon Eclipse.

"The King," she whispers. "Saturn in Capricorn brings the rightful king to rule our hearts." She's eager and ready to meet him.

The sun shimmers off his metal suit while a bright flash stings her eye, reminding her of a similar moment in the cafe when she'd asked the beggar, "Is it even worth it?" and the sun flickered off the metal-binding into her eye.

The armored King bows his head, acknowledging what she'd whispered. Then looks down at her feet, points to her left foot in the frigid water, and tilts his head curiously.

"My foot?" she asks, moving it around in the water. "The pain is much better, thankfully."

He gives her a thumbs up with his metal gloves on and a methodical head nod then points to her heart. He slightly taps it and gives her another thumbs up. Then puts his hand under her chin, guides it up as he stoops his head, nodding.

Whoever he is, she is comfortable and strong in his presence.

He takes his hand back, makes a fist, then opens it slowly to reveal the richest earth in the palm of his gloved hand. She looks at it peculiarly.

He takes his other hand, points to the mound, and softly touches her heart again. A slight zap shocks her chest, and she experiences a flash of her lonely, hard, and sorrowful moments. She is taken back through all her life fears, recalling a similar experience at Apricot Landing.

The King pulls away, points to the soil while she breathes deeply, and an electric spark comes out of his shiny gloved finger into the soil! A seed sprouts rapidly, blooming into a dainty white and yellow flower rising towards her face. She was in awe as it shone brilliant light from within.

He picks the flower, bows his head, and offers it to her. She gratefully takes the vibrant blossom and draws in its scent. Never had she smelled something so wonderful.

The King reaches up with both hands and slowly lifts his helmet off.

She waits in anticipation, not knowing what she will say when long, dirty blonde locks fall out and drape around the King's armor. A wide, loving grin shines proudly for her as her jaw drops in wonder and emotions fill her chest, spurring tears while looking straight into the face of Grace—tears immediately flow and emotions erupt wildly while she tries to compose herself.

The King holds a proud smile, warming her fully and they share deep, child-like giggles while she watches Grace experience her emotions—allowing them, loving them, and encouraging them.

Grace puts her hands on her thighs to compose herself and wipes her tears through the laughter while The King continues snickering, looking at her with joy and compassion.

"You've followed your heart and no one else's, learning to honor your connection with 'self,' and the divine which sustains you." The King brings her hand up, open to the rich dirt, and continues, "You took your desires seriously, no matter what others told you or tried to convince you about yourself. Even after what they did to you or thought of you. No matter what their whispers and judgments were, *You...*" The King points to Grace, "brought me out of the shadows by transmitting darkness into light, allowing the two to work together for your benefit." She closes her hand around the mound.

Grace chuckles quietly with pride and tears for the soul work she's done and continues to have a moment. Knowing it was never *easy,* but it was worth it.

"You met yourself in times of darkness and decided to trust the heavens and its ability to see the bigger picture. You listened to your heart, strengthening your relationship with the soul of God—the energy that created you. *IS* you. Who desires a connection with YOU just as much as you desire it." She taps Grace's heart again saying, "To love *self* is to love *all.*" The King takes both arms out, broadening her chest, and says, "You went after the connection you were seeking, having no idea what the outcome was, trusting your heart, allowing it to guide you with confidence."

"I'm The King of my own heart," Grace acknowledges, smiling softly.

"*You,*" The King nods, "found strength where there was doubt and faith where trust was thought... lost." The King smiles, "*You...*" —She takes Grace's shoulders and turns her towards the sun "are *that!*"

Grace looked at the stunning star, warmed throughout, and thought, *I am loving light.*

The King held up the dark soil and in a gentle tone said, "We are this *too.*" with an expression as to say, unfortunately.

Grace looks at the mound, knowing its nourishing abilities.

"You could also call this… *ugly.*" The King says, moving the lush earth around in her hand, allowing some to crumble away. "It can represent any uncomfortably tough emotion. To truly grow our spirit needs duality."

Grace smiles and glances at the bright sky again, realizing the magnitude of her life's experiences.

"You asked for your story," the King reminded her, "and your story was grateful for your participation."

Grace nods with a smile.

"Everyone on your quest is a mirror to you. We are all trying to grow, seeking to transform emptiness into fullness and darkness into light. We are doing what the rest of the universe is doing… One day we'll be so good at transforming, we won't even notice it as separate from us or that it was once challenging for us.

Without a doubt, you are wrapped in love. Take that through any shadow and you'll grow a part of you which is intelligent love."

Grace leans forward, hanging on to every word. Then a question arose within her.

"My purpose?" Grace asked, curiously.

The King says, "Yours is the same as everyone's, to know you are loved unconditionally. The rest is yours to choose. There's no judgment of your choices and there's nothing you can do that can't be forgiven." she added, holding up her index finger, "Remember that we have *all* the light inside of us, when we have entered into any kind of shadow." Then she adds her middle finger to the first and continues, "Love others and their shadows, forgiveness will come." Then holds up a third finger, ending by saying, "*And*, the hardships don't cancel out the light and beauty, they expand it."

The King opens her arms wide to show expansion, and the sun shines off her armor, so bright and vibrant. She embraces Grace then pulls back, smiles—gives her a giddy, close to her chest wave, and walks upstream.

Grace watches her shimmering soul swirl around to give another supportive smile. She grins back, and The King walks away, turning into a strong elk, a deer, then flickers into everyone else along her journey, ending with the bright loving light of infinite love.

She is whole as she walks away from the river bank. Her life has been restored as she looks back to the flowing waters, realizing that her experiences are all she has, thinking back to the concept of others being a version of herself, embracing the idea that we all are a part of the intelligent universe—which she now sees as vast love. It's as if a veil has been lifted; she has a deeper connection to that which created her, which is what she'd been looking for and wanting all along.

* * *

Once Grace makes it to the top, and back to the dirt road, she takes in a 360-degree view of the canyon and exhales in relief, realizing she is standing at the point of her new beginning.

Special thanks to beta readers:

Sandy F., Taylor M., Jaron K., Kyf V., Chris B., Tama

B., Kandis K., Lance H., Sara M., Keenan S., Alex H.

Editors:

Marnae K. and Chris B.

About the Author

Talia was born and raised in Twin Falls, Idaho and still lives there with her two sons and partner. She's ventured across the States and out of the country but keeps coming back to the wonderful Magic Valley.

She is proud of her unconventional educational background. She spent her first five years of school at home with her mother and two siblings. This is where she gained her lifelong habit of journaling, documenting life, and taking herself through her emotions. From there, Talia went to public school in 5th grade through 9th grade and then left high school. A year later she went to Twin Falls' local community college where she graduated with honors in art and anthropology.

## From the Author

I wrote this story about my life, although it's technically a work of fiction, with a handful of chapters written from my imagination.

To me, it's an edited, embellished compilation of journal entries from 2015 to 2018.

I started this story during a vulnerable phase of my life and I wasn't able to refer to myself by my own name, in first-person, or in present tense. It was too personal, so I thought of the name I had always wanted to name my little girl, Grace, and stuck with that. I expressed myself in third person and past tense in order to keep writing through blockages and processing through emotions.

I realized once I finished this book that my story, which carries the reader through a large portion of my life, *was* my cocoon. I struggled to write it throughout the years. When I finished seven long years of working on it, I experienced the freedom of taking flight. I know I wouldn't have gotten to that point if I hadn't kept going, year after year, chapter after chapter, edit after edit, and word after word.

I continue to see the value in struggling through something you believe in, even if others may not see the value in it—keep going, especially when that something you believe in is yourself.

## Cover

I drew a very feminine woman's silhouette (no, it is not my silhouette) with a pencil then copied it onto clear contact paper with my most loved teal permanent marker and moved it around until I got it to a place I liked. Then I took a photo of it and made the title and description on Canva.

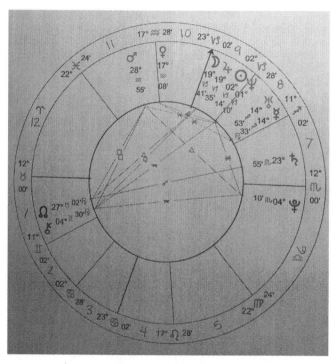

Talia's natal birth chart

Talia started writing Neptune Love Affairs

in 2015 and finally

printed in 2022

neptuneloveaffairs@gmail.com

Made in the USA
Middletown, DE
06 January 2023

18554516R00234